THE GRAVITY MACHINE

THE GRAVITY
MACHINE

ECKART SCHUMANN

authorHOUSE®

AuthorHouse™ UK
1663 Liberty Drive
Bloomington, IN 47403 USA
www.authorhouse.co.uk
Phone: 0800.197.4150

Published by AuthorHouse 12/23/2014

ISBN: 978-1-4969-9972-6 (sc)
ISBN: 978-1-4969-9971-9 (hc)
ISBN: 978-1-4969-9973-3 (e)

To Strelza and our family: Lyal, Linda, Madelin and Beth, Grant, Robyn, Christopher. Thanks for being around and keeping us on our toes.

And to Ken for encouragement and advice on Americanisms.

CHAPTER 1

After such a day Harry needed a cup of coffee.

He picked up one of the mugs in the drying rack, but it was still wet and slipped out of his hands. He grabbed at it, missed, and watched it crash to the floor at his feet.

'Shit!' he muttered under his breath, surveying the shards of glass over the kitchen tiles.

He cleaned up the mess and was still muttering as he tossed the last piece of glass into the bin. His second attempt at making coffee was successful, and he eased into the one big, comfortable chair in his little apartment, his feet on the cushion perched on the low coffee table.

He took a sip, and felt his body relaxing. He smiled, reflecting that the broken mug epitomised life: something would always bring you back down to earth, make sure you weren't getting too cocky.

He took another sip and thought of his work, and what he had just achieved: it had all fitted together so nicely. However, he was on his own, since no-one in the department knew what he was doing. At any rate, no-one he could talk to.

But he had to tell Stephen. He took out his cell phone.

It took a while before Stephen answered: he sounded tired and irritable.

'Harry, why the hell are you phoning now! Do you know what time it is?'

Actually, Harry didn't know, and as he looked at his watch he realised it was after midnight.

'Stephen, it works.'

There was a momentary pause on the other end of the line, 'What do you mean ... what works? What the hell are you talking about?'

Harry was taken aback at the tone of Stephen's reply, and explained tentatively, 'The gravity machine I spoke to you about ... it works.'

'That crazy idea about making things weightless?'

Harry was surprised at Stephen's disbelief and responded slowly, 'Yes, I've made a prototype.'

Stephen's reply took some time coming, 'And this prototype flies, levitates or whatever?' He sounded more interested now, awake.

'Yes.'

'Let me get this right: you've made a gravity machine which is weightless, or you can make it weightless?'

'Yes.'

'And you have it there – with you?'

'Yes – it's in my office.'

'Can I see it?'

'Of course – that's why I called.'

It took a while for Stephen to get his mind around what he had just been told, 'Harry, I don't know whether to believe you – you've either smoked something, or this is the weirdest thing I've heard.' He was quiet again, contemplating his options, 'I've got meetings tomorrow until after three. Can I see it then?'

'That's fine – I'll be in my office.'

After Stephen hung up Harry looked at his cell phone and smiled wryly: he hadn't realised just how improbable Stephen had considered the gravity machine.

However, it was done now, and he could demonstrate it. So they could get on with the next stages.

He remembered a slab of chocolate in the kitchen, and decided he deserved a piece. He fetched it and sank back into the chair, taking a sip of coffee and a small bite of the chocolate, letting it all melt together in his mouth. He felt totally relaxed.

It was after two am when Harry woke with a crick in his neck, still stretched out on the chair. Fortunately his coffee cup was hanging on one finger, keeping the last dregs from spilling. He lay a moment, trying to remember where he was. Then he staggered up and crashed on his bed.

The autumn sun streamed in at the window when he opened his eyes again. The radio/clock at his bedside said nine-twenty-six; he couldn't recall when last he had slept so late.

He was still dressed in his denims and T-shirt, and he lay there awhile, piecing it all together. Now he knew his theory worked his concerns about his assumptions and formulations drifted into the background. He could be concerned with the implications, both for science and for himself. No doubt society would change dramatically.

The room darkened as a cloud cut off the bright sunshine, bringing him back to the present. A long shower served to wake him up, though the sense of accomplishment still pervaded his being. He relished the glass of orange juice and cereal for a late breakfast.

A short while later Harry drove to the university. The sun was high in the sky, though it had lost the sting of summer and the light southeasterly wind added a pleasantly cool touch. It was a magnificent setting, with the university on the lower slopes of Table Mountain, overlooking Cape Town spread out below.

Everything seemed so normal he suddenly felt apprehensive, almost as though the happenings of the night before had been a dream. Then he had been prepared to run through the streets shouting 'Eureka!', but now he felt he had to confirm his experiment.

All the close-by parking at the university was taken, and he had to go to a distant lot. It meant a long walk back to the physics building, however, the grey ivy-coloured buildings reminded him of Cambridge, and he regained some equanimity. There were scattered groups of students standing around in the streets between the various departmental buildings, while others were making their way to lectures. It was still relatively early in the academic year, and there was a palpable intent in the way the students moved around.

Harry Ehlers was a new post-doc, returning to the university after three years at Cambridge. He had been allocated a small back office, but it seemed to be taking forever for all the formalities of his appointment to be concluded.

He hurried up the two flights of stairs in the physics building, hoping to get past the departmental secretary. However, there was little Mrs Shaw didn't notice.

'Oh Harry!' she said as she saw him walking past her office.

He turned back and stuck his head in at the door, 'Yes, Mrs Shaw?'

'Is everything in order for your trip?'

'Yes ... fine.' He hesitated and asked, 'Has Professor Swain looked at my submission?'

'No, not yet – you know how busy he is.' Harry nodded: initially he had been irritated because there had been no response from the head of department to the presentation he was due to make at the upcoming conference in the USA. However, with the subsequent developments and successful completion of his experiment, he was now hoping no-one would ask any questions.

'It's not a problem,' Mrs Shaw continued soothingly, 'we all know how well you'll do at the conference.'

Harry smiled, 'Thanks, Mrs Shaw.' He was grateful to leave and continued quickly to his office.

Mrs Shaw stared momentarily at the vacant doorway after Harry had gone. She had been in the department ever since anyone could remember, and she looked after her brood of students like a protective hen. Harry was one of the best – a bit of a loner, working on his own, and sometimes seemingly on a different plane. That was probably understandable, given his background. Nonetheless, she was glad when he decided to come back.

She smiled – it always took time for her to get used to the way the young people matured into confident adults, becoming part of the teaching and research staff.

Harry reached his office at the end of a long corridor, unlocked the door and closed it firmly behind him. He was aware of the importance of his discovery, but was unsure who should know about it. In particular, he had been given time to write up and publish the results of his PhD thesis, and was too new at the university to have established any collaborative work in the department. He had submitted one paper and was working sporadically on another, which satisfied his superiors.

However, after having completed his degree work at Cambridge he had toyed with some new ideas and started formulating the theory he had now put into practice. Consequently he spent most of his time on these much more exciting ideas. There was no-one in the department who could critically assess what he was doing, and in any case his ideas were fairly radical and he felt they may be scorned.

As he progressed he became more confident in what he was doing, continuing on his own. Then by chance he met Stephen Cambre at the wedding of a mutual friend.

They had been at school together, more acquaintances than friends, and had afterwards taken their own directions at university. Stephen studied law, and was a junior partner in a successful patenting attorney firm. Which was just what Harry wanted to talk about.

'So, how do I go about patenting a new idea or discovery?'

'You have something?' Stephen had learnt to be cynical when anyone asked him about patenting, since it was very seldom anything new came out of a casual conversation.

'Well, maybe – I'm still working on it. At the moment I just want to know the process of getting a patent.'

Stephen's scepticism returned when he found out Harry's idea involved building a machine that could counter the effects of gravity. Nonetheless, he recalled a few occasions at school when Harry had solved intricate mathematical problems with no apparent effort, and seemed surprised when no-one else could understand his reasoning. At times that included their teachers.

So Stephen humoured Harry, saying he would be glad to act as his patent attorney when he completed his invention. He gave him his card, 'Contact me when you're ready.'

It's a common idea that theoretical physicists function with a pencil, a piece of paper and a waste-paper basket, or more recently by being plugged into powerful computers. They are not supposed to have lab space, but to prove his ideas Harry had to have a practical demonstration of their consequences. Fortunately this did not involve large amounts of expensive equipment, and he assembled the bits and pieces for his experiment in his office.

He had the help and cooperation of a departmental technician he had befriended in his postgraduate years at the university. Harry didn't have a formal project requiring equipment, but Dale had managed to obtain a small gamma ray generator, and had helped build the first prototype of his gravity machine.

Everything looked very normal in his office, and Harry put his bag on his desk before going to a cupboard and taking out a small cardboard box. He held the box chest high, and gingerly opened the lid. Inside was a metal ball, in size somewhere between a golf ball and a tennis ball. The bottom section of the ball had been cut off, giving it a flat base, and there were broad grooves extending from this base to the apex. The surface had been roughly filed down to size, and it had the glint of newly-worked aluminium. For want of a better word, he called it the 'glob'.

At his desk he slowly lowered the box with its contents. Nothing untoward happened until the box was about five centimetres above the desk surface and then, as the box went down, the glob remained floating. It hung in the air inside the box as Harry put it down on the desk.

He smiled: it wasn't a dream.

When he left the previous night the glob had been floating perhaps ten to fifteen centimetres above the desk, but it came down by losing energy in the intervening hours. Even in the brighter light of day he could make out the almost ethereal green light emanating from its base, probably using up the energy.

It was a problem that he could, as yet, not remove the gravity energy he had pumped into the glob. His theory showed that extraction of gravity energy had to do with the form and shape of the crystals of the gravity material, but he did not have access to the technology at the university to manufacture the equipment to effect that process. So he had to wait for practical energy loss to take the glob down.

He decided not to pump any more energy into the glob, since he wanted Stephen to view the whole process. By the afternoon it should be down onto the table where he had originally pumped in the energy.

However, he could not help playing around with the glob. He moved it around on its level above the table, marvelling how easily it reacted to the slightest touch. Then he pushed it away from the table towards the farthest wall: it moved slowly and purposefully through the air, until it hit the wall with a gentle 'thok'.

He retrieved the glob and put it back into its box and into the cupboard, closing the door slowly. He mused about his immediate future: the first thing he had to do was update his abstract to the American Physics Association – the APA – who were hosting the conference in San Francisco. He had already been given the statutory fifteen minutes for his presentation, with an allocated slot after lunch on Thursday – a typical low-profile time, suitable for a new post-doc.

He read through his previous abstract. It was already close to the maximum five hundred words allowed, and it took some time to decide what to leave out and what to modify. When it was finally finished he attached it to an e-mail to Dr Flugle, the APA conference chairperson.

In his covering note he requested permission for a short demonstration. Such a practical application was unusual, in part because theories were debated, but also because most of the experimental verifications of modern physics require vast setups involving expensive equipment and often teams of experimenters.

However, in his case the glob and energy transfer apparatus could fit easily into his luggage, and indeed the actual energy transfer was quick. Harry felt it was important as a verification of his theory, but he would have to see what they allowed.

Having completed what he wanted to do, Harry decided to go to lunch. He had had little to eat over the last couple of days while refining the gravity energy transfer to the glob, and moreover his light breakfast had done little to satisfy his hunger pangs

Though it was still relatively early there were quite a number of students around, and while he stood in the lunch queue he looked around for a table where he could sit. Most were occupied by one, two or more students, eating, drinking or just talking. He didn't want to sit at a big table in the centre with a whole lot of others, and preferred a smaller table near one of the windows.

He noticed a girl sitting alone at a small window table. She had caught his attention on a previous occasion when she was in an animated discussion with a couple of other students. She wore the regular student denims and t-shirt without any attempt at further makeup, yet somehow she was decidedly attractive and interesting.

By nature he had always been shy with the opposite sex. It was not that he lacked the desire to go out and 'have fun', but he just couldn't make the small talk that seemed to be a requirement of that scene. He became tongue-tied when he tried to make conversation, which just worsened his embarrassment. So, in a typical nerd-fashion he rather concentrated on his work

However, he had to eat somewhere and at worst she could just ignore him. In any case, he was on a bit of a high: hell, he had just invented the gravity machine!

He waited for his selection of food, paid, took some cutlery and moved over to where the girl was sitting. When he approached her table she was staring out the window, and his resolve almost left him. But she turned and saw him coming, so he couldn't back out.

'Mind if I join you . . .?' he asked hesitantly.

She looked at him impassively, and it was apparent he had disturbed a deep introspective train of thought. Her marked brown eyes seemed distant, inspecting him.

'No, fine,' she eventually said.

She looked down at her plate as he pulled out a chair and sat down opposite her. Not exactly the welcome he'd been hoping for, but then she did look up and half smiled at him. Her mousy-blonde hair was cut quite short, seemingly uncombed with one curl wisping over her forehead, and others sticking out like short pieces of straw at the back. She was wearing a loose-fitting, faded blue T-shirt with an abstract yellow design visible above the table.

Harry smiled back. She had an open, beautiful face with a cute nose and pert mouth with no make-up. He didn't know what to say, and then also looked down at his plate to start eating. When he raised his head again he found her looking at him.

'You're a post-grad?' she asked.

'Just started a post-doc in physics.' Harry hesitated, finding the words to respond, 'And you?'

'Finishing a masters in botany.'

Her tone was curt, and having dispensed with the preliminaries, she appeared disinclined to continue the conversation.

'What aspect of botany?' he eventually asked.

'More environmental management, with emphasis on the botany.'

Again she was quiet, not encouraging any further conversation. Harry felt awkward, though at the same time intrigued with his lunch companion. She didn't seem to deliberately want to ignore him: she appeared to have her mind on other matters.

It had been some time since he had tried to chat up a girl, and somehow as he looked at her eating he wanted to know more about her.

'I guess I should have introduced myself,' he tried to keep the conversation going. 'I'm Harry.'

She looked up again, with another half smile, 'Hi, I'm Tracy.'

He suddenly realised she was finishing her last mouthful.

She leaned back, wiping her mouth on her serviette, 'Harry, I'm sorry if I appear rude, but will you excuse me? I have a whole lot of things to do.'

'Of course . . .'

He watched her leave: she was slim, and moved with an easy elegance between the tables. She dumped her plates and cutlery, and then moved up the sloping entrance walkway. At the top she turned briefly, and Harry imagined he caught her eye, but she turned abruptly and was gone.

Now he found himself looking out of the window, wondering about her. He smiled wryly: so much for his ability to charm girls. He shook his head and concentrated on his lunch; he had the meeting with Stephen to look forward to.

CHAPTER 2

Stephen arrived around half past three, muttering about students and parking. He was a big man, and his jacket was open with his tie hanging loose. The day had warmed up, and Harry could discern flecks of sweat on the pale blue shirt, while there was a slight roll above Stephen's patent leather belt. He was putting on weight thought Harry, but perhaps that happened to lawyers when they went to work in the city.

They shook hands in greeting, and Harry closed the door of his office. He indicated to the glob now sitting on the desk; in the interim it had lost the last bit of gravity energy.

'That's the glob I told you about,' he said. Stephen nodded briefly, going across to the desk and picking it up. It was quite roughly made, and when he turned it over he saw it was hollow with a small hole in its base. He looked inside, and could discern streaks of yellow.

'That's crystalline gold,' Harry informed him. 'That's the gravity material I'm using.'

Stephen looked around him: so this was where the brilliant Harry Ehlers spent his time. The sparse office had only the bare essentials: the desk and chair plus a second chair for a visitor, a cupboard, a bookcase and a filing cabinet. The bookcase was half full of impressive-looking tomes, while there were a few files scattered around. A notebook computer was lying shut on the desk, adjacent to some instrumentation.

A window to his right afforded a view of the back of the physics building, as well as the back of the adjacent departmental buildings. Not much inspiration there, though in the distance pine trees on the slopes of Table Mountain were discernable, their dark green counteracting the bright sunshine.

Stephen turned back to where Harry had moved across to the desk. He hardly looked like an international scientist, but then again, what did a scientist look like? He was slim, of medium height, with a dark rather than swarthy face that was at the same time boyish and serious, and his black hair tended to be long, curling slightly at the ends. He wore a pair of faded denims, a grey T-shirt and sandals: typical student attire. It occurred to him Harry probably hadn't grown out of his student mentality.

'Not very impressive for what you claim,' Stephen said, indicating to the glob.

Harry smiled, 'It depends what it can do.'

He motioned to Stephen to give him the glob, which he turned so that the hole in its base fitted neatly over a small round extension on top of a little pedestal on the desk. Harry clipped a loose arm attached to the pedestal over the glob to hold it down.

He indicated to the wires going from the pedestal to a small control unit, 'I was lucky to get this gamma ray generator – it became available from another project.'

He hesitated, 'Perhaps I should first tell you what all this does.'

Stephen nodded, interested but sceptical, uncertain what to expect.

Harry was not sure how much clarification was needed. 'You see,' he started, 'if you pick up an object, and raise it, you give it energy.' As an example he picked up a pen, holding it above the desk.

'Then, if you let go, it falls and loses all that energy again, changing it to noise, heat and such like.' He dropped the pen onto the desk with a small thud.

'So all I'm doing is giving the gold in the glob gravity energy, which will raise it up to the appropriate level. Because it's given internally, the gold doesn't lose the gravity energy like this pen did and it stays at that energy level. So it doesn't fall down.'

Stephen nodded: it seemed reasonable.

'I can attach other matter onto the gold, which will bring it down a bit,' Harry continued. 'That's what the aluminium cover of the glob does, though it doesn't affect the gravity material inside.'

Harry stopped, but Stephen didn't say anything. 'Anyway,' he continued, 'the generator pumps the energy into the gold – effectively taking it up to a higher energy level.'

He indicated to the little arrangement on his desk, 'It's all ready to go.'

'That's it?' Stephen couldn't believe this simple little arrangement might be part of a ground-breaking experiment.

'I'll add the fanfare later.' Harry paused, and added, 'All that has to happen is the transfer of energy.'

'Okay – go for it.'

Harry switched on the generator, producing a slight hum in the office. He fiddled with the dials on the little control box, and Stephen discerned a slight change in the tone. Besides that, nothing seemed to happen.

'Look at the glob,' Harry advised him.

As he gazed at it, Stephen noticed a slight green light emanating from its base.

Harry switched off the generator and continued, 'I've transferred the energy – not too much. I have to hold the glob down to keep the transmitter over the hole in the base, and when I unclip it the glob will float up to its new energy level.'

Stephen nodded, intrigued by the show, and anxious to see the next stage.

Harry unclipped the arm, holding the glob down. Then he gently took away his hand, and the glob jumped up in the air, oscillating quite wildly about a new level some twenty centimetres above the desk. After a few seconds it settled at the level, just hanging there, and with the green light now seeming to envelop it.

Stephen stood for some time just looking. He moved closer, glancing at Harry: "Can I ...?" he indicated to the glob.

'Of course.' Harry smiled broadly now.

Stephen touched the glob gingerly. The push made it drift away, but he quickly pulled it back. He could feel the inertia of the object, yet it moved about easily at his touch. He put his hands all around it, inspecting the office around him.

'Do you mind if I take it out?' he suddenly asked.

'No, not at all,' Harry replied after a moment, as he realised Stephen still needed proof it wasn't some sort of gimmick in the office holding up the glob. 'Just make sure there's no-one about.'

Stephen opened the office door, saw an empty corridor and pushed the glob out. It carried on floating serenely, and after doing an around turn he came back into the office, closing the door behind him.

He sat down on the visitor's chair, looking at the glob hanging in the air in the middle of the room.

Finally he turned to Harry, 'It's for real, isn't it?' It was stated rather than asked, and Harry nodded briefly.

'I'm sorry I doubted you. I guess I should've known you always come up with the goods.' He looked at the glob, 'That is the most incredible thing I have ever seen. The potential there is absolutely unlimited.'

'There is one thing still lacking,' Harry eventually said. Stephen looked at him questioningly, and he continued, 'At the moment I can't get the energy out of the gold again - a reverse transfer to get the glob down.' He paused, 'I've worked out the theory, but don't have the facilities here to make the equipment.'

Stephen went back to the glob, and pulled it down slightly. He turned to Harry, 'You mean you can't get it down?'

Harry nodded, and Stephen turned again to the glob. 'I hadn't thought of that ... I more or less assumed it was part of the process.'

He grinned, 'That would be fun – having all sorts of objects floating around, and we couldn't get them down again.'

Harry returned the smile: it did seem a bizarre concept.

Stephen tapped the glob and it moved across to Harry. 'Why have you shown this to me?'

Harry stopped the glob and left it hanging. He was serious now, 'You're a patent attorney, and we've spoken about patenting. I want to know about patenting this.'

Stephen stared at the glob for a while, 'I was hoping that's why you contacted me. This is big, really big – this is the kind of thing one can only dream about.'

He stood up and looked out the window: 'It must be formulated very carefully. One can't have any loopholes.'

A thought struck him, 'You haven't published it yet?'

'I've sent in an abstract to a conference in San Francisco in about two weeks. Which is why I wanted to get the experimental side working. It will be published in the proceedings.'

'That doesn't give us much time – we need to have the application lodged before you go, otherwise it becomes public property.' He explained the patenting procedures briefly, indicating the first step would be to take out a provisional patent. Thereafter more detailed patents would have to be lodged in all the relevant countries.

He paused again, 'When can we get the patent description finalised? Tomorrow is Friday, and I have appointments the whole day. I'm going to tell my partners about this – see whether I can have time to concentrate on just this.'

He saw the look on Harry's face. 'Don't worry, it's safe with us – we deal in new ideas the whole time – that's what we do. This is so big . . . we'll have to handle it very carefully.

What about the weekend?' he continued.

'I guess I can make it,' responded Harry.

'Good,' said Stephen, '... that's settled. We'll work Saturday and Sunday, see how far we get. When do you leave?'

'Thursday. I have the weekend in Boston, and then go to San Francisco on Tuesday – the conference starts on Wednesday.'

'So we'll have a few more days to finish off.'

A thought occurred to him: 'Don't worry about costs at this stage, provided we handle all the patenting aspects.'

Harry nodded, 'Sounds fine to me.'

Stephen took Harry by the shoulders; he was half a head taller, and his eyes were shining, 'There is so much money in that little thing – that glob – that you'll be swimming in it. It will affect transport, society, everything... and we'll have control of it. The world will be coming to our doorstep.'

He looked at his watch. 'I have to get back to my office.' He went across to the glob, pushed it down and watched it bob up and down around its energy level. Shaking his head in disbelief he shook Harry's hand.

'Fantastic!' He smiled, 'I'll contact you tomorrow to make arrangements to get the patent description drawn up.'

Harry watched him go, and then closed the door behind him. He sat down on his chair, put his feet up on the desk and wondered about the future.

When Harry left to go home he stopped briefly at Mrs Shaw's office.

'I've made some changes to my abstract for the APA conference,' he said as nonchalantly as possible. 'Do you think Professor Swain would like a copy?'

'He probably won't have time to look at it now ...,' she started, 'but send it through anyway, we should have the latest on file.'

She looked at Harry, conscious he must be getting irritated at the delays and unresponsiveness of the departmental head. 'You must understand, Professor Swain wants to be more involved with physics. However, Council matters take up a lot of time, and the department must have good representation at the highest level in the university.'

'Yes, I know,' Harry agreed, hoping he sounded sympathetic. However, it was with some relief that he left: he had done what he had to do, but it wasn't his fault if Professor Swain did not read his submission. In particular, he was fearful his superiors may demand some acknowledgement if they knew what he was doing – it happened in such situations that heads of department demanded co-authorship of important papers. That was not something Harry wanted.

Proceedings of the APA conference were also to be published. This meant speakers had to submit completed papers of their presentations within a month of the end of the conference. These would be sent for rapid review, with the objective to have the Proceedings out within a few months to ensure they didn't become dated.

Now that he had finalised the experimental aspects, Harry completed the draft of his paper; he would finalise it once it had been presented, since there may be additional aspects coming out of the conference.

Moreover, he needed confirmation from Stephen in case the patent rights could be infringed, and in any case submission of a paper would probably require approval by the department.

Harry arranged to meet Stephen at his office on Saturday morning. Being weekend, Stephen had no appointments, and they could work undisturbed.

The offices of Allen, Nyoka and Associates were situated on the top floor of a Wynberg centre. After getting the go-ahead from Stephen, building security allowed Harry through to the elevator, and Stephen was waiting for him when the doors opened again.

They went through to a luxurious, functional office. A large picture window in one wall framed Table Mountain, while the curved desk allowed Stephen to work with clients while at the same time having immediate access to his computer and ranks of files behind him.

Harry sat down and put his draft paper on the desk. He did not know what was required, and had brought his computer and additional notes.

Stephen looked at the paper: *Identifying Gravitational Field Potentials: Practical Applications*. He started reading the Abstract, gave up, and turned a few of the subsequent pages. He put it on the table and looked at Harry.

'Look Harry,' he said, 'we are going to have to write something down which is understandable to a bunch of lawyers. I can't begin to comprehend this, so you will have to come down to my level and explain the concepts in nice, easy, non-mathematical terms. The most important thing is to define clearly the new processes being used to store gravity energy. These must be worked into the patent application to cover all the ways in which this can be done, so no-one can circumvent the patent through some slight technical innovation. So, let's start at the beginning: what is gravity?'

The process turned out to be a new experience for Harry, quite frustrating and even annoying at times. The concepts involved were those at the forefront of gravity theory, and the people in the world who could properly understand the formulations probably numbered no more than a few hundred.

Harry initially found he was at a loss to explain his theory without recourse to equations. Stephen was sympathetic and led the discussion with a series of well thought-out questions. As they progressed and Harry discovered what was required, he became better at the descriptions. In fact, he had to admit approaching gravity theory in the terms demanded by Stephen served to clarify his own ideas. He had accepted many of the concepts embodied in the standard equations, but to describe these in non-mathematical terms required a much greater understanding of the basic physics.

The very question of what gravity was in reality, as opposed to the familiar mathematical descriptions, took on a new meaning. When he returned late that night to his room, he lay on his bed for a long time wondering about all sorts of new ideas. A quote from Bertrand Russell took on new significance: *'Mathematics may be defined as the subject in which we never know what we are talking about, nor whether what we are saying is true'.*

On the other hand, Stephen entered what for him was a completely new world. He had never understood what Harry was doing, apart from the fact he found obscure meanings in complex mathematical expressions. The results seemed to bear no relation to the real world.

Now he encountered a beautiful system of thought which delved into the essence of the natural world around him. It tried to explain in rational terms things he took for granted; in fact, things he hadn't even thought about. How did one body affect another across seemingly empty space? What was space itself, that it was deformed in a complex interaction by a mass within it? And how did time fit in?

However, one thing he did know, and that was there were millions – no, billions – to be made out of this new theory. He had landed with his bum in the proverbial butter, and he would make sure he received his due share of the proceeds.

That night in his apartment he stood for a long time gently bouncing a tennis ball: watching it fall, hit the ground and come up again. He marvelled someone could dream up a theory involving space and time which caused the ball to fall towards his floor. It sounded like a fairy story, and yet Harry had used it all to make a very practical machine. What was gravity really?

He looked around his lounge. Everything stood in its place because of the distortion of something around him he couldn't see or sense. Even that ugly vase standing on the mantelpiece which had been given to him by Pam ... or was it Samantha? Anyway, it didn't matter now - it would form the basis of a scientific experiment.

Standing on the ceramic tiled square in front of the fireplace, Stephen took the vase gently down from its resting place. He raised it to a level above his head, grimaced at the odd shape and strange pattern, and let go. He watched carefully as it fell and crashed onto the tiled floor. Then he stood looking at the shattered remains - the work of who knows what - sighed, and went to bed.

It took them the rest of the weekend to formulate the general aspects of the patent application to Stephen's satisfaction. The patent was held by Harry Ehlers, and all the legal affairs would be handled by Stephen Cambre, in the legal firm of Allen, Nyoka and Associates.

On Monday Stephen finalised the whole provisional patent application, and in the afternoon Harry joined him to refine the details. It was late that night before all the documentation was complete, ready for Stephen to lodge on Tuesday.

They went out to a nearby coffeehouse to celebrate. There were few other patrons, and the coffee arrived quickly. Stephen took a deep sip and leaned back.

'You're extraordinarily lucky the way this has worked out,' he said. 'This gravity theory is actually not what your PhD at Cambridge was about, so they can't claim patent rights. Then you had that travelling stint ...'

He looked at Harry, 'What was that all about?'

'It was just something I had to do, after finishing my degree,' Harry replied slowly. 'In January I had two weeks at an Austrian ski resort with some Cambridge friends. It was a great holiday after the stress of finishing my thesis.'

'I had made no further plans of where to go from there.' He stopped for a moment, recollecting his thoughts. He stared at the street lights off to the side, before turning back and continuing.

'Everybody was just pushing where to go, who to work with to continue their careers. I had some offers, but it all seemed so pointless. I just had to get away for a while, to see what I wanted to do.'

'My father had always harped on the importance of history, in particular the ancient cultures in the Middle East. I had some inheritance money, so I spent the first couple of months travelling around there, moving onwards to India.'

Again he stopped, taking a sip of coffee. 'The ancient cultures are incredibly interesting, where one can find them. However, most of it's just people – millions of them. And they've destroyed those civilisations – or are busy selling them off bit by bit to ignorant tourists.'

'So I needed space, and ended up in Nepal.'

He looked at Stephen, 'What a fantastic place. It was the end of the dry season, and the warming weather meant I could get to some high altitudes. Right into the snow and ice, with the mountains all round.'

'The local people are very genuine, and I moved from one village to the next, going where they said it would be amazing. But it was all amazing.'

Stephen frowned: 'So where did you work on your theory?'

Harry paused, taking another sip of coffee, 'I guess I had a lot of time to think about things. All sorts of things. Mostly about whether the universe is a rational thing, and whether we can understand that rationality. Perhaps the mountains give one the right to think big.

Anyway, the whole question of gravity is part of how the universe fits together on the large scale. The ideas in this theory are an extension of some of the concepts I had generated in my thesis, but I was surprised to see how neatly my new assumptions worked into established theory.'

He smiled, 'Suddenly I was excited. I was up in one of the high valleys when I wrote down the equations in a notebook I carried around. I knew what it meant, and thought I should get back to so-called civilisation.

There were still lots of details to be worked out, but it seemed a working model could be made quite simply. For that I thought I should get to a university or some such institution. However, I'd made no plans, and the places I would want to go overseas have long procedures for choosing post-docs.

So I thought UCT may take me on at short notice as an ex-student. In any case, I had a hankering to come home.'

Harry downed the last of his coffee. It wasn't often he spoke to anyone so freely, but he had now been working with Stephen for the last few days, and he felt relaxed after completion of the patent.

'Even in the upper reaches of the Kathmandu valley I found an internet connection. I sent an e-mail to the department, and they responded within a day. I think they were very surprised, and said I should come. We could work out the details of my position once I was back.

So I did just that.'

Stephen raised his eyebrows, 'And now you've been here almost two months and they still haven't given you a contract to sign?'

'Nor paid me any salary,' Harry added.

Stephen nodded. He was quiet for a while, then continued: 'Amazing story.' He looked down at the table, moving a menu so it lined up with a fold in the tablecloth. He looked up again at Harry: 'The fact that UCT haven't paid you means you probably aren't employed by them. Or at least one can argue that.'

'You also haven't officially worked with anyone here.' It was more of a question than a statement.

Harry nodded, 'To be fair, there isn't anyone here directly involved in my line of physics, and I've been told I can start something new.'

'Whatever,' Stephen responded. 'The point is they have no right to your work, since the ideas were generated before you arrived here, or were in their employ. Though it is my guess they will try and prove otherwise.'

The sequence had not escaped Harry, but he was cautious about the legal profession: often decisions seemed to be made which defied a rational cause and effect. 'On the other hand,' he added, 'all theories are based to some extent on what has gone before.'

Stephen smiled, 'Always a contentious issue, the reliance on past work, and the novelty of the new. I think without doubt your ideas are new, otherwise why aren't there gravity machines flying around? They will have a lot of trouble trying to show the theory has been out there.'

He drained his cup.

'Another coffee?'

'No thanks,' Harry replied. 'I think it's bedtime.'

Once home, Harry had a quick shower before getting to bed and a deep, dreamless sleep. For the second time in a week he awoke to find the sun streaming into his bedroom.

He had a leisurely breakfast, taking his time getting to the university. Once in his office he sent his amended abstract to Mrs Shaw for forwarding to Professor Swain; he hoped she was too busy to read it herself.

Then he refined his actual presentation. He had worked out which ideas and equations to include, making sure each slide was clear and specific and not too cluttered. In his schooldays, when his parents had been alive, they had helped him organise his class presentations, and he never forgot the finer details.

Around midday a loud knocking interrupted his thoughts, and his door was brusquely opened. 'Hey, Harry, you coming to lunch?' Andile Mangope stood there with a couple of other post-graduate students.

'Sure.' Harry happily dropped his work and joined the group.

'So, when do you get back from the States?' Andile took him by the arm in a vice-like grip: not intentionally, it was just normal for him. He was finishing his PhD in experimental physics, but the great passion in his life was mountaineering and rock climbing. For that he exercised daily to strengthen his hands and arms so he could do pull-ups on the fingers of one hand. A small man, but his T-shirt strained over his biceps.

'Wednesday, three weeks.'

'Good, so you can join us in the Cederberg on Saturday, three weeks.'

Harry smiled, 'I'm not doing any climbing with you.'

'We'll get you on some easy routes.'

'You don't know what an easy route is.'

Andile grinned, 'You can go walking with the girls.'

'Now that sounds good – am I invited?'

Andile looked at Craig, a Masters student, 'I don't think you'd keep up with our girls.'

The banter continued to the cafeteria, where they momentarily had to wait for other students to exit. As they came out Harry recognised Tracy in the group.

'Hello Harry,' she said pleasantly as she passed. He managed a short 'Hi Tracy' in response.

'Nice,' said Craig, looking back at Tracy. 'So, Harry, how did you meet her?'

'I ... uh ... we had lunch ...'

'And there I thought you were a devoted physicist. Meanwhile, you're out there getting the girls – does she have a sister?'

The greeting from Tracy lifted Harry's spirit: at least she had remembered his name. While it was irrational such a small thing should improve his whole demeanour, somehow it did. Back in his office he half thought of trying to contact her, but realised he didn't know her surname. With only two days before his trip, he let it slide.

On Thursday morning he was in his office, getting everything together before his flight that evening, when his cell phone rang.

'Dr Ehlers?' the voice sounded distant, with an American drawl.

'Yes?'

'Ken Flugle – I'm chairman of the organising committee for next week's APA meeting.' Harry sat up, recognising the name of the prominent physicist on the other end of the line.

'I'm interested in the abstract you submitted on gravity energy fields – it seems like a remarkable new approach.' Harry did not respond, waiting to hear what the call was about.

'Now, you've said you want to present a demonstration of the theory. Have you actually built something?'

'Yes, that's right. It's quite primitive, but it does show the theory working.'

'You mean you can transfer energy? Get a mass to a different energy level?'

'Yes – it's quite quick, and I can carry it in my luggage. It won't take much to set it up.'

'So what happens? Does it fly?'

'Well, it sits at the new level...'

'Just floats there?'

'Yes.'

Flugle was quiet a moment. 'So what you are saying is this is the proverbial anti-gravity machine?'

'Not anti-gravity – it just utilises a different aspect of energy in a gravity field.'

Flugle chuckled, 'I'm using science fiction terminology.'

Then he continued, 'We've got a problem with a keynote speaker, and I would like to reschedule your talk to be the opening presentation of the conference.'

Harry swallowed, 'Okay ...'

'Harry ... can I call you Harry?'

'Of course.'

'Well, Harry, I'm taking you at face value. I've spoken to Fred Morton – your Cambridge supervisor – and he was most surprised at your work. He says you don't say anything you can't back up.' Harry remained quiet.

'So, as far as I can judge, if you've done what you've just said, then this will probably be the most important presentation since ... since ... relativity. That's about where I'd put it.' He paused to let the import of his statement sink in.

'I'm going to invite a few members of the press. Do you think you can handle that?'

'I hope so ...'

'When do you arrive in San Francisco?'

'On Tuesday evening at six-ten.'

'You've left it pretty late – are you flying from South Africa.'

'No, I'm leaving this afternoon. I've got the weekend in Boston.'

'That's good, so you'll get over some jet lag. Where are you staying in San Francisco?'

'At the *Uptown Residence.*' It was one of a number of hotels offering accommodation to delegates at reasonable rates. Harry had taken the cheapest he could get, knowing a conference hotel would offer all the basic essentials.

'I'll have you picked up at the airport. Would it be possible to give me a quick demonstration on Tuesday evening?'

Harry hesitated, 'I'd like to, but it depends on the heights of your place and the auditorium. You see, I can't take out the gravity energy at the moment.'

It took a moment for Flugle to digest the information. 'We can arrange the height – I thought your theory showed the energy can be extracted?'

'It requires a low frequency energy source, which I don't have. It will also need some manipulation and calibration.'

'Fair enough. Does that mean this mass will just continue floating?'

'I've called it the glob – it's a bit bigger than a golf ball. It loses energy quite quickly through a green glow.'

'Fantastic! This gets better and better. UFO's are supposed to have such a green aura around them. You can put on a real sci-fi show. Only this time it will be for real.'

He paused a moment, and continued slowly, 'Harry, you probably don't appreciate fully what you've done – I don't think anybody can. I'm looking forward to meeting you – and the glob.'

'Thanks Dr Flugle. I hope it all works out.'

'Call me Ken. I'll be in contact beforehand.'

Harry sat for a long time after Ken Flugle hung up. It seemed the dye was cast, and his life would be changing. In many ways it was exciting stuff, and he valued the opinion of the president of the APA.

He had done the proper thing in submitting his abstract for approval, and attendance at the APA meeting had gone through as a matter of course. Funding was coming from the South African Science Foundation – the SASF – so the university had no expenses in that regard. Yet he was disappointed no-one in the department had even talked to him about his visit to the USA, and in particular he had had no communication from Professor Swain, head of the Physics Department.

He smiled: perhaps he should consider himself fortunate with the whole question of the patent to be considered.

CHAPTER 3

The visit to Boston was a nostalgia and remembrance trip for Harry: he hadn't been back since his family returned to South Africa after the change to democracy. At the time he had only just started school, so his recollections of America were vague.

His father, Dr. Robert Ehlers, had been a young lecturer in the department of history at Rhodes University in Grahamstown. As one of the liberal English universities in South Africa, they had continued to admit students of colour, in spite of threats from the apartheid government.

Clare Grootboom was one of his students, a beautiful girl from the so-called coloured community in the neighbouring city of Port Elizabeth. They fell in love, but there were strict laws against such love across the colour-line. They could not be seen to consort, let alone have any ideas of marriage. They managed a discreet relationship, and none but their closest friends knew what was happening.

However, the relationship caused problems in both families. Robert's parents were in the process of emigrating to Australia, because they foresaw the demise of white rule and there would be no future for them under a black government. His one brother was busy establishing himself in Canada.

'For God's sake, Robert, there are other women in the world who are more suited to you,' his father told him in exasperation. 'Come with us to Australia – forget your coloured girlfriend, because this country is going down the tube.'

But love doesn't work like that. Robert could be very obstinate, and he said goodbye to his parents and went back into the arms of Clare.

On the other side, her uncles, aunts, brother, sister and cousins warned her against such white men, telling her she mustn't look outside her community for a husband. In particular, she was the first one in the family to go to university, and now it seemed she thought she was above them by having an affair with a 'whitey'.

He would just use her, and when he was finished, she would be thrown out like a dirty washrag.

Only her mother supported Clare. She could see beyond the confines of her immediate community, recognising her daughter had an opportunity to improve her situation. The old lady helped where she could, in particular when the couple decided their only chance for a future together lay outside of South Africa. However, before that happened she insisted Clare had to complete her degree in classics and mathematics. It was a difficult year or two for the young lovers as they continued their liaison in secret, keeping out of the watchful eye of the security police.

Robert applied for positions at overseas universities, and eventually obtained a suitable position at Boston University in the USA. They made arrangements to travel as soon as the academic year finished, buying separate tickets to fly out of Cape Town. Only once they were in the air did they feel safe, and they managed to persuade a fellow traveller to change seats so they could sit together.

An unpleasant interrogation session followed at the customs and immigration sections at Logan airport before they could finally embark on American soil. Robert had arranged rental of a small house in Allston, an area with a strong student and university community. They found a cab driver to take them to their front door, and finally they were together in their new, sparsely furnished home. Clare burst into tears from relief and exhaustion.

That was where Mary Sinclair, their new neighbour, found them.

'Land sakes, you two,' she said. 'We can't have you crying here on your first day in America!' She called her husband, Charles, and they organised a take-away supper. For the first time Robert and Clare felt they owned their own lives.

Mary took over and explained how the American system worked, where the closest shops were and what they sold. She told Clare about the public utilities and what they provided. More than that, she was always available for help and advice.

At that stage Robert and Clare were not married and Mary arranged for a civil marriage. However, none of Clare's family could afford the cost of a trip to the USA to attend the wedding, while Robert's parents had only just arrived in Australia, and could not, or did not want to, travel at short notice. His brother living in Canada flew to Boston, and was the sole family member present to witness the ceremony. Of course, the Sinclair's were also there.

After a few years Harry arrived. His mother had been teaching at a local school, and had been sending as much money as possible back to her family in Port Elizabeth. With the new arrival she could no longer work on a full-time basis, and the new mouth meant there was no longer money available to send back to South Africa.

Harry found out later this caused a lot of unhappiness 'back home', since they had become used to the regular supply of dollars. His uncles, aunts and cousins accused his mother of forgetting her roots and the people who provided her education. Only his grandmother steadfastly supported her daughter in her new life in the USA.

Nonetheless, when change came to South Africa his parents started talking of 'going home'. A campaign was launched to bring back South Africans, and his father managed to obtain a tenured position at the University of Cape Town.

Life in Cape Town turned out to be not too different to Boston. Harry went to school in a predominantly white community, and gradually lost his American accent. His parents encouraged a questioning attitude, and it soon became apparent that young Harry was blessed with a remarkable ability to approach problems in novel ways. His mother's mathematical background ensured a numerate competency, while the books his father brought home gave a wide perspective on the development of society over the ages. It was a happy time in his life.

In many ways it was fortunate they were not closer to Port Elizabeth, because the family immediately started requesting support. Harry heard his mother explaining they were not an infinite source of money, and indeed on one occasion he heard his father saying adamantly 'No more!

We also have a life to live.' He did find out later from his grandmother that she continued to receive a small monthly amount from her daughter.

Clare continued to keep close contact with the Sinclair's, a contact that became easier as social networking sites became available. After his parents were killed, Harry continued the communication, but it became limited to once-a-year Christmas letters. Nonetheless, when he indicated he would be coming to the USA the Sinclair's insisted that he visit.

So it was when Harry landed at Logan International in Boston they were there to meet him. He wasn't sure he would recognise them, but being friends on *Facebook* meant they had followed him and seen the occasional photo on his site.

As he entered the arrivals concourse Mary came forward and embraced him.

'Harry!' she said, 'my, but you've grown.' She held him at arms distance to look at him.

'It's more than twenty years, Mary,' Charles chuckled as he came forward to shake Harry's hand. 'That's what they do.'

Harry was surprised to see how old they were. He realised after a while they had taken in the young Ehlers' many years before almost as surrogate children, since they never had any of their own. In that sense they doted on Harry as a grandson, and that evening over dinner he had to tell them all about Cambridge and his position at the University of Cape Town.

'I always knew you'd do well, Harry – you had such wonderful parents,' Mary enthused.

There was an awkward silence for a moment, but then Charles broke in, 'It must have been very painful for you Harry, but what happened to them?'

Harry was expecting the question, but even so he swallowed heavily before he could answer.

'I don't know – I've never found out the full story,' he replied softly.

Mary and Charles gave him time to compose himself.

'I know they went to visit gran in Port Elizabeth,' he eventually continued. 'I was in Cambridge at the time, but my dad said they were going to sort out some money problems – the family was always asking for more money.' He looked up and they could see the tears in his eyes, but he quickly blinked them away.

'As soon as I heard the news I returned to South Africa. I got there five days after it had happened. All I was told was they had been killed by a gang – the area is notorious for its gangs, and the police don't have much control. In fact the police couldn't tell me anything.' He hesitated a moment and then continued, 'Or didn't want to.'

'And the family?' Charles asked.

'Nothing ...' Again he paused. 'That was the worst of it. I didn't know any of them, and they were just sullen and didn't want to talk at all. What made it worse is that I know very little Afrikaans – which is what they all speak.

One uncle – who my mother always said was the best in the family – said there was bad blood and advised me not to push it.'

'I only saw my gran a day later – I think they were trying to keep her away from me. She became hysterical when she saw me – just held on to me saying "my baba, my baba". I couldn't find out anything from her.

She died a few months later.'

The story had come out in a rush, and left Harry empty. He sat in his chair, staring ahead, recollecting a part of his life he did not want to think about.

'And anything more?' Charles asked quietly.

Harry shook his head. 'The police advised me not to look at the bodies. I've always regretted it - not being able to say a final goodbye.'

Mary and Charles said nothing, and after a while Harry continued: 'They were cremated, and I left immediately after the funeral. It just felt like such a hopeless, desolate place – I don't know how my mother could have lived there.'

'They've never caught the murderers?' Mary asked.

Harry shook his head, 'It's not uncommon in South Africa.'

That evening Harry lay awake in his bed, listening again to the distant traffic on Commonwealth Avenue. Talking about his parents' deaths brought back all the dormant memories. He had always been a loner, and the loss of the two people dearest to him just made him withdraw even more.

When he returned to Cambridge he started looking for other answers, which sometimes saw him walking the streets in the early hours. It was a quiet time when he could think, and somehow he hoped he would find some solace in all the dark old streets and edifices, steeped with the memory of all those wise men who had lived there through the centuries. But nothing came of it, apart from some odd questions from strangers.

He wasn't religious, nonetheless attended a few services in Kings College Chapel, hoping for he did not know what. He was always in awe of the magnificent structure and enjoyed the singing, but the sermons seemed contrived and superficial. So again he drew a blank.

It also affected his relationship with Melissa. Pretty and very bright, she started her PhD in organic chemistry in Harry's third year. They drifted into a relationship which suited them both, where they had a partner for all the Cambridge functions, especially the May Balls. It was Melissa who organised their social calendar, with Harry happy to follow.

While they were both fully involved in their work, they made time to have regular lunches and coffee at the Graduate Centre. They had similar attitudes to their future careers, eschewing the one-upmanship attitudes which seemed to pervade many of the students and lecturers.

On one particular weekend he was invited to her home in Yorkshire. It raised the eyebrows of some of his fellow students, 'That's dangerous, Harry – you never know what it means.' He decided it was worth the risk.

While he enjoyed the time with her, he found the family formal and quite a strain. They seemed to put tremendous store in family origins and history, and somehow Harry didn't quite fit those expectations.

On the other hand, Melissa was deliberately otherwise about such matters, being more interested in a renegade ancestor who was shipped off to Australia than any of the others who had made the social scene. In fact, Harry suspected he had been invited specifically to shock her parents' middle-class English sensibilities. She sometimes compared her white English skin to his brown African skin, 'You look so much healthier,' she complained.

However, after Harry had been back a few weeks Melissa confronted him.

'You've changed, Harry,' she lamented. 'I'm sorry your parents died, but you need to get over it. You've got your life to live.'

Harry couldn't argue about it, because he wasn't able to vocalise precisely what was wrong. So he found consolation in his work, and he withdrew more and more from social interactions. He had the excuse that he was in the final strait of writing his thesis, and he saw Melissa less and less: they drifted apart in the same way they had drifted together.

She didn't join him when he went skiing in January after handing in his thesis. He said goodbye to her, and they both knew they would be going their own separate ways.

He was still friends with her on *Facebook*, and over the last month noticed she had changed her status. There was a new man in her life, and she was now 'attached' to Sidney. It occurred to him that they had never been formally attached on *Facebook*, which probably explained why he could wish her well without any rancour. She had written back to thank him for the good times they had had together, and hoped he would find what he was looking for.

Another phase of his life was over.

For the rest of the time in Boston Harry enjoyed trying to remember how things were and how much they had changed. Walking around Allston brought back pleasant memories. They drove to Cape Cod and did all the touristy things. As a child Harry did not remember Martha's Vineyard though he could recall being on a ship. He enjoyed the beaches and the markets in Provincetown.

On Monday evening Ken Flugle phoned to confirm the arrangements for the following day, and on Tuesday afternoon the Sinclairs took Harry to Logan airport for the flight to San Francisco.

Then he was back in the real world. It had been such a relaxing, uncomplicated weekend he was loathe to leave, but on the other hand he was ready to switch into conference mode. He had to get his mind right and focussed on his presentation.

A car was waiting for him at the airport.

'Dr Flugle said to take you to your hotel, and afterwards to his hotel,' the driver informed him in a nasal monotone. Fortunately he said little more, leaving Harry with his own thoughts. The sun had not yet set and he could watch the city passing by on the drive north. Even though he knew the glob worked, he couldn't help feeling anxious about the next few days.

The conference was to be held at the Deteten Convention Centre, situated in the heart of San Francisco. The hotels were clustered in the area, and they went first to the Uptown Residence, where Harry registered. He found his room and dumped his suitcase on the bed, taking out a small separate bag where he had packed the glob and associated equipment. He took it with him to the waiting car.

The chairman of the APA was staying in one of the upmarket delegate hotels, close to the convention centre. The driver had obviously informed him when Harry would be arriving, because a concierge was waiting at the door and he was taken to a secluded coffee table in the hotel lounge area.

Harry recognised Ken Flugle from photographs. A soft-spoken man in his late fifties, his receding hairline gave the impression of someone bull-dozing forward, but his eyes were somehow curious and incisive. He stood up and smiled as he shook Harry's hand.

'Welcome Harry,' he said. He indicated to two others at the table: 'Let me introduce Caroline Fraser and Ferdi Livicki – I hope you don't mind that they join us?'

'Of course not.' Harry recognised the names of the other two physicists: he was in elite company. He shook their hands and they sat down.

'Now, before we carry on - can I offer you something to drink? We've already got our drinks, and there are some snacks on the table.'

Harry ordered a fruit juice. He put his bag on the table, which immediately drew the attention of the others.

'Is that it?' Caroline asked with some disbelief.

Harry nodded, and took out the glob. They took turns to inspect it.

'It is not much to see,' said Ferdi, turning the rough aluminium ball around in his hands.

He smiled, 'I look forward to seeing what it can do. Can it perform here?'

Harry nodded, 'I need an electricity supply. I also need to know the approximate height above sea level.'

'I have that,' Ken said. 'This morning I used my GPS to check on the height of the auditorium and this area – the podium is about nine metres higher.'

'That's fine,' Harry smiled.

'There's a plug behind the curtains,' Ken continued, indicating to the wall behind him. 'I've arranged for an extension cord.' He bent down and picked up the cord lying at the base of his chair.

'Okay, then we're ready,' Harry responded firmly. There was an air of expectancy, though Harry could sense some scepticism as they watched him take out the gamma-ray generator and the little pedestal for the glob. He had remembered to bring a small transformer for the lower US voltage.

Harry's juice arrived, and he stopped his preparations to take a sip. Now it was happening he enjoyed getting his little display ready for these famous people. No need to rush, take his time and drag out the expectations.

When he had everything ready he picked up the glob, indicating to the hole: 'I've used crystalline gold as my gravity material because it's dense and will easily be able to lift the aluminium casing.' He hesitated and then added: 'It was actually a Kruger Rand my parents gave me.'

Caroline smiled, 'That's a fair investment, what with the price of gold nowadays.'

He put the glob in place on the little pedestal, clicking on the small arm to hold it down. He did a quick calculation using the height value Ken gave him, and set the dials on the generator.

'It's ready.' He smiled at the three watching him intently.

'Go ...' Ferdi said under his breath.

Harry turned up the power for about a minute, during which time nobody said anything. Under the bright light in the lounge it was not clear anything had happened.

Harry turned off the power.

'And now ...?' Ken asked.

'There should be enough energy to lift it about a metre above the table,' Harry replied. 'I just need to unclip the arm to set it free.'

'Do it ...' Ken said quickly.

Harry smiled and unclipped the arm, holding the glob down. He looked at the other three and let it go. It lifted quickly, overshooting its new equilibrium level and oscillating wildly up and down.

Harry caught it, and brought it slowly down to a position where it hung in the air at about eye level. The green glow became apparent.

'That's its new energy level ...?' Ken stated rather than asked. He moved to take the glob, and inadvertently knocked it forward. It moved over to where Caroline was watching, and she caught it gingerly as it came to her.

'Can I hold it ...?' she asked, and started moving it around.

'Incredible,' she ended, as she pushed the glob back to Ken.

All three scientists played around with the glob, pushing it around to each other. It moved so easily, and Caroline directed it into the central reception area of the hotel. It moved silently past one of the guests, who stood looking at it in amazement until Caroline quickly retrieved it.

'Wow!' she giggled as she came back to the other three, 'this is fun!'

Ken turned to Harry, 'This is the most amazing thing I've ever seen. To have such an advance in theory, combined with experimental verification – well, it boggles the mind. I just didn't believe you'd done it.'

'I want a copy of your paper, Harry,' Ferdi said.

'And me,' Caroline added.

'Congratulations, Harry,' Ken continued. 'I don't know how else to say it. We're privileged to have seen what you've shown us tonight.

Tomorrow is going to be a momentous day.'

CHAPTER 4

It was early Thursday morning. Harry leant back on the reclining chair, his feet stuck out against the low railing of the porch. The rising sun cast long shadows into the hotel suite behind him, while twenty-one floors below San Francisco was still dark, though already the traffic was building up.

He didn't register the city or the sunrise as he stared into space. His mind was too occupied with everything that had happened over the past twenty-four hours. The turmoil in his emotions meant he had been awake early, and by five am he could no longer lie in his bed.

He made a cup of coffee in his luxuriously-appointed kitchenette, which probably alerted the hotel staff that he was awake. They phoned to inquire if he would like the daily papers.

'I'm sure you will want to see them, sir,' the man added.

The pile they brought him would have taken a whole day to read, and he skimmed through the headlines. There was just one story, and it added to his whole sense of unreality, of something happening to someone else.

The discarded newspapers lay at his feet. The headlines on *World Today* were three inches high, bold and black and screaming out: '*YOUR WORLD HAS CHANGED*'. Below there was a picture of Harry, standing at the podium, a slight smile on his face. The caption read '*and this is the man who has done it*'.

The *San Francisco News* lay off to the side, its headlines blaring '*AMAZING GRAVITY MACHINE*'. There was a close-up picture of the glob, and the photographer had even managed to capture the slight greenish glow – unless it had been added. It made it look like the best science fiction UFO. There was another picture of Harry, just his face, with the query below: '*Harry Ehlers: Is this the new Einstein?*'

His day had started normally enough in the Uptown Residence. With his body not yet entirely out of South African time, he had woken early and lay in his bed thinking about his presentation, wondering how his theory would be received. The commendations of Ken, Caroline and Ferdi the evening before did much for his confidence, but he was still nervous.

He was glad to be talking early, since it meant his direct involvement would be over quickly. He wasn't sure what would happen, but thought he could then enjoy the rest of the conference.

After a shower and getting dressed, he checked all the equipment in his bag. The receptionist directed him to a nearby fast food joint for breakfast, where he ordered and ate slowly, watching the passing crowd. He didn't see anybody he recognised, which wasn't surprising since he was new in the field. There were some Cambridge colleagues coming later, and he had made arrangements to have supper with them.

He was at the conference venue well before the opening, and found Ken Flugle waiting for him.

'Ah, Harry, all set for your presentation?'

Harry smiled and gave him the memory stick with his presentation slides, and it was quickly set up in the projector.

'You're the first speaker, so we can set up the generator and glob – it won't take long for the energy to be loaded.' Ken looked at Harry: 'I can't wait to see the reaction of the audience, in particular the press.'

He hesitated a moment, and then continued: 'After last night I took the liberty of spreading the word amongst reporters.' Harry nodded, it didn't matter as far as he was concerned.

'Come, I must introduce you to Ian Nathan – he's the first session chairman.'

Professor Nathan was one of the world famous mathematicians at the conference. A Nobel Prize winner, he was deliberate in everything he did.

'So, Dr Ehlers, Ken tells me we can expect an exceptional talk from you. With a practical demonstration?'

'I hope so,' Harry replied diffidently.

'You'll be doing the keynote presentation – you know it's a half hour slot?'

'No ...' It was something that had escaped Harry. 'I've prepared for twenty minutes.'

'I'd forgotten that,' Ken said quickly, 'but I don't think it's a problem. Give your prepared talk – the glob will easily take up the rest of the time.'

'The glob?' Professor Nathan didn't understand.

Ken smiled, 'In an hour's time the whole world will know about the glob.'

Flugle and Professor Nathan were called away to attend to administrative duties, and Harry was left to set up his demonstration. There was an electricity supply in the podium, and it did not take long to get organised.

When he finished he found Caroline Fraser waiting for him. She smiled broadly, like a fellow conspirator who knew more than everyone else.

'Ready?' she asked. He nodded, and she continued: 'I'm looking forward to this – you're gonna wow them this morning!' Harry smiled back nervously.

She looked up at the auditorium, 'Pretty full already. Lots of people with cameras – must be the press. Ken said he'd spread the word.'

She turned to Harry again, 'I hope you don't mind, but I've also ...' She indicated to a small camera in her hand. She added quickly, 'Don't worry, just talk normally.' She gripped his arm and smiled, 'You'll be great.' Then she went off to a seat right in front of the podium.

The speakers had seats in the front row on the one side, giving them easy access to the stage when it was time for their presentations. Harry was introduced to the following two speakers, and Dr Wi sat down next to him. The conference was about to start.

The opening welcome by Ken Flugle was formal, structured and brief: the delegates were there to listen to new developments, not long-winded welcomes. Before handing over to the first session, he mentioned he was expecting an exceptional conference.

Professor Nathan took his place at the front.

'As you may know, we have had a change of schedule, since our previous keynote speaker is unable to attend. However, I believe our replacement will do more than fill the gap.'

He paused before continuing, 'Dr Harry Ehlers recently completed his doctorate at Cambridge with an exceptional thesis. However, his talk today is on something completely new. It is titled *Identifying Gravitational Field Potentials: Practical Applications*. The abstract promises groundbreaking results, and I, for one, am anxious to hear what he has to say.'

He looked around at the audience and continued, 'I've been told by Dr. Flugle to look out for the glob. That's particularly for the members of the press.' A buzz went around the auditorium, as the delegates also realised the press corps was bigger than usual.

With the scene set, Harry swallowed heavily and took his place behind the small lectern on the podium. A sip of water from the glass eased his dry throat. He looked down and saw Caroline Fraser smiling encouragingly, her camera in her hand.

Once his first slide was up he gained confidence, and he briefly described his theory, going through the main equations. The listeners were interested, though there were few who could follow all his discussion points. He worked his way through to where he could demonstrate a practical application of all his equations.

'And now,' he continued, looking at his audience, 'I've built a small prototype of the gravity machine – I'd like to give a short demonstration'. He put the little generator pedestal onto the lectern, and extracted the glob.

He paused a moment, and then held it up. He was gaining in confidence, beginning to enjoy his presentation. He smiled at the audience, 'This is the glob Professor Nathan mentioned.' A murmur went around the auditorium as people sat forward, though in truth the glob was too small for most people to see properly.

He set it up on its little pedestal, 'I'm now going to supply energy to the gravity material in the glob.'

It was deathly quiet in the auditorium as he applied power, but when nothing apparent happened a few muttered questions could be heard. Harry switched off the generator.

'There's now enough energy in the glob to lift it up about half a metre,' he explained. 'I just need to unclip the arm holding it down.'

He did that, and guided the glob to its new energy level, leaving it floating on its own, the strange green light below barely visible, but still giving it an ethereal aspect.

The audience didn't quite know what to expect. As a spectacle it wasn't that much, and yet they could somehow sense this was something very unusual. A babble of voices ensued, and some in the audience were standing up, craning to get a better look.

'Is that thing floating in the air?' someone asked. Harry nodded.

'Let us have a look,' someone else shouted. For a moment Harry hesitated, and then gently pushed the glob forward, away from the podium.

As it moved away, quietly and serenely floating in the air, people began to get an appreciation of what they were seeing. Suddenly cameras flashed and a spotlight highlighted the glob. The visual evidence of a freely-floating object served to persuade the audience this was more than just a theory: it was a demonstration of the mythical gravity machine.

The reporters present made the most of it. The *News* science correspondent wrote: '*This was an historic occasion, and no doubt yesterday's events will be played over again and again. I was privileged to be there.*

We had been given some indication by Dr. Ken Flugle, President of the APA, that the first lecture by Dr. Ehlers would be exceptional. One of my colleagues asked: "Dr. Who?", and decided to come later. I think he will regret that decision for the rest of his life.

Yesterday Dr. Harry Ehlers was unknown. There is no doubt there will be few people in the world who will not have heard of him by the end of this week. That is how fundamental his discovery is, and also underlines the impact his gravity machine will have on just about everything we do.

After a short lecture on the physics – of which I understood little – Harry Ehlers pumped gravitational energy into a cut-off metal sphere, a bit bigger than a golf ball. He christened it the "glob".

The process took less than a minute, with only a slight electrical hum during the transfer. There was total silence as the glob rose up from the table. There seemed to be a green glow around it. After a few wobbles it settled about two foot above the table, just sitting there, floating in the air.

Of course, magicians have done levitation before, and that little demonstration didn't prove anything. Someone to my right shouted: 'Let us have a look.

Ehlers looked up with a slight smile, and pushed the glob towards the audience. It stayed at the same level, just gliding through the air, completely silent. Nobody said anything, everybody just stared at it.

I was lucky, because my seat was at about the same level as the table on the stage. I watched the glob come over, slowing down in the air. Eventually it stopped in front of our row.

Everybody was mesmerised, and it was a moment or two before someone stuck out a hand and gently touched the glob. It moved away and she made a grab at it.

That caused pandemonium, and suddenly everyone wanted to touch and feel the glob. I had my turn, and I can definitely state this is not a trick. There were no wires, mirrors, magnets or anything else. The glob was floating at a particular energy level.

Somebody stuck a pen onto the glob, and it floated slightly lower, carrying the additional weight.

Physicists still have to give their opinion on the theory proposed by Dr Ehlers. It is groundbreaking stuff, and it will probably take a few days to digest what he has done. Moreover, other laboratories must be able to replicate the gravity machine.

In my book this works. I can see no other reason why the glob could float like that.'

The story carried on, with words such as 'amazing' and 'fantastic' littering the commentary. Other reporters wrote similar stories. Dr Flugle had made sure Harry's talk was recorded, and it had probably been shown on every newscast around the world. It was available on YouTube, Facebook, Google, Yahoo and every other fabric of the internet.

Comments were coming in from all sides. It was derided as a scam, called irreligious, and calls were made to ban its use. There were also claims that the ideas had already been published before, and it was not a new discovery.

However, perhaps the most emphasis was on the possible implications of the discovery. *World Today* had gathered a team of experts to speculate on what the future held.

'What this all means', the article ran, *'is fundamental change. Not just in some of the things we do, but in just about everything we do.*

At a fundamental level, it appears the gravity machine will conserve power. This is because the energy that is pumped into the gravity machine to raise it up will be available again when it comes down – minus a small percentage because nothing in nature is ever 100% efficient.

So we can expect a marked decrease in the demand for fossil fuels. It will mean a re-alignment of world power structures, with the world oil hegemony losing a lot of its control. This is also welcome news for all the climate change proponents ...

However, there is very little good news for many of our established industries. Change will be everywhere, and listed here are some of the implications that come immediately to mind, though no doubt every day there will be new applications.

Transport: Forget about cars, boats, trains and planes. This will mean a totally new way of getting about – everywhere. There will be no need for roads, harbours, stations or airports as we know them now. And the massive industries associated with all these activities will need to adapt dramatically.

The whole structure of our society has been built on the automobile. We will no longer need streets for cars and the planning of new cities and suburbs will take on a totally different aspect. It will require innovative thinking.

The enormous areas of our land taken up by roads, highways and cloverleaves will become available for other uses. Perhaps we can plant trees again.

People will be able to go anywhere: The one big thing the gravity machine promises is mobility. Border posts built around roads, airports and harbours will be meaningless – gravity machines will be able to cross anywhere, at any time. Countries will need to devise other means to identify their territories and their people.

This will also mean access to inhospitable and sensitive areas. Tropical jungles and Antarctica will be areas where you can zip in over a weekend. New kinds of control will be necessary.

Space travel becomes entirely feasible to everyone: The essence of the gravity machine is that the enormous amounts of power needed to escape Earth's gravity will not be needed – energy can be applied at a continuous low level, and slowly take a spaceship out beyond the atmosphere.

We will be able to buy a spaceship from the dealer on the corner, and head off for the moon. It will herald a new age of discovery and settlement, with all the problems and excitement associated with such activities. There will be the inevitable claims, conflicts and questions about who – or what country – owns what. No doubt there will be numerous deaths, because space is a very inhospitable place.

At a fundamental level, people will have to retrain. There are going to be enormous stresses and problems, but also enormous opportunities.'

The *Business View* had already picked up on the financial aspect. The headline in a special late edition proclaimed: *CHAOS ON THE MARKET.* Trading on most of the world's stock exchanges had been suspended as all the major motor manufacturers took massive hits. The values of Toyota, GM, Ford, Mercedes, Volkswagen, Audi, BMW, Nissan, Tata, Kia, Fiat, Peugeot, Renault ... were all down by more than 40%.

The CEO of Mercedes appealed for calm, saying the motor industry would adapt. People would still need transport, and all the gravity machine meant was a new kind of motor. It led to some rethinking, with a more positive sentiment evident.

The aircraft and shipping companies had not been as badly hit, as investors tried to assess the future. Aircraft seemed to be ahead of cars since they were already using the air, though wings would become superfluous. Could gravity machines be made big enough to transport the vast cargoes of ships? And where would they discharge their cargo? It would all take time, and in the meanwhile life would carry on as before.

However, those companies involved with road construction and maintenance were running for cover. The bottom had dropped out of their market.

The oil price had also plunged, though not to the same extent as other commodities because people realised it would continue to play a major part in modern society. In particular, uses in agriculture and chemicals would not diminish. Nonetheless, OPEC called for an emergency meeting.

The article in *Business View* ended: '*It is not clear when markets will reopen. The gravity machine is going to change our lives, and investors need to know what those changes will be, and how quickly they come about, before they commit themselves.*'

Harry could not complete his lecture, and Professor Nathan tried to restore order with little effect. Everyone wanted to inspect the glob, to handle it, push it up and down and photograph it. In desperation Nathan eventually prised it out of a reporter's hands, and marched it up to the podium where Harry was watching the proceedings.

'Take it down,' he ordered, not realising that Harry couldn't do that. However, Harry just put the glob into his bag with the other equipment, the weight of it all keeping it in place. The audience quietened as Harry came down from the podium.

Professor Nathan looked around from his position on the podium. 'This has been a momentous lecture, and I am sure we will hear a lot more about it all.' He paused, and continued slowly, 'No, that's probably an understatement – this will be news around the world.' He smiled at Harry.

'However, we have a conference program, and we need to get on with it,' he continued briskly. 'Our next speaker is Dr Wi from Columbia.'

Harry thought of taking his seat for the lecture, but Ken Flugle intercepted him.

'The reporters want a lot more information. Would you mind going to another lecture hall to answer questions?'

Harry looked at the horde of reporters around him, all of whom had ignored Professor Nathan's call for Dr Wi's presentation. There were cameras flashing and microphones being pushed at him.

It was a circus. He smiled, 'Not at all.'

Dr. Flugle escorted him out of the hall, and half the audience went with them. Science correspondents were sending their stories and their photographs to the world's press. Already the hype was building up.

A short while later Harry stood at the front of another lecture hall. It filled up rapidly, as word spread about the gravity machine. It was also apparent that it was not only science correspondents who were present: some big cameras and lights appeared.

Fortuitously the new lecture hall was higher than the big auditorium, so Harry could energize the glob again, under close scrutiny at every step. Photographs were taken from every angle, and the glob passed from hand to hand, turned around, pushed up and down and inspected minutely. If it could be taken apart, it would have been lying in pieces.

Eventually it became clear that questions also had to be answered. The hall quietened as Harry stood in the front, the glob hanging in the air to one side.

'Has your theory been tested by anyone else?' was the first question.

'No,' Harry replied, 'it will be published as part of the proceedings of this conference. It will enable anyone else to comment on it.'

'And to build a glob?'

'Of course – that's the ultimate test of the theory.'

'How long will that take?'

'A few days, maybe a week ...' Harry shrugged his shoulders. 'It depends what resources they put to it.'

'Will you help?'

'If they want me to.'

The newspaperman smiled, noting such a test would probably be the most eagerly-awaited result in history.

Harry motioned to Ken Flugle not to take another question. 'I want to add something at this stage – something nobody seems to have noticed.'

He paused, 'At this stage I don't have the means to take out the gravity energy again.'

He pointed at the glob, 'So it's just going to hang there, slowly coming down as it loses energy through the green light.'

There was a moments silence as the import sank in. 'You mean you can't take it down?'

Harry grinned broadly, 'That's right. The theory shows how to do it, but I didn't have the equipment to do it. It was also too much of a rush.'

It was light relief for the audience, and there were chuckles and laughter all round.

'It is also something which will have to be verified experimentally,' Harry added quickly. 'However, as I've said, the theory does show how to do it.

There were two or three further questions on the theory, and then the topic changed.

'There are obviously a lot of implications with this gravity machine. It is going to change our society. As such, there will be a lot of money tied into it.' The questioner paused, then continued, 'What have you done about patents?'

Harry smiled, slightly self-conscious. 'It has been patented,' he said quietly.

There was a buzz in the hall. Harry seemed such a non-worldly scientific type that few would have expected him to consider the financial aspects.

'Who holds the patent?'

'I do.'

The newspapers all picked up on this aspect. It was labelled the biggest get-rich-quick story in history as the financial experts tried to estimate what the potential earnings would mean for Harry. The numbers of dollars mentioned were obscene as they described the various options that were open in terms of patent rights. It also depended on how tightly circumscribed and comprehensively the patent application had been written.

The provisional patent had been accessed, but it required an understanding of the theory before any sense could be made of it; it would take time to analyse. Harry hoped again that he and Stephen had covered all the bases, or indeed that his theory didn't have extensions he hadn't thought about and that could be exploited.

It was late morning when the session ran out of steam as it became clear that expert comment was needed on the theory, and other globs had to be built before the gravity machine could finally be accepted. Proceedings were brought to an end by Dr. Flugle and the audience was asked to leave as no more questions would be answered, and indeed Harry was human and needed to eat and rest.

While Harry was packing up the glob, a man and a woman came up to him.

'Dr. Ehlers,' the man introduced himself, 'Jim Spriggs, and this is Angie Hathaway - we're from *World Today*.'

Harry shook their hands, and Spriggs continued, 'Amazing story, we were privileged to be here.' He had quite a florid face, with incisive eyes searching Harry's face.

'You do know what you've done?'

Harry frowned, 'What do you mean?'

'Well,' he hesitated. '... where are you staying?'

'The Uptown Residence – it's conference accommodation.'

'You'll have to move,' Spriggs said decisively. 'As of now you'll have no time to yourself if you stay there. There are going to be a million people wanting to talk to you, and to ask you favours.'

'It's the price of fame,' Hathaway added, responding to the questioning look on Harry's face.

Ken Flugle came over to join the group: he obviously knew the reporters.

'Ken,' Spriggs said, turning to Flugle, 'we were just explaining to Harry here how his life is going to change.'

'We can also help him,' added Hathaway.

Flugle raised a questioning eyebrow, and she quickly explained, '*World Today* has a suite at the Beverly Rose hotel – for important people who need privacy. I'm sure we could get it for Harry.'

They looked at Harry, who shrugged his shoulders, 'I'm hoping to go to some other sessions today ...'

Ken looked at his watch, 'Which reminds me, I have to get back to the conference as well. I didn't realise the time.'

Spriggs turned back to Harry, 'You can have the suite in the Beverly Rose – no strings attached. I really do mean it: after today you will have no privacy.'

'I'm sure you could also do with some spoiling,' Hathaway smiled at him.

'Jim and Angie are good science reporters, Harry,' Flugle came in. 'They probably have a much better idea of where this is all heading. I would take up their offer.'

Harry looked at them, and shrugged his shoulders again, 'Okay,' he said, 'but I'll have to fetch my things.'

'I'll get them for you,' Spriggs volunteered, 'you can go with Angie to the hotel.'

Harry was embarrassed by all the attention. 'It's okay. I'll need to pack up...'

'We'll take you,' Spriggs said firmly. 'Hopefully there won't be anyone at your room yet.'

With the decisions made for Harry, Hathaway phoned the *World Today* office to confirm the arrangements. Harry could hear his name mentioned, and he thought she said something about a 'major scoop'. She returned, smiling, 'It's all done.'

'We'd like to take you to supper this evening, Harry,' she continued, '... at the hotel.' She turned to Flugle, 'You're also invited, Ken ...'

Flugle smiled, 'I'm sure I can make it. What time?'

When Harry hesitated, Spriggs broke in quickly, 'How about reasonably early – say seven? You're going to be plenty tired, Harry, and jet-lag is still a factor.'

'Anything for a free meal,' Harry responded. He hoped his Cambridge friends would accept he had other commitments that evening.

Spriggs and Hathaway had a newspaper car, and they quickly drove to Harry's hotel. There were few people about, and he quickly packed his suitcase.

When he handed in his room keys, the receptionist quickly told him, 'No refunds. It's not our problem you're not using your booking'.

'Keep it,' Spriggs quickly cut in, ushering Harry away.

On the way to the Beverly Rose they stopped at a Burger King for a quick lunch. Though flattered by all the attention, Harry wanted some space and spoke little while downing his burger. The two reporters did not push him with questions, but sought rather to assess him as a person, someone they could bring to their readers.

'What are you going to do this afternoon?' Hathaway asked.

Harry smiled, 'Well, I am attending a conference, and there are some talks I want to go to ...'.

She looked at Spriggs. 'Today may still work,' she said slowly, 'tomorrow – I doubt it.'

'What she means is you're news, Harry,' Spriggs added. 'Particularly now.'

When they arrived at the Beverly Rose Harry's suitcases were quickly commandeered by a bellhop. The manager was on hand as Spriggs and Hathaway brought him to reception.

'Dr. Ehlers,' he said, 'we are privileged to have you stay with us.' He reminded Harry of Julia Roberts' hotel manager in *Pretty Woman*: someone who was familiar with celebrity, and knew precisely what was expected of him. On the other hand, Harry was overawed by the understated luxury of the reception area.

'We'll leave you now, Harry,' Spriggs said. 'They'll look after you here.' Unobtrusively he pushed some cash into Harry's hand: 'For the bellhop,' he said quietly and smiled.

'We'll see you at seven,' Hathaway added as they turned to leave.

Harry turned to the manager, who smiled broadly: 'You have the *World Today* suite on the twenty-first floor. I suggest you unpack and make yourself comfortable. We are here whenever you want anything.'

He turned to the bellhop, 'Make sure Dr. Ehlers is comfortable.'

The suite was enormous. It had its own lounge area and kitchenette, a bedroom bigger than his whole apartment in Cape Town, and a porch looking out over the city. The bellhop explained the modcons and services available, and was very happy with the tip Harry gave him.

When he was finally on his own, Harry lay down on the big double bed and stared at the ceiling: morning was a long time ago. Then he sat up, looking at the TV screen which seemed to occupy half the opposite wall space. For a moment he thought of switching it on, but quickly looked at his watch: he wanted to attend a conference talk at 2 pm. He had about 15 minutes to get there.

He quickly packed his conference bag, but when he reached the hotel foyer he realised he had no idea how to get to the conference. As he stood for a moment pondering his options the hotel manager came up to him.

'Can I help you, Dr. Ehlers?' he asked quietly.

Harry explained his situation, asking if there were busses he could catch.

The manager smiled, 'We have a much better solution.'

He turned to the reception counter, 'A limousine for Dr. Ehlers.'

A minute or two later he was sitting at the back of a luxurious limo: stretching out, his shoes couldn't even touch the front seat. He had been given a small remote, with instructions to find a convenient stopping place and then to push the button. It had a GPS, and they would fetch him within ten minutes. He smiled to himself, times had certainly changed.

Even so, the talk had already started when he entered the auditorium and sat at the back. He tried to concentrate on the subject, but became aware of other delegates turning around to look at him, whispering. The woman next to him caught his eye, 'Fantastic talk this morning,' she said, smiling. He nodded.

He stayed for another talk, and moved on to another session. Later he went to the communal area for coffee, and was overwhelmed by the number of people who wanted to talk to him. A few even asked him to sign on the programme.

A big man with a cropped beard and wearing a white shirt with a blue and red bow tie came through the crowd; it was an American image, and didn't seem out of place with all the denims and sneakers worn by most delegates. Harry immediately recognised Professor Abel Finwych from an inspiring presentation given at Cambridge the year before.

'Harry,' Finwych said, taking him by the one shoulder and steering him away from the people standing around him, 'we need to talk.'

Finwych led him into one of several small offices situated close to the communal area. There were already a lady and a man sitting around a small table, and Harry immediately recognised their names when he was introduced. All famous physicists. They indicated he should sit down.

Finwych occupied the Chair in the Physics, Mathematics and Astronomy Division at Caltech, and he had a simple proposal for Harry.

'From what I understand, you will be prepared to assist in building another glob.' He looked keenly at Harry.

'Yes, that's the way to prove it works.'

Finwych looked relieved, glancing quickly at the other two. 'We would like that to happen at Caltech. I've already spoken to the Provost, and he has agreed every possible facility will be put at your disposal.'

Harry looked at the three sitting around the table. He was being invited to the place where Hale, Millikan, Feynman and other luminaries had spent their days.

'Of course ...' he replied.

'It needs to happen ASAP,' Finwych continued, 'can we leave tomorrow?'

It was clear Harry would not participate much longer in the conference, and he nodded agreement. Finwych arranged to pick him up at his hotel the next morning.

There was only one session left in the late afternoon, with nothing that Harry was keen to attend. In any case, he wanted time to himself.

He buzzed the limousine from a suitable spot and 15 minutes later he was in his suite at the Beverly Rose. He dumped his bag on the bed, and wandered out onto the wide porch. He could see right out over San Francisco. It was late afternoon, though the summer sun was still quite high in the sky.

Below him there was movement everywhere, people doing things, important and unimportant, but mainly down there. He wondered how his discovery would change all that: in particular, would one still have peace if there were vehicles whizzing past at every level?

He sighed, and went back inside, sitting on a chair opposite the lounge TV. Everybody had told him his invention was the top story all over the world, and so he decided to see for himself.

The first channel he tried was CNN, and they had just opened a panel discussion. The first words he heard were: '... feasibility of this gravity machine. Bill, what is your take on it?'

The camera panned onto one of the panellists, someone Harry did not recognise.

'Well,' he said, 'if it's a fake it's very good. We have seen how reporters and photographers have inspected the glob. There are no wires or anything else involved. It was presented at an APA conference, which gives it tremendous credibility. Moreover, the theory is published, which means other physicists can analyse the basic assumptions.'

He paused, 'The biggest test is whether other labs can build a glob. Dr. Ehlers has said he's happy to help with such a construction, so we should know definitely within a week or so. Certainly he is entirely open about it all, which makes me believe it's genuine.'

'Then there's this rather funny situation where Ehlers can't yet take out the gravity energy he's pumped in. He says the theory shows how to do it, but we don't want to end up with all sorts of objects hanging around in the sky.' He grinned broadly.

The camera moved back onto the anchorman, 'And Ehlers – where does he come from?'

One of the other panellists, a woman, took up the cue, 'He graduated from Cambridge earlier this year with a PhD in theoretical physics. So he's got the right background. I found one of the referee's reports on his thesis: it said he had an unusual acumen for original thought. It forecast an exceptional future for him.'

'Well, that certainly seems correct!' There were smiles of assent from the other three panellists.

'Interestingly, he was born in Boston,' the woman continued.

'So he's an American citizen!' the anchor interrupted.

She smiled, 'Also a South African. His father was a history professor at Rhodes university, and married a so-called coloured woman. That was during the apartheid era, so they had to leave. He got a job in Boston, and that's when Harry was born. They stayed until the transition to democracy in 1994, then moved to Cape Town, where Harry received most of his education.'

Though it was all personal, in a way it was distant and Harry felt as though they were talking about somebody else.

'Harry has had some traumatic experiences,' the panellist continued slowly: 'While he was at Cambridge his father and mother were murdered. It seems it was some sort of family feud.'

Suddenly it was no longer distant. He felt a sense of grief, remorse and anger welling up in him. Damn, what right did they have to air all those personal details? He jabbed at the remote and the TV went blank.

He went and lay on the enormous bed and stared at the ceiling. So they were going to analyse his whole life in public. He had anticipated some interest, however, this was all way beyond anything he had imagined. He didn't like it, but realised there was little he could do about it.

After a while he packed out his clothes, which filled a small corner of the closet space. He had a luxurious shower, trying out all the different body washes, rinses and hair shampoo. It made him feel a lot better.

While dressing his cell phone rang. It had to be someone he knew, so he quickly picked it up: he saw the name "Stephen". He felt a sense of relief and elation at being able to talk to someone who had been with him from the start.

'So, Harry, this has really taken off!' Stephen sounded excited.

'Yes, I had no idea it would be like this.'

'Everybody believes in the gravity machine. It's the main talking point on every news channel.'

'I'm amazed. I thought it would take longer. That people would assess it first, and only accept it once other labs showed it worked.'

'It's the glob,' Stephen added by way of explanation. 'That little ball did it, as I said it would! It's the symbol of the future. People want to believe.'

Harry filled Stephen in on what had happened, and told him about the reporters from *World Today*, and his new accommodation at the Beverly Rose. 'It's luxury you cannot believe,' he ended off.

'Well, you better get used to it. There's a lot of money involved here.'

'I've been asked to go to Caltech to help build another glob.'

'What does that mean? That's a good university ...'

'The best, you don't know who all have been – and are – there. I'll have all their facilities at my disposal, so can't see it taking more than a day or two to build another glob. And add in the energy reversal.'

'That's excellent,' Stephen enthused. 'The sooner the basic principle is accepted, the better.'

'I've got a dinner date with two reporters from *World Today*,' Harry continued.

Stephen was quiet a moment, 'Be careful what you say to the reporters. They will dig up everything they can.'

'They seem pretty good types, and I guess I have to pay my dues for this suite.'

Harry could hear Stephen chuckling. Then he was more serious, 'I'm thinking of flying over to join you – what do you think?'

Stephen's presence would certainly help, particularly as Harry could foresee a good likelihood of all sorts of legal issues coming up.

'That would be great.'

'OK – I'll see what flights I can get.'

Stephen hung up, and Harry stared for a moment at the receiver: he looked forward to having Stephen's support.

He continued dressing, and switched the TV on again: a close-up of the base of the glob filled the screen. They were speculating on how energy was transferred to the crystalline gold evident inside. He switched off the TV.

It was almost seven, and he was hungry. He wasn't sure about the questions he would face from the two reporters, although he was reaching the stage where he didn't care. To hell with it, he would enjoy the food.

The hotel people seemed to know exactly what he was doing, and he had hardly exited the elevator when there was someone to show him to the dining room.

'Dr. Ehlers,' he was greeted at the entrance, 'it's a pleasure to have you dine here.' The others were already seated, and stood up as he came. His chair was pulled out for him to sit down.

'How are you feeling?' Ken Flugle asked the question, and Harry could sense amusement in his voice.

He grimaced slightly, 'Okay, I guess – I'm not used to all this attention. Not at a personal level. It's pretty disconcerting.'

'You had a look at the news channels?' Spriggs asked.

Harry nodded, 'Everything seems to be about the gravity machine ...'

'Not surprising,' responded Hathaway, 'considering what it means.'

Harry looked at her, and she continued, '...you know, it's going to completely change society. You must have realised it, particularly seeing as you took out a patent?'

'In a way,' he replied slowly, 'I spoke to a friend about it, and he advised me on the patent.'

'Stephen Cambre?' Harry nodded: she had obviously done her homework.

The dinner went by quickly. The two reporters didn't push their questions, while at the same time they tried to extract everything they could to try and find out more about this new world sensation, this inventor of the gravity machine. Harry enjoyed the food and the conversation, but before ten o'clock he excused himself: it had been a long day. The reporters were happy with that: they had deadlines to meet.

The personal scoop was on page three of *World Today*. Titled '*Dinner with Harry*', it had a picture of Hathaway and Harry in deep conversation at the dinner table. It was a fair article, painting Harry as a serious young man with exceptional mathematical vision and grasp of physics. He was reserved about his personal life, and in particular did not want to discuss his family.

Being the sole patent holder, he would have to make some very important decisions in the future. Decisions that would affect society as a whole.

On the other hand, society would have to adapt, and adapt quickly. Apart from the patent rights there were a myriad legal questions that the mobility of gravity machines raised. International agreements would have to be negotiated, and there were aspects such as the rights to privacy which could easily be infringed. Space beyond the Earth was now in question, with all the legal conundrums that involved.

CHAPTER 5

Harry drifted between reading the papers, watching the TV news channels and getting used to the idea that he was the man they were all talking about.

When his phone rang he recognised the UCT number: it was afternoon in South Africa.

'Hello ...' he said tentatively.

'Harry! What have you been doing!' He recognised Mrs Shaw's voice. 'Everybody's going crazy here. Why didn't you tell anyone?'

'I did, Mrs Shaw.'

'Well, Professor Swain wants to talk to you. I'm putting you through.'

He heard the clicks of the exchange, and Professor Swain's voice.

'Ehlers, Swain here.'

'Hello, Professor.' Harry wondered for a moment about titles: he was on first name terms with Caltech professors and Nobel prize winners, but with Swain everything was formal.

'Ehlers, why wasn't I informed about this gravity machine?'

'You approved my conference presentation, professor – it's all in there.' Harry was feeling peeved: no congratulations were forthcoming from anyone in South Africa, just accusations.

Swain was quiet a moment, 'I would have expected you to discuss this with me beforehand, not go behind my back and get a glob – or whatever you call it – made in our laboratories.'

It was true that he had not had official approval to build the glob, though he was told just to go ahead, particularly since it was a small job. Get a technician with time, and carry on. In fact he had done much of the work, and growing the gold crystals from his Kruger Rand had been fun, once he got used to the idea of destroying the coin. The gamma ray generator came from a completed project.

'I was told I could, professor.'

Swain switched to another tack, 'And there is the whole question of the patent rights. As an employee of the university, the patent belongs to the university.'

'As you know, professor, I have not yet received my contract.'

'You've been paid your salary, so you are an employee of the university.'

'I haven't been paid. Mrs Shaw said I could get a loan from department funds, but I've actually used my own money until now.' It was a sore point for Harry, using his savings for daily expenses. When he approached Swain about it the professor was not particularly interested.

'That is of no concern. Do not claim the patent rights again.'

Harry didn't want to continue the conversation. 'I'll think about it, professor. In the meanwhile, you'll have to excuse me – I have things to do.' He hung up.

Harry was seething. He had no doubt Swain himself had been asked by his superiors to explain the situation. He had probably blustered his way through, and had now tried to take it out on Harry. Stephen had warned him that the university would try and claim the patent.

He went and sat on the porch again. The contrasting emotions were getting to him.

A few minutes later his phone rang again: he had been warned that his phone number would soon become public property, and that he could expect to receive unwanted phone calls. He looked and didn't recognise the number, and he wondered whether to answer. Eventually he did.

'Dr. Ehlers! I'm Jeff Anslin from the *Broadsheet*. Fantastic achievement! Can I ask you a few questions?'

Harry hesitated, and decided no. However, he had no reason to be rude, 'Sorry Jeff, I can't talk at the moment.'

'Some other time – just let me know ...'

'Sorry.' He hung up, and decided only to answer numbers he knew. He had to have a filter put on his cell phone.

Abel Finwych called soon after seven am.

'Harry, how're you doing? How soon can we get going?' It was obvious he would have everyone hopping to get construction started.

Harry didn't want to be rushed. 'I must still have breakfast – I'll be ready about nine.'

'Right ... We'll pick you up at nine. I've arranged accommodation for you in a hotel close to the university.'

After a shower, Harry went down to breakfast, and was ushered to a table on one side of a half-empty breakfast hall.

'It's a buffet, sir. Help yourself to anything you like, and the staff are there to help prepare any cooked breakfast.'

It seemed everyone knew who he was, and as he was getting his fruit and yoghurt he had to respond to calls such as 'Fantastic invention!' and 'You're certainly going to change things.' Fortunately, most just required a smile or a 'Thank you' in response; the last thing he wanted was to start a conversation.

However, while waiting for his cooked eggs a woman came up behind him.

'You know, Harry, you're going to have tremendous opportunities to do good with your invention.'

He looked around: she was smiling at him. Very attractive, with short blonde hair, little make-up, probably in her late thirties. She was calm and at ease with herself, holding a plateful of food.

'You actually have the chance to change history, which very few people can do.'

She saw she had his full attention, and continued, 'There are a lot of powerful men out there. They're going to pressurize you to accept their way of doing things.'

He was intrigued, and his eggs weren't ready, 'Go on.'

She was suddenly more intense, 'They want the system as it is, and your invention is going to change things. They won't like that, and they'll do everything they can to keep the status quo. You know, the power distribution – men in control.'

She paused, sizing him up, 'You seem reasonable. Don't be taken in by what they can offer. Just remember they're a bunch of greedy pigs only interested in themselves.'

'Ultimately, they need you - you don't need them. Decide for yourself what you want to do. Do it for humanity.'

With that she smiled, and went off to join two other women at a nearby table. They all looked at him as she turned around and indicated to where he was standing. He smiled back.

When his food was ready he went back to his table to finish breakfast. He was getting a lot to think about – things that were not in his normal horizon.

Abel Finwych was waiting for Harry at nine in a chauffeur-driven limo. It seemed a pity to desert his luxurious suite after such a short stay, but packing up his few belongings did not take Harry long. He kept a few of the newspaper articles.

'Fortunately one of our donors has a jet in San Francisco, so we don't have to wait for a commercial flight to LA.' Finwych grinned at Harry, 'You're going to have to get used to all this moving around.'

They took off as soon as they were comfortably settled on board the private jet. It was a short flight to Los Angeles, and Finwych took the opportunity to quiz Harry on what was required for a glob.

'I've looked at your paper, Harry, and I must confess some of the conclusions are not entirely clear to me. Please explain the process.'

After describing what was required, Harry added he thought they should continue with gold as the gravity material as it had been shown to work.

'Makes sense to me,' Finwych replied.

'It doesn't seem very complex to make such a glob,' he continued. 'When do you think it should be ready?'

'If everything is there, it shouldn't take more than a day or so.' Harry paused, 'It obviously depends on the size, I presume something small is still OK?'

'Perhaps a bit bigger than your glob ... the press have to see it!'

Harry was quiet a moment. 'It would be nice to be able to do the reverse energy transfer – take the energy out again.'

Finwych nodded.

'That'll take a bit more experimentation,' Harry continued.

'Would you say Saturday is a reasonable time to get it all organised?'

'Putting the energy in – yes. Getting it out again - I don't know.'

They were quiet, each with their own thoughts. The low drone of the plane was unobtrusive, and Harry looked out the window: clouds obscured any view of the land below.

'You know the world's going to be there?' Finwych suddenly interrupted his thoughts.

Harry nodded: it had occurred to him.

'I don't know how we're going to organise that ...' Finwych mused. 'Our PR department will have to sort it out.'

Then he was more definite, 'We've arranged you stay in one of the hotels near the campus – it's more convenient than anything we can offer. In particular, they can ensure you aren't pestered by reporters – and others.' Harry nodded: he would go where they told him.

A Caltech car was waiting when they landed and they were whisked through the university campus in Pasadena.

The President insisted on welcoming Harry to the university. It turned out to be quite a formal occasion with the world's press invited, and after the requisite handshakes and photographs the obvious question came up.

'When will the next glob be built?'

The President looked at Finwych for an answer.

'I've discussed the matter with Dr. Ehlers, and we hope it will be ready by Saturday.'

'Will there be a formal announcement and demonstration?'

'Yes, our public relations department will organise the event – you will be notified of proceedings in due course.' Finwych had committed them to a deadline, and the President had committed the university to organising an event that would attract world-wide attention.

Nonetheless, it was apparent Finwych had accepted that the theory worked and there would be no problems with building another glob.

The newspapers picked up on the attitude, and some touted Saturday's demonstration as a non-event; nonetheless it would serve to clear up any remaining uncertainty around the gravity machine.

The deadline was tight, and Harry was introduced to some of the PMA staff before being taken to the Instrument Shop. Anything he wanted was at his disposal, and he was amazed at the range of equipment available and being developed. As such, the following two days were both exhilarating and stressful.

His demands were relatively modest, and construction went quickly, in particular since they had the glob as a prototype. They decided that *Glob Two* would be precisely the size of a baseball, with a circumference of twenty three centimetres. It had an aluminium outer surface as in the original glob, but smooth and polished this time, and one of the technicians with time on his hands contrived to simulate the stitching on a baseball.

On Thursday evening Harry registered at The Pasa hotel, situated on Del Mar Boulevard and within easy walking distance of the campus. He had a suite on the fourth floor, and again the luxury of the situation made him smile: his mother would have tippy-toed around, not believing ordinary mortals had access to such affluence and service. It seemed he would have to get used to it: probably not that difficult, he thought.

By Friday afternoon the first tests were conducted. Under Harry's guidance the glob rose up half a metre above the test bench, to the applause of the watching technicians and research staff. They spent the next few hours playing around with it as it gradually lost energy. Harry had to pose for photographs, on condition none of this information went outside the lab.

Initially, Harry found he could walk around Caltech and its environs without getting attention. However, the hype started building up with TV coverage and press arriving and people began recognising him in the street, with reporters tailing him to the hotel. Once inside he was assured of privacy.

On Friday evening Stephen arrived, having booked into a suite at The Pasa adjacent to Harry.

'So, how's the world shaker?' Stephen greeted him. Ever the lawyer, he wore a fine new suit.

'I bought it for the trip,' he explained. 'You know, in the kind of negotiations I anticipate, you've got to have the right image.'

He looked at Harry. 'You're actually lucky. You can wear what you like because that's you – you've made it your image, and in any case everybody knows who you are. I'm the support staff, so got to do things right.'

Harry smiled: it seemed inverted logic, but if that's what Stephen thought, well that was fine.

'South Africa's gone crazy about the gravity machine,' Stephen chuckled. 'Nobody had the faintest idea it was going to hit the world stage.

'Poor Professor Swain,' he continued. 'He's been interviewed on a couple of occasions – claims it's all a departmental thing, though it's obvious he didn't have a clue.

'I've been lucky. I've managed to keep a low profile, and left before anyone realised what part I played in the patent.'

'What are you going to do here?'

Stephen hesitated, 'Well, I hope you agree, I'm seeing some people about the patent to assess the demand.'

Harry nodded, 'Sounds like a good idea – it's not something I'm interested in.'

'I'll report back. You need to be informed.'

The newspapers, TV and the web were full of expectations, though it seemed the news of *Glob Two* had already been leaked since there were quotes from 'confidential sources' that it had already flown. A reliable report stated NASA had put any further rocket construction on hold.

However, Harry wanted to get the reverse transfer finalised, and was in the lab early on Saturday morning. Abel Finwych found him there with some of the technical staff.

'So, Harry, I hear everything is going well.'

'Reasonably, but I'm not sure about the reverse transfer. It seems that when the transfer starts, it will probably work like a chain reaction, releasing all the energy in a burst of gamma rays. Up to now I haven't managed to initiate it.'

'You'll have to be careful with gamma rays.' Harry nodded.

Finwych broached the subject of the presentation, 'PR have booked an auditorium that will seat about one thousand five hundred. Various groups have been allocated space, with the press and TV channels right in front.

You'll do the actual presentation, the President will introduce the show, and I'll also have a chance to say something.'

He smiled as Harry turned to look at him, 'It will be a show – that is what they all want. There will be cameras, big screens the whole lot. Afterwards there will be questions – are you happy with all that?'

'Do I have an option?'

'No, I guess not.' Finwych hesitated a moment, and continued, 'You will be paid for your work, probably about fifty thousand dollars.'

Harry's face lit up, 'Fifty G? You serious?'

'Considering the occasion, that's actually very little. The audience will be billions, and it's history in the making. And it's all your doing.'

Harry smiled, 'Thanks – that's great!' It was more money than he had ever had in one lump sum, and the first real indication of rewards from his invention.

However, Harry was more concerned with his experiment. He had energised *Glob Two* and put it onto a low frequency modulator, with an arm extending into the hole in its base.

'I don't want to be too close if it discharges gamma rays,' he said. 'Can I get a long lead attached, so I can operate the system from a distance?'

'Of course.' Finwych immediately organised the lead, and a short while later a group clustered around Harry as he varied the low frequency modulator. A gamma ray spectrometer had been set up to measure any emitted radiation, since they would not be able to see it.

It took a while, and suddenly there was a low 'whooof' and a clunk as *Glob Two* dropped down onto its pedestal. A collective sigh rose from the watching group, and one technician quickly fetched the spectrometer.

'Not bad,' he said, looking at the instrument. 'I wouldn't want to be too close.'

Harry was elated: the last hurdle before the presentation had been crossed. However, it was almost noon, and the presentation was set for two in the afternoon. He gave instructions for everything that needed to be set up in the auditorium, including his old glob.

Harry returned to the hotel for a quick shower and put on clean clothes; he was glad he had brought more than one good shirt, otherwise he would be wearing the same one he had at the APA presentation.

He found Stephen waiting for him, and after a quick lunch they were picked up and taken to the auditorium. A throng of people surrounded the building, with cameras and microphones everywhere and the auditorium nearly full. There seemed to be an admittance policy, and Harry was quickly whisked through while Stephen went to find a seat in the upper stalls.

The Caltech President and Abel Finwych were already there, and they quickly informed Harry of the procedures to be followed. There was a table on the stage with both globs and their associated equipment. He checked whether everything was set up, and took his seat behind the table, watching the chaos getting some order.

Soon after two pm the mc tapped on the microphone, and gradually the audience quietened.

'Ladies and gentlemen,' he started, 'welcome to Caltech. I extend a particular welcome to the press and TV channels, because this is going out to the world. We are the lucky ones to be here to witness what is going to happen this afternoon.'

He called on the President to say a few words. He was brief, being aware that people were not there to listen to him. Nonetheless, he managed to point out the important part Caltech always played in major scientific discoveries, this being one of those major events.

Finwych took his place in front of the ranks of microphones. It was obvious he enjoyed the limelight.

'Ladies and gentlemen,' he began slowly, looking across at the throng in front of him. 'We are here today because of a remarkable presentation given by Dr. Harry Ehlers, only three days ago. Three days that have literally changed the way our world will function in future.'

'Harry provided a demonstration of a gravity machine. Of course, with the scams in the world today, what he did on Wednesday had to be shown to be real – a consequence of the major development his theory represents.'

'As the President has already said, Caltech has been asked to substantiate Harry's theory.'

He smiled, and continued, 'You wouldn't be here today if it was a scam, because we wouldn't have anything to show you. So, yes, I can confirm what the news media have already been telling the world – it's for real. The anti-gravity machine of science fiction is no longer fiction.'

At the back of the auditorium someone started clapping, and this was quickly taken up by the rest of the audience. Then someone stood up, and soon everyone was standing and clapping.

Finwych was grinning broadly as he calmed the audience. 'This is the first time a scientific theory has had such a standing ovation.'

'I must now hand over to Harry and Glob Two. Or perhaps it should be called *baseball glob*, because it is precisely the size of a baseball.' A titter went through the audience at the implication in terms of the US participation.

Harry had been watching the audience in amazement, and now stood up to do his thing. In fact, it all went easily, being essentially a repetition of his previous demonstration. He was wired up with a microphone and said little new, pointing out the original glob and proceeding to work with baseball glob, a name that seemed to have met with immediate favour.

Everybody in the audience had watched Harry's original demonstration at least once, and so knew precisely what was going to happen. The only difference was the lighting, the cameras and the TV screens, picking up every little movement that he made.

A short while later, baseball glob floated amongst the audience. As before it was photographed and pushed around, with the imitation stitching on the surface getting maximum exposure. However, attention soon palled, and the glob was returned to Harry on stage in expectation of something new.

He stood looking at the audience as it gradually quietened, his left hand resting on baseball glob as it floated alongside him.

'There is still one thing missing,' he eventually said, 'and that is the reverse transfer. In other words, getting the gravity energy out again.'

'The theory does show how it can be done, and with all the expertise here at Caltech we have managed to put something together to extract the energy.'

He paused, and continued, 'It worked this morning, though it wasn't very controlled. In fact, it's almost like nuclear fission, where a kind of chain reaction sets in, and the energy is released in a split second. Mainly in the form of gamma rays.' A buzz went around the audience, as the import of the words set in. Later news headlines showed it to be an unfortunate choice of words.

Harry looked around at Finwych, who nodded, indicating he should go ahead.

'Okay, so what I'm going to do is set up the table in the centre of the stage, and control the process with a long lead.'

Now the audience was really interested, with something new and the possibility of fireworks.

The table with all the equipment was moved back from the front of the stage, away from the front row of the audience. Harry clipped baseball glob onto the low frequency modulator and positioned himself some ten metres away from the whole structure.

'You won't see much,' he said as he started the modulation process. 'Gamma rays have a very high frequency, so there won't be a flash of light. Perhaps some noise.'

It took a few moments and then there was a loud 'whoomp' and smoke enveloped the little structure on the table. Baseball glob fell down on its pedestal, which itself fell over, allowing the glob to roll off the table with a thunk onto the stage floor.

The audience erupted as cameras zoomed in. Harry and Finwych both moved forward, Finwych to pick up the glob and Harry to inspect the pedestal: he found the top arm melted away.

'Strange it didn't do it this morning,' Harry said to Finwych, pointing out the molten arm. Everybody heard him, and cameras zoomed in on the still smoking pedestal.

'More energy ...' mused Finwych. 'The glob must have been higher, with more energy.'

'That's right!' Harry responded, '... makes sense.'

He turned to the audience, smiling and holding up the pedestal, 'Well, that's the end of the experiment for today ...' There were some chuckles from the audience.

Finwych, still holding baseball glob came forward. 'Harry's right. You've seen the confirmation of the gravity machine, so that's essentially the end of the demonstration.'

He turned to Harry, 'However, Harry has agreed to answer some questions.'

A small podium was set up, with ranks of the various news media's individual microphones. Harry was positioned within the rank, and Finwych designated the first questioner.

'It seems the gravity machine is not available for immediate use – would you say there is still a long way to go before we can buy a gravity car from a dealer?'

'It depends what you mean by 'long',' responded Harry. 'This is all new. I didn't know how the energy would be released again, though I did suspect something like we saw this afternoon. We are going to have to work out how to release the energy gradually.

Then there's the gravity material – both these globs have used gold, but it's probable there are other more suitable elements. That is going to require research.

As far as actual vehicles are concerned, there will have to be an energy source on board to raise them, and to store the energy again when they come down – probably batteries. Otherwise there is no energy saving.'

He shrugged his shoulders, 'So still lots of work to get all the practical aspects operational. I imagine there are going to be many groups working on this.'

There were a few other questions on the gravity machine itself, and then the tack changed.

'The University of Cape Town has issued a statement that the question of the patent rights are still under discussion. What is your take on that?'

'Well, I haven't signed a contract with anyone and I certainly haven't signed anything relating to patent rights. I'm not a lawyer, but I believe they will have a problem showing I did any of this work under their auspices.'

'Where and when did you work out this theory?'

Harry paused a moment before answering. 'After finishing my PhD I took off about three months. Went through the middle-east, and had more than a month in the Kathmandu Valley. I had time to sit and think. With my theoretical background I could try different options – play around at my leisure. There was no pressure and this just worked out. I first wrote it up in the snow.' He smiled.

The audience was silent a moment. It seemed a strange way for a new theory to be born – out there, away from any normal academic structures.

There were a few more questions, then Finwych closed the proceedings. It had been a momentous afternoon.

CHAPTER 6

With the stress of the demonstration over, Harry slept late on Sunday morning. He found Stephen at their breakfast table, reading a newspaper.

There was only one story, and Harry was on the front page, holding up a smoking pedestal. The headline read: *PROBLEMS GETTING IT DOWN* and the story continued *Massive release of energy melts gravity machine apparatus.* It continued that there were problems utilising the gravity machine, and extracting the stored energy could be likened to a nuclear reaction.

'That's not what I meant – why do they always get it wrong?' Harry moaned.

Stephen smiled, 'It's what you said – you have to choose your words carefully.'

After the demonstration there had been an informal celebratory dinner with the President of Caltech and selected staff. A large screen was erected, and the whole event was re-shown. Harry was getting used to seeing himself in the news, and chuckled with the others when he saw the look of apprehension on his face anticipating the release of gravity energy from baseball glob.

The demonstration had been beamed around the globe, and was watched by billions. The gravity machine was a proven reality, and utilisation was the main story. People wanted to know when they could buy their own gravity car.

They were interrupted by Abel Finwych coming into the breakfast room. He had more or less free reign in the hotel, and marched over to their table. He nodded to Stephen in greeting, and sat down at their table.

'Harry,' he said, coming straight to the point, 'we have to work out some sort of a schedule for you. You've obviously got a filter on your phone, but it's bedlam out there. The university's inundated with calls for information and access to you. They don't seem to believe in Sunday any more.

But first, do you have a draft of your paper?'

Harry nodded, and Finwych continued, 'We can't wait for the Proceedings to come out. You need to submit it to the APA so they can put it on the web.'

He shifted his big frame on the chair, 'However, there is another request ...'

Harry looked at him, and he continued, 'Most of the calls have been for more information – from corporations, state institutions and individuals. All want to know how the gravity machine works.'

He chuckled, 'Quite a few have come from fellow physicists: they've suddenly found themselves in high demand, because everybody thinks they're the ones who can explain it all, and can help companies make gravity machines. But they also have to learn, and reading your paper won't be enough.

So, what everyone wants to know is if you'll conduct a workshop on your theory.'

'Hell, Abel,' Harry replied slowly, 'I don't know the answers. There's still a lot of practical work that needs to be done on other materials and elements. And there's the reverse transfer ...'

'Agreed, but you're streets ahead of anyone else. It's a whole new way of thinking, and people need to be taught – there's nothing like direct contact and answers to questions.

So, what's your schedule for the next week or two?' Finwych asked.

Harry was quiet for a moment, 'I don't have a schedule. I intended going to the canyon-lands, just drifting around. My flight back to South Africa is on Tuesday - in nine days.'

Finwych looked relieved. 'The workshop is very important, and you can do the canyon-lands next time.'

He thought a moment, 'We'll probably need a week to set it up. So how does Monday-week sound?'

'I want to leave on Tuesday,' Harry responded. 'Let's see how it goes.'

'I'd like some input into this,' Stephen suddenly interjected. Both Finwych and Harry looked at him.

'The companies attending will want to manufacture gravity machines. So they'll be subject to patent rights,' Stephen continued.

'What does that mean?' Finwych asked.

'They'll have to sign an agreement to use the procedures in Harry's theory.'

'With what implications? Are you talking about charges?'

Stephen smiled: Finwych was quite belligerent in his questioning. 'Nothing specific yet. I've worked out some general structures, but we'll have to refine it when the whole process becomes clearer.'

Finwych didn't respond, and looked at Harry.

'Patents are standard for new discoveries,' Stephen added. 'Charges will need to be negotiated.'

'You'll have to talk to PR about the arrangements,' Finwych said eventually. 'Of course you're right, in the end it revolves around money. The physicists coming to a workshop will be hired by the big companies, wanting to know how the gravity machine can be exploited. So they'll be paid.'

'They'll be paid well,' Stephen responded. 'The companies are there to make it work, so people can buy their gravity machines. It's what the eventual users want.'

'And they'll make a lot of money.'

'Of course,' Stephen said irritably, 'That's how the system works. Whoever gets there first will make the most money. The companies will be throwing billions into research, and will want to get it back. With a profit.'

He looked at Harry, 'And you are the one who deserves most of it.'

'There's a lot of work that still needs to get done before a practical gravity machine is available,' Harry said quietly. 'It will need more than just physicists: engineers, chemists, the whole lot ...'

Finwych looked at him, 'Well, you're at the top of the list of every company wanting a physicist to guide them. You can name your price.'

Harry frowned, 'That's actually not what I want to do. I'm quite happy to help generally, but I don't want to become involved in details of production.'

Finwych smiled broadly, 'Fortunately you can choose what you want to do.'

They decided on an all-day workshop on the following Monday, starting at nine in the morning and ending at five in the afternoon. Details would be worked out by PR, with input from Stephen.

Harry also had something else on his mind. 'I've been dabbling in some other extensions to the theory, and thought I need to publish it. It won't take more than a few days to write up. Perhaps I could do that here as well.'

Finwych looked at him in amazement: 'Something else? Along the same lines?'

'More cosmological - dark matter and things.'

'Fantastic! Ferdi is actually editor of the *Journal of Cosmological Research*. He'll be happy to publish something from you.

Perhaps you could give a colloquium to the department?' Finwych continued. 'I know you're going to be busy, but it would be fantastic – you could include the new developments.'

Harry thought about it, 'Okay ... later on in the week.'

Finwych stood up to go, but then added, 'Just a word of warning, Harry: there are mobs of reporters, press, TV etc. out there. Not a good time to go for a walk.'

He smiled, 'Enjoy the quiet while you can.'

When Finwych had gone, Harry turned to Stephen: 'What charging structure do you envisage for the gravity machine?'

'It's not that obvious,' Stephen replied slowly, 'but it's important the correct structure is set up at the start. This is a fantastic opportunity, and you need to make sure you make the most of it.'

'I don't want to profit unnecessarily – it has to be fair.'

'Harry, there's no such thing as an unnecessary profit. Everyone will be very happy to pay, and we need to use the opportunity fully.'

Harry didn't answer, and Stephen continued, 'We'll probably have charges per unit, but there are a large variety of uses, from cars to ships to space travel. Then there are the different users, from individuals to companies and countries.'

'Incidentally,' he added, 'you can be sure the defence forces of the world will be very interested in your workshop. This is going to have a major impact on the way wars are fought in the future. However, I don't know how to check on armies or air forces and make them pay. International patents can be complex.'

As expected, Harry was kept busy and he was allocated an office in the PMA Division. It was well-appointed and functional, and he couldn't help the comparison with his office at UCT; he wondered for a moment if there would be changes when he went home.

When Harry was engrossed in a particular problem he worked to his own rhythm, which often meant midnight and early morning sessions and sleeping whenever he was tired. He found an all-night café where he could get a coffee at any time, and it was convenient to be able to order food at the hotel on a 24-hour basis.

In the Division he enjoyed the interactions with students and staff in the cafeteria. While he was accorded immediate respect, they had seen it all before, and everybody was treated as an equal.

His top priority was to complete the paper on the cosmological ramifications of gravity potentials, and for that he had to use the library. He obtained accreditation, but found unwelcome interest in him from other library users. He was used to working on his own without interruption, and now it seemed whenever he looked up he found people staring at him; in particular, pretty girls who smiled at him were the most disconcerting.

Initially he tried to avoid the host of photographers and journalists who were always waiting at the door of the hotel, but on the second day he walked outside, sat on the steps and asked them what they wanted.

They took their photographs, and he answered questions. The query quickly came up, 'Why don't you twitter, or have a blog?'

Harry hesitated, 'It's not something I've even thought about – or something I want to do. Why would anyone want to know what I'm doing the whole time?'

The questioner stared at him: 'Because that's the world out there. People want to know.'

'Well, you can tell them, not me.'

His response was widely reported, and he was amazed to find there were some people who thought he had an obligation to be a part of their lives. That they somehow had a right to know what he thought and what he was doing.

He said he would be available to answer questions if anything major turned up, and in return asked that they respect his privacy. However, the attention didn't decrease at all, since he was now seen as a relatively soft target and there were many paparazzi looking for sensational news. With his odd hours he worked a lot in his hotel room.

He signed in to his g-mail account, but soon stopped as more and more e-mails rolled in: obviously his address was common property. Out of interest he opened a few, and they ranged from congratulations from complete strangers, to others who asked questions about what he was going to do, and some asking for largesse. He didn't reply to any, and after a while swapped to Facebook.

At least there was some filtering, and he knew the friends who offered congratulations and comments. He could laugh at some, and enjoyed responding, mainly to the effect that he was as surprised as anybody at all the reactions.

He saw the comment from Melissa: '*Harry, sweetie, what have you done? Congratulations – you've turned the world upside down!*' He smiled as he thought of her saying that: it was so like her. In her independent way she would have relished being a part of it all. No, that wasn't right – she would have taken control of everything.

He wrote back: '*Nothing much Melissa – just some equations. Don't know why everyone is making such a fuss.*'

His colloquium was set for Thursday afternoon. He had more or less finished his paper: it was actually quite short, building on his previous results and speculating about cosmological consequences.

The auditorium was packed, and it was clear there were some people who attended just to see him. Abel Finwych suggested he start by going through the fundamentals of his theory: it was all still very new, and would bring his audience on board. So for Harry the preparations for his lecture were based a lot on what he had already done.

He was proposing all matter resided at a basic zero gravity potential, and that applied energy could lift it to higher levels – it was similar to adding heat energy to raise the temperature of a body. In the initial stages of the big bang at the origin of the universe the large amounts of energy available raised the gravity potential of the early matter, and he speculated that the so-called *dark matter* in evidence was actually not matter at all, but rather elevated gravity potentials. Its effect on the space-time continuum acted as though it was matter, and this also explained the lack of radiation emanating from such sources.

Afterwards, the audience was invited to snacks and cocktails, and Harry found himself talking to some of the department's post-graduate students.

'Harry,' one of them asked, 'tell us where you really got these ideas.'

'Yes,' another added, 'you can't expect us to believe all that crap about Kathmandu. That you sat in the snow and enlightenment came.'

For a moment Harry was dumbstruck. Then he asked, 'How do you get ideas?'

They looked at each other, 'We talk, bounce ideas around. Work on things. The best place is right here where we get stimulation – where we can ask others.'

Before Harry could respond Ferdi came and grabbed him by the arm. 'S'cuse,' he said. 'Harry, we need to talk about paper.'

'That's fantastic ideas,' he continued enthusiastically when he had Harry alone. 'Such a nice explanation. When can I get the paper?'

'I've got a draft ready – I can send it to you tomorrow.'

Later, when Harry walked back to the hotel he wondered about new ideas. In many ways he had always been a loner, and his most productive times had been when he could think without interruption. It took time to connect all the dots, but it was easiest when he alone had the pencil.

Stephen hadn't been to the colloquium, and arrived back later. He had been doing his own things over the last few days, and Harry knew he was in communication with other patent attorneys and talking to various interested parties. He was also heavily involved in the preparations for the workshop.

'The university is having a lot of pressure put on it in terms of who to invite,' he complained. 'In particular, the government here is trying to exclude any involvement from countries which could be regarded as hostile, or who could get an economic advantage. I don't think any representatives from China or North Korea will come.'

It again made Harry realise just how all-encompassing the interest was in the gravity machine. As always, politics had to intrude.

'Who will be there?' he asked.

'Mainly companies, with first allocations to US firms. As expected, there will be a large contingent from the US army, air force and navy. I found that out by accident – you probably won't know the difference. Also NASA.'

'Incidentally,' he continued, 'I've arranged a payment of two hundred and fifty thousand dollars for your services.'

'You're joking ...'

'Harry, you just don't know what the implications are. We could have asked a hundred times the attendance fee, and they would have been glad to come.'

'Three hundred thousand dollars in a week! That's over three million Rand.' Harry smiled, 'but I'll take it.'

'Get used to it.'

Stephen paused and added, 'I had no idea how big this would become. I hope you don't mind, I've put myself up as a contact between you and outside.'

'That's great – I appreciate it.'

Stephen nodded, he thought Harry would agree.

'Fortunately I could point most of the queries to the workshop,' he continued, 'and they've got a whole secretariat doing the organising.

There are others – non-profit groups, and I've even had queries from some UN bodies.'

'Why?'

'Well, some of the UN structures could be affected by the gravity machine. The economic implications have already been substantial, and the way countries react could affect payments and the way business is done – a whole new power balance. They are putting out feelers in terms of what the machine can do. I really couldn't comment – they wanted to talk to you.

To give you an example of the kinds of thinking going on: there is speculation that vast ships will be able to take fresh water into the deserts. They'll hang there, gravity-feeding water to all sorts of cultivations. So land values in those areas are suddenly taking off, though I don't think any sales have been made.

Droughts could also be a thing of the past, which will affect a number of UN agencies. It will impact on countries and the movement of people and the establishment of new cities. This part of California could benefit enormously, though the ecological implications are unknown.

Nonetheless, preparations have to be made for all possibilities...'

Harry sat there, amazed. While he had been working on his paper and the colloquium he had not been following the news, and had avoided TV and newspapers. It seemed there were many people who were seeing all sorts of possibilities opening up.

'There are some other smaller items ...' Stephen added.

'Such as?'

'The Smithsonian wants your glob as a display item.'

Harry smiled, but Stephen continued, 'You may think that is mundane, but any museum displaying your glob will have thousands pouring in to see it. So it means money and prestige.'

Harry remembered his discussion with Professor Swain, 'I guess it depends on UCT – they probably have first rights. Though that's my Kruger Rand!'

Stephen nodded: 'The Smithsonian is already negotiating with Caltech for the baseball glob, though I guess it will be displayed here first.'

He paused. 'Finally, there is one more thing ...'

Harry looked at him questioningly.

'You're a public figure, and you know what happens to public figures nowadays.'

'What?'

'They go on talk shows...'

'Nooooo.' Harry had thought about the possibility, though it was not something he wanted to do. Particularly not after some of the analyses of his life that he had seen.

'Yes! I've had calls from every major channel in the US and elsewhere. Essentially it's up to you.'

'What do you suggest?'

'It could be fun – depends how you handle it. You've been comfortable with TV at your presentations. You can decide what topics they can't raise. It will be a big coup for any network that gets it, so they won't want to antagonise you. Most of all you're not a controversial figure.'

Harry thought for a moment, 'It may work,' he said slowly. 'But I don't want the topic of my parents' death brought up.'

'Anything else?'

'Nothing I can think of now.' He added, 'Not longer than half an hour.'

'I'm sure they'll accept that. Can I go ahead and organise it?'

'Who will you get?'

'I'll see who Caltech PR recommend – probably time it for Saturday night.'

On Friday Harry joined Stephen in the workshop preparations. To ease Harry's load, Finwych would start by working through the basic theory, assuming a reasonable level of mathematical ability and familiarity with physics and atomic structure. Harry would take over when it came to his new ideas.

Many specific questions had been raised by the proposed participants, and the agenda was designed to try and answer these as best he could. However, there were as yet no answers to many of the questions, and Harry could only suggest proposed directions of research to try and find solutions.

In the afternoon they returned to their apartment and had coffee on the porch. Stephen took a call on his mobile, something about a meeting the next day.

'You'll be interested in this, Harry,' he said after he had hung up. 'I've got a meeting tomorrow with Sir Richard Straithwaite. He's chairman of a group called B2O, standing for Beta to Omega. I've looked it up on the web, and they apparently control a large group of international companies, or otherwise companies and organisations have a voluntary association with them – not clear which.'

'Anyway, they claim to cover all aspects of man's endeavour. The group is called B2O and not A2O – standing for Alpha to Omega – because god should be at the start, and they can't control Him.' He chuckled.

'However, there's no doubt they are extremely powerful, and should be taken seriously. He specifically asked that you also be at the meeting – think you can make it? It's at ten at his hotel.'

'Do I have to?'

'It'll give you some idea of the kinds of negotiations that lie ahead. You're going to have to make decisions.'

Everything else seemed to be in order. 'Okay,' he responded.

That evening they had supper at the Finwych's. His wife Harriet turned out to be a famous photographer, who hugged Harry when he arrived, exclaiming, 'Ah, at last I get to meet this famous person!

But,' she continued, 'no physics this evening. I do not want to listen to things I don't understand.'

Nonetheless, she took some photographs of Harry – because that was what she did. Another invited couple were also not scientists, so conversation covered a variety of topics from art to politics. As was his norm, Harry listened rather than talked, relaxing in the exuberant company.

Midway through dessert Stephen received a call from the Caltech PR manager: it was arranged that Harry appear on the show *Thommo Talk* the following evening.

Harriet clapped her hands, 'Fantastic, Harry! He's good, and you'll enjoy it. You must just relax and give as good as you get.' She punched the air to show what she meant.

Harry had heard of *Thommo Talk* since it was syndicated in many countries. However, he had never watched it, and had no idea what to expect.

CHAPTER 7

Sir Richard Straithwaite was an imposing figure. He wasn't particularly tall, but he was obviously strong and fit, which, as it turned out, was all part of his belief of a 'healthy mind in a healthy body'. His short, greying hair, tailored grey suit and upright bearing gave the impression of someone not to be trifled with.

'Ah, Harry,' he said shaking Harry's hand in a firm grip, 'it's good to see a fellow Jesus man doing so well. I went down a few years before you.' His smile showed a perfect set of teeth.

It took Harry a moment to realise that he was referring to Jesus College in Cambridge, where he had been a student. Obviously also Sir Richard's old college.

'Of course ...,' Harry smiled back. '... it's a good place.'

'And you must be Stephen Cambre,' Sir Richard said, turning to Stephen and shaking his hand.

'Thank you for coming, gentlemen,' he continued, leading the way to a small boardroom in his hotel suite.

'I've arranged for any kind of tea, including your South African *Rooibos*. Or anything else you want.' He turned and looked at them, 'Just not alcohol at this time of the morning.'

Stephen decided on *Rooibos* tea, while Harry settled for coffee: good, fresh filtered coffee. Sir Richard only drank Earl Grey. A waiter on hand returned a short time later with the order and fresh scones and strawberry jam.

They settled into the comfortable chairs around the table, and Sir Richard came straight to the point.

'Harry, you've done something quite extraordinary, something most people can only dream of doing. Your discovery will change the course of human history – you've probably realised that from the interest in the gravity machine.'

He paused a moment, and continued: 'However, there are all sorts of ramifications that flow from your discovery. Such abrupt changes can destabilise the order we have in our society, an order that has taken centuries to establish. We must guard that the power balances are not upset, otherwise untold strife can ensue.

There are power blocks – not only countries, but international companies and groupings. Some of these power blocks ... well, I regret to say it, are basically evil. Their intent is to destroy our western civilisation, and replace it with narrow-minded undemocratic systems. We cannot allow that to happen.'

He looked keenly at Harry and then at Stephen. Stephen nodded, but Harry looked down at his coffee: he had always been wary of generalisations, and this seemed to be one of those.

Sir Richard leaned back and took a sip of tea before continuing.

'The gravity machine represents a hiatus, a definite break, in the way our society has been developing. We must recognise there are forces out there who are seeking a new world order. It's similar to the development of the atom bomb during the second world war: there is going to be a rush from companies and countries. The one's who win will have an enormous advantage, and could destabilize our society'

'I'm sure we agree with you, Sir Richard.' Stephen looked at Harry.

Harry was uncomfortable with the direction the conversation was heading. His father had always told him to treat people as individuals, and not to categorize them into groupings, on whatever basis.

'I would hate to see the gravity machine used as a means of gaining power,' he eventually replied.

Sir Richard leaned forward, 'Then you must ensure the technology doesn't give them an advantage. You must fight these evil forces with us.'

Harry didn't want to be browbeaten, 'The technology is out there for everybody. I firmly believe that making it freely available is the only way to stop anybody from gaining an advantage.'

Sir Richard took another sip of his tea, studying Harry and Stephen.

'Possibly – provided everybody plays fair,' he responded slowly. 'What concerns me is that somebody – or some group – could get an advantage and force their opinions on society.'

Harry shook his head, 'I don't see it that way at all. Not as far as the gravity machine is concerned, anyway. If the basic knowledge is provided to all, I have no doubt advances will occur over a wide front. People have different ways of exploiting a situation, and in our free society ideas will flow. It is only in regimented societies that structures could be developed to suppress people.'

'It is those regimented societies that are the danger.'

'Then we can't be prescriptive, and be regimented ourselves,' Harry replied. That is why I think it's such a good idea to hold these workshops and get the new ideas out there – to everybody.'

'I think you are being idealistic,' Sir Richard replied. 'In the real world people don't play fair.

Only the future will tell,' he continued after a moment. 'Nonetheless, Harry, you must realise you have the knowledge at the moment, and all I ask is that you are careful how you use your expertise, and who you help... You cannot be too careful.'

'I agree. But I do believe that putting ideas out there for everybody is the way to go.' It was not in Harry's nature to be confrontational.

Sir Richard smiled, 'Possibly... But have another scone – the strawberry jam is a speciality.'

Indeed, Harry could not resist another scone, and put blobs of butter on it with lots of jam. It tasted good. Stephen still had a piece on his plate, which he ate slowly.

Sir Richard sat back, 'That is the one subject I wanted to broach, and in the end it will depend on the detail and how it is done. Harry, please consider carefully to whom you give knowledge. The stakes are very high.'

Harry nodded, his mouth full.

'However, I also want to talk about something different,' Sir Richard continued. He waited a moment to collect his thoughts.

'You may not have heard of B2O, because it generally operates in the background. Basically, it is a coming together of like ideas, and our members join on a voluntary basis because they accept the framework and the beliefs we espouse. We extend throughout the civilised world, and we have members in governments and corporations at all levels. So it is true to say we have an influence on many decisions that are made both nationally and internationally.'

'I am the designated spokesman of B2O, and I have been asked to put a proposal to you – specifically on the way ahead for the gravity machine.'

He waited a moment for any response from Harry or Stephen. When none was forthcoming he continued, 'Firstly, we want to make sure that some – shall we say "undesirable" – groups don't take advantage of your good intentions. We have already touched on some of those aspects, and we trust, Harry, that you will be careful about disseminating the secrets of the gravity machine.'

Harry nodded briefly, and it seemed to satisfy Sir Richard.

'The next aspect concerns the patents themselves, and here I believe we can definitely help you,' he continued slowly.

'You see, the patent is only the first stage, and actually collecting your rewards is another story entirely.'

'I'll give you an example of what I mean. You've patented your discovery, but any proceeds from that patent depend on companies and countries actually recognising the legal right given by such patents. Not all countries are signatories, and you are going to find there will be many who will ignore any rights you have flowing from the patents. You need to maintain the present structures, and have the clout to enforce them.'

Stephen nodded: he had obviously identified such possibilities.

Sir Richard let the import of his statement sink in, and then continued, 'That is why it is important to maintain the present social order, something to which B2O is committed. We would like to see the proper utilisation of the gravity machine for the benefit of humanity.

We propose taking over the control of the patent, ensuring all the rights are properly administered. Harry, I want to emphasize it won't stop your involvement in working on the gravity machine, – in fact it would probably mean you could spend more time doing what you want to do, and not have to worry about patents and finances.'

He turned to Stephen, 'And you could join us in administering the patent.

For this privilege – and I use that term because I mean it – we would be prepared to offer an immediate down payment of eight billion British pounds. This would not preclude your involvement, Harry, and you will be a member of the Board. We also envisage additional future payments when we see how things develop.'

Harry looked at Stephen, raising his eyebrows: eight billion pounds, over one hundred billion Rand, more money than he could ever dream of.

It took a moment for Stephen to answer, 'Thank you, Sir Richard. That is a most generous offer, particularly in terms of the administration of the patent. I'm beginning to find it's quite a minefield.'

They both turned to Harry. He was unsure of what to do, and didn't like being pressurised. 'Well, yes,' he eventually responded. 'It is a lot of money. But we can't make decisions yet. Give me time to see what happens.'

Sir Richard nodded, 'I don't expect an immediate answer, though we must know soon. There are developments where we need to be involved from the start.'

They concluded their tea on that basis.

Harry had some minor items to clear for the workshop on Monday, and afterwards met Stephen at a restaurant near the university for a light lunch.

'So, what do you think of Sir Richard?' asked Stephen, as they waited for their order.

Harry took a while to answer, 'Eight billion pounds is a lot of money.' While the newspapers had speculated on his possible earnings, it was the first time such a definite amount had been identified.

'It's reasonable in terms of what the patent is worth. But remember there will probably be more, much more.'

'I'm not sure about B2O,' Harry continued slowly. 'On the one hand they want to stop other groups from getting control, but it's essentially so they have control. Who's to say their ideas are the best?'

'Well, we don't know. It's becoming apparent we'll have to get help to administer this thing. It's big, and it's international.'

Harry nodded. He chewed on a mouthful of food, and continued, 'You know, I met people like Sir Richard at Cambridge. They're born into privilege, and they have this natural air of superiority ... they expect people to accord them respect just because they were born.

It actually pissed me off at times,' he added vehemently.

Stephen looked at Harry in surprise: it wasn't often he expressed emotion so forcefully. But he didn't elaborate.

'So?'

'So I think we should wait. See what else comes up.'

'Okay. However, I think Sir Richard is an impatient man.'

Stephen changed the subject, 'You ready for this evening?'

It took a moment for Harry to realise he was referring to the talk show.

'Not really,' he replied diffidently. 'I wish I hadn't agreed.'

You'll do fine.' Stephen assessed him and added, 'You should get some new clothes for the occasion. It'll boost your confidence.'

Harry hated buying clothes because he always seemed to buy the wrong thing. However, after lunch Stephen steered him to an exclusive-looking men's tailor. Harry was immediately recognised, and when Stephen dropped the word that he was going to wear the clothes for his live show with *Thommo Talk*, the whole store buzzed.

'I just want something casual,' Harry protested at all the attention.

'Dr Ehlers, I can assure you we have just what you want.'

After 30 minutes even Harry had to admit the result was very comfortable. A V-necked light purple T-shirt with some highlights, dark slacks and brown shoes made him feel good. It was all packed into an exclusive-looking bag.

'You can put it on after you've had your hair done,' the tailor said. He gave Harry his card, 'Remember to give it to Thommo for the credits.'

'So,' Stephen grinned when they had left the shop, 'to which hairdresser do you want to go?'

'I'll wash my hair myself, thank you,' Harry retorted.

At five pm a limousine came to pick Harry up for the short drive to Los Angeles. Tom Hallman, alias Thommo, was there to meet him.

'Welcome, Harry, and thank you for the opportunity to have you on board. I'll introduce you to the other guests, and we'll go on for the first half hour. Then you come on for the next half hour.'

There were three other guests on the show, and Harry was relieved to see the familiar face of Ken Flugle; the other two were Jackie, a local politician, and Chris, an industrialist. Harry was left with a PR person, watching from a lounge area while the others set the scene for the first half hour.

The panel discussed the advent of the gravity machine, and Ken told of his first contact with Harry, 'I needed a replacement keynote speaker, and read the abstract of this recent PhD graduate from Cambridge.'

'Harry Ehlers?'

'Yes. He made some unusual claims, and I contacted his ex-supervisor. He told me if Harry said something, then I could believe him. The most amazing thing was his claim to have built a gravity machine. Completely matter-of-factly as though it was nothing unusual.'

'When did you first see it?'

'On the Tuesday evening before his presentation. I knew this was something big, and informed the press.'

'And the rest, as they say, is history.' Tom turned to the others for their opinions.

Chris was the first to respond, 'You know, the most striking thing about this development is that nobody knew about it. Not a clue. Then suddenly there it was. And it had all of us ducking for cover, not knowing what the hell was going on. We still don't know. But everybody is speculating.'

Tom smiled, and turned to Jackie.

'I agree,' she said, 'politically it has enormous consequences, and we actually don't know the details. It's going to touch every facet of our lives, but we can't plan because we don't know. Power balances are going to shift, and the movement of people will put all sorts of pressures on countries and their national boundaries.'

'And what about space?'

'Yes, well, that is truly exciting,' Jackie continued. 'It opens up all sorts of possibilities for exploration. A whole new frontier. But a political quagmire, and very dangerous.'

There were a couple of ad breaks, and then Harry was steered out onto the set. He found himself in front of a wildly clapping audience as Tom led him to his seat.

After they were settled, Tom asked, 'How does it feel to be the centre of attention all over the world?'

'Weird.'

Tom grinned, 'Yet we know so little about you. You're a theoretical physicist – I have trouble saying that – but what does it mean?'

Harry described briefly what he did, and it calmed him somewhat. He didn't particularly enjoy the next questions on his personal likes and dislikes, particularly when Tom leaned back in his chair and looked at the audience, 'Now, the question all the girls want to hear – are you in a relationship?'

Harry shook his head, 'No, not at the moment.'

There were screams from the audience, and one girl in front shouted out, 'I'm free tonight, Harry!'

Tom looked at the audience again, 'Anyone on the horizon?'

Harry grinned, 'No.'

Tom also smiled, waving at the audience, 'All you girls have a chance. However, you'll probably have to be able to think.'

The ad break came, and Tom indicated they would continue with more general topics involving all the guests.

It became clear both Jackie and Chris were uncertain why Harry thought it would be some time before gravity machines were available to the public. After all, it had taken Caltech less than two days to build baseball glob.

'It depends on what you call a long time. It won't take long for other globs to be built, and much bigger ones as well. I'm talking about commercially – being able to go to the local shop and buying one off the floor. I could be wrong, but getting a controlled reverse transfer will take time. Remember it will need energy storage on board,' Harry responded.

The overall impact of the gravity machine was unclear, since new opportunities seemed to be opening up every day. However, it was important that industry, local laws and international agreements as well as society itself adapted. Moreover, the changes were required before any gravity machines came generally onto the market, and in that case it would be fortunate if all the utilisation problems were not solved quickly.

'Well, I'm sure we are going to see a lot more vehicles in space from different countries which won't give a damn about patents or human rights,' Jackie added. 'The UN is going to be fully occupied trying to legislate. So time is good.'

Tom summed it up at the end, thanking all the participants, and commenting that 'the world will be watching and awaiting developments.'

Afterwards, on the way back to Pasadena Harry contemplated the evening. It was more of the same thing, people expecting him to be part of their world. He wasn't sure whether he liked the idea.

Sunday was spent in preparations for the workshop. Each of the participants would be issued with an information pack, which included Harry's paper and some additional documentation. The emphasis was different to his previous presentations, being directed more at the possibilities of future research to enable utilisation of the gravity machine.

Abel Finwych would help in organisation and presentation. Nonetheless, the prospect of seven or eight hours of intense lecturing was daunting.

'Harry,' Finwych told him, 'we are going to have a wide range of knowledge and mathematical abilities out there. So I suggest we start with some basics to make sure everyone is one board. That's where I can help you.'

And so it proved. It was a diverse group of people who registered on Monday, and it was apparent language could also be a problem. Some of the groups knew each other, though everyone was there to get as much advantage for themselves as possible, because in the end they would be competitors.

Finwych's imposing figure served to set some discipline in a group not used to taking orders, and he began proceedings. He had brought himself up to speed with Harry's paper, and for the first hour or two he went over the basics required for an understanding of the later theory.

Harry watched from the side, and while the majority seemed appreciative of the approach, there were some in the audience who were irritated with a repetition of established theory.

After a tea and coffee break Harry started developing his own theory. He deliberately progressed slowly, in part to keep everybody with him, but also because he was wondering how to spread it all over the allocated hours. He invited questions as he went along, knowing it would indicate if his message was getting across.

At the end of lunch he was approached by a man in military uniform, who introduced himself as Colonel Alan Winburger from the US Air Force. He came straight to the point.

'Dr Ehlers, I must congratulate you on your incredible work. However, you're an American citizen, and you should think about what you owe America. Not only America – the whole free world.'

'I'm also a South African.'

'Yes, I know that. But you were born here. That must mean something.'

'It means a great deal to me,' Harry replied slowly. 'I'll always be grateful for what America did for my family.'

'Why don't you stay here? You can help us develop the gravity machine. You can help the free world maintain its freedom. There are threats out there, and we cannot let them get ahead of us.'

'Colonel, you have some very good people here – people I'm proud to call my friends. I'll help them as much as I can. I don't want to get involved in international politics, or take political sides.'

'It's not a matter of politics as much as maintaining democracy. There are autocrats and religious fanatics out there who want to impose their thinking on our society. We cannot let that happen.'

'Colonel, I believe in democracy as much as you do. I'll certainly help as much as I can, but I don't want to join any side. Believe me.'

It was not clear whether Colonel Winburger believed Harry or not, but fortunately the call came to continue with the afternoon session and Harry excused himself.

Harry now introduced baseball glob to the participants. As before it was pushed around and inspected, and everybody was allowed to take photographs. The function of the crystalline gold was explained.

However, Harry and Abel Finwych made sure they only put a limited amount of gravity energy into baseball glob, so the reverse transfer could proceed without damage to the new pedestal.

'Gravitational energy is absorbed by the nuclei of the atoms,' Harry explained, 'which is why the wavelength of the generating radiation has to be so short – hence the gamma rays. On the other hand, it is the crystalline structure of the molecules which interacts with the modulating radiation to release the energy – hence it has a much longer wavelength.'

'I believe changes in the crystalline structure, for instance the addition of other elements or impurities, will enable a more controlled release of energy.'

The rest of the afternoon was involved with discussions of what was required in such a modified crystalline structure. Harry was the first to admit his knowledge of molecular and crystalline structure was limited, and that there were many in the audience who were much better at identifying possible structures which would work. However, it also became clear that discussions were restrained, since the different groups were not prepared to provide information which might benefit competitors. The directions for research had been identified, and they would be able to return to their laboratories with ideas of where to go.

Later, after the last participant had left, Harry felt totally drained: he had worked hard for his money.

'That was well done, Harry.' Abel Finwych came and sat down next to him. 'It's been a long day, and you deserve a rest.'

Harry smiled at him, 'Thanks Abel – a lot was your doing.'

Stephen came and joined them: he had been working in the background with the Caltech PR. 'All very successful,' he said. 'I've heard a lot of positive comment. Even some suggestions of a follow-up ...'

'No thanks,' Harry replied vehemently. 'Let's get something to eat, and then I'm going to crash.'

Later, when they were back at *The Pasa* Harry told Stephen: 'My flight to Cape Town is tomorrow – I'm going to be on it.'

CHAPTER 8

On Tuesday morning Harry packed his bags. He had done everything he had to – the conference presentation, building baseball glob, confirming his theory, the colloquium, talk show and the workshop. All in two weeks. It seemed he had been away an age, and he felt the need to be on familiar turf again.

He contacted the airline, and changed his flight to depart from Los Angeles and not San Francisco. Then he called Abel Finwych, confirming his decision to leave.

'I can understand, Harry. The last two weeks have been a roller-coaster for you, and you did indicate you wanted to go back today. What about lunch before you leave?'

'That would be welcome.'

They had lunch in the university cafeteria, with a number of staff members from the division joining them. Harry suddenly wondered about his decision: these were stimulating, intelligent people with whom he enjoyed interacting. What would he find in South Africa?

'I have no doubt we'll see you here again,' was Finwych's parting comment.

Stephen had a number of meetings arranged for the next few days, and he intended spending some time on the east coast. He would keep contact with Harry, and in any case would probably return to South Africa within a week.

A university car took Harry to the airport in the early afternoon. He didn't want any special treatment, and was relieved to stand in the ticket queue, pushing his own suitcase forward as the queue advanced. Nobody recognised him, or if they thought they did they quickly erased the thought: Harry Ehlers would not be queuing there with everybody else.

At the check-in counter he had to hand in his ticket and passport. The girl took his documents, and as she started typing she stopped with her fingers in the air. She looked at him, back at his passport, and brought her hand to her lips in amazement.

'Oh my god,' she said, 'You're Harry Ehlers – you're the gravity man ...'

'Please,' Harry said urgently, trying to keep her quiet, and looking around whether anyone else had heard. '... just give me my boarding pass.'

She quickly realised he did not want his presence advertised.

'Of course, Dr Ehlers.' She hesitated, and took a piece of paper off her desk.

'Just give me your autograph – nobody's going to believe me.'

Harry took the piece of paper. 'To Millie,' she smiled, indicating where he should sign.

He quickly wrote the requested *To Millie* and signed his name. Happily she produced his boarding pass.

But if Harry thought he could continue incognito he was mistaken. The airline had rules about nefarious or important passengers, and any employees recognising such passengers were duty-bound to inform their manager. They could then decide whether it required further action.

Harry's case required further action. They couldn't let such an important world figure travel in economy class, and a little later when Harry was sitting at the boarding gate two airline officials came up to him.

'Dr Ehlers,' the first one announced rather loudly, so that other passengers turned to stare. 'we're honoured to have you fly with us. Please allow us to upgrade your flying experience.'

'I'm fine ...' Harry began lamely, realising his cover was blown.

'You'll actually have more privacy,' the second official added quietly, understanding Harry's predicament.

Harry grimaced, but the second official had already picked up his hand baggage. He stood up and followed them to the VIP lounge. He could feel the stares of his fellow passengers, and heard his name mentioned.

In spite of what he felt, Harry had to admit the VIP lounge was more comfortable. He sat in an upholstered chair, and in the short time before boarding enjoyed some juice and a couple of snacks. More than that, his privacy was respected, and he could carry on reading his magazine.

Boarding was easy, as he and the few other first class passengers were ushered in first to the front of the plane. He had a wide window seat with correspondingly wide armrests. The air hostess smiled broadly as she helped him to his seat.

'Good to have you on board, Dr Ehlers,' she said in a broad southern accent, 'I guess you're going to change flying for us.'

He smiled back, 'I hope for the better.'

'We'll see.' She went to help another passenger.

The man in the adjacent seat had heard the conversation, 'You're Harry Ehlers?'

Harry nodded.

The man was quiet for a while. 'That's a hellova thing you've done,' he eventually said.

Harry shrugged his shoulders, but the man continued, 'No, really. I'm involved with banking and investment, and you've turned our world upside down.'

He smiled, 'If I had known what you must have known, I'd have made a fortune in the last week. That knowledge was worth billions.'

Harry turned and looked at him: fit looking, of indeterminate age, balding with hair greying at the temples. This was another unthought of consequence of his discovery.

'Really? Billions?' he asked.

'Yes,' the man replied. '... while others have lost billions. You're not very popular in some parts of the world. Not your fault, but most people don't like change, or having to adapt.'

Harry didn't answer, and the man continued, 'I guess you haven't been following the financial pages - there's red all over some industries. In many ways it's what business is about, though generally industries get some warning. This came from one day to the next. Good companies have gone to the wall just because they were in the wrong business.

As I say, it's not your fault, and it's exciting stuff. Most of the stories have been about opportunities, and there are enormous possibilities. But it's knocked some companies totally.'

The man considered Harry keenly, 'You're not going to be short of money – have you thought what you're going to do with the money from the patent?'

'What do you mean?' Harry responded. 'What do you do?'

'I run my family's business – mainly investments.'

'Inherited business?' Harry said it with a touch of cynicism, feeling peeved he should now feel guilty for the changes caused by the gravity machine.

The man looked at Harry, deciding not to take offence, 'In a way yes, it depends what you do with what you're born. Life isn't fair – some people have a lot and others very little. You've used your mathematical abilities to develop your theory. I inherited money, and I've used it to build a thriving company.'

Harry felt embarrassed, 'Sorry, I didn't mean it that way ... what I meant was, people need to work, to earn their rewards. It's just some people I've met feel they're entitled to rewards, just because they were born.'

'No offence taken.' The man smiled again, 'I agree with you entirely. People just start at different levels – whether they move up or down depends on them.'

The announcements indicated they were ready for take-off. Harry was surprised how quiet it was at the front of the plane, and he sat back to enjoy the experience.

'Is this your first time in First Class?'

'It shows?'

'I have a cousin who's a scientist – he doesn't fly first class.'

'They bumped me up here.'

The man hesitated. 'That's one of the strange things about money,' he said, and added quickly, 'and, of course, fame.

It's the same old story,' he continued, 'unto them that hath shall be given. You'll find now you have enough money to buy anything you want, you won't have to because people will give it to you.'

When Harry didn't respond he continued, 'You need to understand money, because you'll have a lot of it in future. It's alive, and it needs respect. It's got emotions, and it doesn't like greed – it'll kick you in the teeth if you want too much of it.

So accept what money can give you, but don't be ostentatious – don't abuse it.'

The train of thought intrigued Harry, 'So what should I do?'

'That depends what you want to do.' He studied Harry seriously, 'You're in a unique situation, it could make or break you. My guess is you're fed up with your new situation, and you want to get back to what you consider normality.'

Harry nodded, attentive now.

'Don't,' the man said. 'Accept this is normal now. Don't fight it, or you'll be very unhappy. There are millions who envy your situation, but they're probably the ones who would squander it all and achieve nothing.

You're intelligent, you must decide what you want to do – not what other people want you to do. And what you want to do mustn't have the sole objective to get more things or money – that's when greed kicks in, and money kicks back.'

He hesitated a moment, but the look on Harry's face made him continue. 'Money and wealth will support you if you have greater objectives. You must control it, work with it. That all presupposes stupidity is not involved.'

He smiled, 'It looks like supper is served.'

Harry looked up and saw the stewardess hovering around, waiting for their orders.

The supper was delicious, and the conversation didn't continue. Afterwards the man went to the toilet, and Harry asked the stewardess who he was.

'That's Hamish Prentiss: probably one of America's richest men,' she replied. 'Very pleasant, not showy at all. You've heard of him?'

Harry shook his head.

'Not surprising,' she continued. 'He doesn't flash his wealth around. Also a philanthropist, I've heard.'

Harry relaxed as the realisation came that he shouldn't fight first class. He was accepted, and didn't have to prove anything to anybody.

Prentiss came back, and Harry suddenly thought of something.

'Do you know the B2O Group?'

Prentiss stopped where he was clipping in his safety belt, 'Sir Richard Straithwaite?'

Harry nodded.

Prentiss continued with his safety belt, 'Why do you want to know?'

'We've had an offer from him.'

'To take over the gravity machine?'

Again Harry nodded.

Prentiss didn't respond immediately. He completed adjusting his safety belt and made himself comfortable, looking straight ahead.

'That's a powerful group,' he eventually said slowly. 'They have interests all over the world ... in all sorts of fields. Stands to reason they would want to control the gravity machine.'

'Is that good or bad?'

'I can't tell you, I've always avoided dealing with them.'

Prentiss was serious now, 'You must do what you think is best. This concept ... this gravity machine you've invented ... it's big. You know, I don't believe anyone can conceive how it's going to change society. Controlling all that will give tremendous power.'

'Snacks or something to drink?' The stewardess smiled at them.

Harry ordered a cappuccino, one up on his normal cup of coffee; he saw Prentiss order a glass of water.

When the stewardess went to another passenger, Prentiss turned to Harry again.

'Harry – you don't mind if I call you Harry?' Harry shook his head and Prentiss put out his hand: 'I'm Hamish.'

Harry smiled as he shook the proffered hand, 'Yes, I know, the stewardess told me.'

Prentiss looked up briefly to where the stewardess was standing in the cabin, and continued, 'I can't hope to understand what you've done, but I can understand some of the consequences. Moreover, I doubt whether there will be any total control over what people ... companies ...

countries do with your gravity machine. However, within the structures of our society what you decide to do with your patent will have vast ramifications.'

Harry didn't quite understand what Prentiss was driving at. The older man looked at him intently.

'Whatever happens, you'll be unbelievably rich and famous. Don't rush into anything until you can see what's happening.'

He paused, and continued slowly, 'Something like this needs to be for the benefit of humanity. More important even than that, it needs to be for the benefit of our planet. Do you know what I mean?'

'Climate change?' Harry was aware of the arguments around the topic, though he hadn't followed the details.

'Much more than that. We are on the verge of wiping out so many different species that in the end we will wipe out humanity. The gravity machine offers a chance at a massive change to everything we do. Along the way there'll be different options, and we need to ensure we make the right choices.'

He stopped and looked at Harry, 'You'll no doubt be involved in making some of those decisions.'

Harry felt uncomfortable. All his life he had made decisions where he understood the options and felt he could choose logically what was best. Moreover, the consequences essentially involved only himself, and he accepted that responsibility. Now it seemed Prentiss was implying the whole of humanity would be affected by what he decided; no, he actually included the whole planet.

Harry shook his head, 'I can't control how people use the gravity machine.'

Prentiss smiled, 'You may think so, but that's another strange thing about money: if you're rich people automatically think you know the answers to everything. And your name is associated with the gravity machine, so you'll be involved. Even if you don't know anything about the other topics.'

The stewardess arrived with their drinks and some snacks, and their conversation stalled. Prentiss took out an Ipad and became immersed in his work. Harry mulled over what he had been told, and fell asleep in the wide, comfortable chair.

He awoke with the announcement that they were about to land in Miami.

'Sleep well?' Prentiss smiled at him. Harry nodded.

'Harry, I didn't mean to preach earlier,' Prentiss continued. 'The decisions you make are very, very important. For everything we do – and there aren't many people who can claim to be in that position.'

'Most importantly, don't rush into anything without knowing precisely where you're going.'

The plane landed, and while they were taxiing to the terminal buildings Prentiss caught Harry's eye.

'If you need any support at any stage, I'd be glad to help.'

Harry considered the offer, involuntarily wondering if there were strings attached. He had enjoyed their conversation, and in any case the man didn't need any money – he was rich enough.

'Thanks, I'd appreciate that.'

Prentiss took out his card, and then held back a moment, 'Please don't give this to anyone else – it's got private numbers.'

Harry nodded.

'Well, good luck.' They shook hands, and Prentiss left as soon as the doors were open. Harry followed slowly: he had some hours to kill before his next flight.

News of Harry's flight was carried on to South African Airways, and he soon found himself in the corresponding VIP lounge. However, he didn't object and let himself be carried by the flow. As Prentiss said: enjoy it.

His flight was scheduled for a late take-off, and he had a few hours in the lounge. He found a wi-fi area, and went onto Facebook. However, he was now getting overwhelmed with friends' requests and some contacts who seemed to be writing something every few hours.

He saw the response from Melissa: '*Harry, sweetie, you need to visit Cambridge and tell us all about the equations.*'

He thought for a long time how to respond. The memory of Melissa excited him, although passion had not been one of the great hallmarks of their relationship: in many respects she had been too controlling. He wondered for a moment if her parents would still find him wanting.

However, he had moved on. The three months travelling had matured him, and the student-life in Cambridge was past. Moreover, the last two weeks had been another lifetime in the making, and he was moving in spheres that beforehand he didn't even know existed. On the one hand it was exciting stuff, but on the other hand it irked him that everyone wanted a part of him. His new mantra said he should move with it, accept it all but move with it and keep control.

He wrote back: '*Thanks Melissa – yes, it would be good to visit. Not now – there is just too much happening.*'

When his flight was called he again made his way to the exclusive area at the front of the plane. He avoided conversations with other passengers, and fortunately the seat next to him was unoccupied. After a midnight meal he had a good sleep, and awoke to a breakfast spread.

He was drinking his coffee when the steward came over with an urgent message.

'Dr Ehlers, I have to tell you the Deputy Minister of Science and Technology will be welcoming you when we land in Cape Town.'

The cup of coffee stopped in mid-air. 'Why ...?' he asked. His peaceful return home had received an unwelcome jolt.

The steward smiled, 'For what you've done – for South Africa.'

There was nothing he could do about that, and he spent the time mindlessly watching movies and playing computer games. After lunch the steward came to him again.

'The Deputy Minister is the Honourable Angie Ramabola, and she will receive you in the arrivals concourse.' Harry hoped he wouldn't be expected to make any speeches.

There were a few clouds around as they approached Cape Town, and as always he found himself entranced with the whole Table Mountain massif and the way it rose out of the Cape Flats.

After the plane landed he was whisked out to a separate entrance to the terminal building. As he entered the concourse he saw a low stage had been set up, on which some official-looking people were sitting.

Flashes started going immediately from a phalanx of reporters who had gathered at the entrance: the news of his return had obviously been broadcast. He was ushered straight onto the stage. Curious onlookers stopped to stare at the proceedings, and it occurred to Harry denims and a T-shirt were probably not the appropriate clothes to wear; at least his mother would have fretted over the choice.

Deputy Minister Angie Ramabola was a large lady, dressed in a bright floral dress. She laboured out of her chair and enveloped Harry in an embrace. Then she turned to a lectern rigged with microphones at the front of the stage.

'Dr. Harry Ehlers, we welcome you home,' she began. She looked around at the members of the press and media, happy to be the centre of attention.

'This is indeed a proud moment for South Africa and all Africans' she continued. 'Congratulations, Dr. Ehlers: you have used the wisdom of Africa and built a gravity machine which will change the world.' She turned and smiled broadly at Harry, who stood behind her, wondering what he would have to say.

'The world will sit up and take note now of what Africans can do. You have been born and raised here, living proof our education system is world class.' Obviously no-one had told her of his past.

She paused a moment and continued, 'What you have done will shake the world. No one anywhere had any idea of what you were doing. As a true son of Africa you have built this new gravity machine – that will enable us to fly without wings or jets. It is an amazing invention, one that will change history.'

She turned again and gestured at Harry, 'You see – this is the talent we have in South Africa. We don't need foreigners to teach us anything.'

Harry blanched: now what? South African politics and prejudices coming into the mix? The deputy minister smiled at him, a large conspiratorial smile, and continued, 'Dr. Ehlers has been raised in

Africa, he has learnt the African wisdoms and the African truths. These are much better than anything we can get from the west.

Now, this gravity machine will be for the benefit of all Africans. No longer will we have to beg for assistance from anyone – they will come to beg at our door. It will change everything, and from now on we must be taken serious.'

She paused a moment, indicating to the reporters and the microphones and cameras, 'You will see Africa will take its rightful place as a leader in the world. Dr. Ehlers has shown what we can do.'

She stopped rather abruptly and beamed at him, and Harry realised he was expected to respond. She vacated her position in front of the mikes, indicating he should take her place. He moved forward reluctantly, wondering how to answer and not offend anyone.

'Thank you Minister ... uh ... Deputy Minister,' he began slowly. He looked at the faces in front of him: 'Indeed, I have benefitted from my upbringing here in Africa ...' He was learning quickly about the platitudes of public speaking.

'I have just given the ideas – people all over the world will use the ideas to build gravity machines. It will benefit Africa, but not only Africa. I hope it will ultimately benefit humanity as a whole.

More than that, it should benefit our planet,' he added as an afterthought, remembering what Prentiss had said. He hesitated, not quite knowing how to continue.

'Does that mean it won't be under the control of big business?' a reporter demanded.

Harry was happy for the interruption, 'I hope not – nothing has been finalised yet.'

'When can we buy a gravity machine car?' another query came up.

'I don't know – there are still lots of details to be worked out. The workshop on Monday indicated potential directions for research.'

Other questions followed, which Harry answered as vaguely as he could. In particular, he could not clarify whether UCT had a claim to the patent rights, or for that matter whether he actually had a position at the university.

'You have to stay in Africa,' a journalist added. 'The Deputy Minister has indicated it's very important.'

Harry looked at the speaker, a young woman in her twenties or thirties. Why was there this insistence on nationalism, or some sort of continent-wide identity? It was a cloying sentiment stifling a world-wide humanity.

'I live here because this is my home,' he replied. 'The gravity machine is just an idea – and that idea doesn't have a home. It can be used anywhere in the world.'

'The rights must remain here,' a man responded forcefully. 'How will they be controlled?'

Harry shrugged his shoulders, 'I don't know – no decisions have been made yet.' The continued insistence on controls and rights was becoming tedious.

'What are you going to do with all the money?'

Harry smiled wearily, 'I haven't seen any – I'll let you know when I do.' He was now getting fed up with the situation, and continued, 'You all need to understand I don't know how this will pan out. There are still lots of decisions to be made, not necessarily by me. So that's all I can say.'

He stepped back, looking at the Deputy Minister. It took her a moment or two to take up the cue.

She quickly came up to the microphones, 'eh ... yes, Dr Ehlers. Thank you for your contribution. I think you can see how we value your work.'

However, it was apparent she had concerns about some of his replies, 'You must understand it's important that something born in Africa must always remain in Africa. So the gravity machine must remain African.'

She looked at him and he nodded: it was not something he was going to argue about. In any case, he didn't see he had any way of dictating what would happen.

There were still some journalists who wanted to ask more questions, but Harry felt his arm taken firmly, and he was guided through the throng.

'Come, ladies and gentlemen,' a voice said at his side, 'Dr Ehlers has had a long flight. Allow him the opportunity of some privacy.'

The reporters opened up a passage, respecting the man guiding Harry. When they were through Harry looked at him: he was quite short, in his late twenties or thirties, and beginning to show a bit of weight. He was wearing a smart grey suit, and in the manner of African men had shaved his head. He had a wide congenial smile, and Harry smiled back, 'Thanks.'

'I'm Mac,' he said, shaking Harry's hand. 'We have a lot to talk about. But first: how're you getting home?'

It was one of those things Harry never organised specifically, since there was always some form of transport available. 'Oh ... probably bus ... or taxi', he replied.

Mac shook his head, 'Not good enough – come with me, I'll take you.'

Harry found his bags had been taken through customs, and his entry documentation had been cleared.

It turned out Mac was the leader of the national youth league. Harry was introduced to two other league members, who took their places in the front of the new BMW taking them back to Cape Town. Harry and Mac sat in the back seats, and Harry thought wryly he should get used to being chauffeured in expensive cars.

'Now, Harry,' Mac said when they were on the main road out of the airport, 'the Deputy Minister was serious when she said this gravity machine of yours must remain in Africa.'

Harry frowned. 'How can it remain in Africa? It will be built and used all over the world.'

Mac smiled patronisingly, 'Yes, it will be built all over the world, but the benefits must come to Africa.'

'Some benefits will certainly come to South Africa ... and Africa.'

'No,' Mac repeated, 'most of the benefits must come to Africa.' He was serious now, leaning towards Harry. 'I've been thinking about this, and how we can help our people here in Africa. They're the ones who've been suffering since colonial times, and they're the ones who must get the benefits.'

'How ...?'

Mac smiled again, leaning back in the seat. 'As you know, we have a successful system here in South Africa to benefit previously disadvantages people. It's called black economic empowerment or BEE, and it's helped a lot of our people to share in the wealth of the country. We can have the same thing for Africa – anybody who wants to build your machine will have to have Africans on their management boards.'

'Only black people?'

'Oh, you know what I mean – not the whites.'

Harry stared at him. He recollected why the name 'Mac' had been vaguely familiar. He was not a political animal, but did remember reading about Mac Manyi, who had used BEE to get himself onto various corporation boards, milking the laws requiring equity in business. He was using the system to make millions for himself.

Mac sensed some reticence, 'Don't believe what you read in the press – it's all lies about the system being corrupt. We are actually empowering our people, and the whites don't like the way black people are succeeding – they want to keep us down.'

He was silent a moment. 'You must have had it in the USA – being a coloured person.'

Harry thought of his parents, and the way they had tried to keep racism out of their lives.

'How will you select the people – the Africans – who benefit?'

'We have systems in place to find the most deserving cases. You must know it's not only for individuals - whole communities benefit.'

'Why can't deserving groups be identified anywhere in the world?'

'Harry, it's all in history. Africa has been downtrodden for so long it deserves first chance.'

'You give people a chance who show they deserve it. You don't give people money just because of skin colour or because they were born somewhere.' Harry was irritated by the whole entitlement argument again.

Mac looked at Harry, 'I can see you don't understand the situation. People have to be empowered – they have to be given a chance to prove themselves.'

'That's fine. One can support schools and institutions where people learn to do things themselves. That enables them to progress – you don't just give them things.'

'You need to have people in the controlling boards of all the big companies who can see the policies are implemented. Otherwise it's all just talk, and the companies won't comply with the requirements.'

'What will they have to do?'

'Who?'

'The people appointed to the boards?'

'Well, attend board meetings, I suppose. They can check they get what they're entitled to.'

They reached Harry's apartment, and he was relieved to see there were no reporters around. He took his bags out the boot of the BMW, and Mac lowered his window to take leave.

'Harry, think about what I've said – it's important for Africa. I'll come around next week and we can finalise the details of how this works.'

Harry went slowly up the two flights of stairs to his apartment. Why did people think they were entitled to wealth for no other reason but that they were born into specific groups or parents?

CHAPTER 9

Thursday dawned blustery and wet, with the first rains of the winter bringing cold weather. It matched Harry's concerns about the coming day: he would have to see Swain at the university, since his arrival back in South Africa had been on TV and was no doubt in the morning papers.

He deliberately put on his oldest denims, a pair of well-worn running shoes and a bleached T-shirt that had at one stage been grey. It was cool, so he added a floppy sweat shirt. Then he had a slow breakfast, contemplating how his life changed from minute to minute.

When his doorbell rang he wondered for a moment whether to answer since he wasn't expecting anyone. Whoever it was must have got past the apartment security doors, although that wasn't difficult. His worst fears were confirmed when a camera flash greeted him when he did eventually open the door.

'Dr Ehlers! We want to congratulate you on your achievement! Can you answer a few questions?'

Two women and a man, about his age. Smiling at him, just doing their jobs.

He decided to be straight with them, 'Look guys, I appreciate what you're doing. But I actually have nothing more to add to what's been said.'

However, one woman stepped forward marginally – she was very attractive, with her black hair in tight braids on her head. 'Dr Ehlers, will you be staying at UCT? And will the gravity machine remain in Africa?'

Harry smiled as the microphone was pushed at him, 'I haven't been to UCT yet. And all I've done is describe the process of storing gravity energy. I can't say where gravity machines will be built, but presumably by companies all over the world. Hopefully.'

'What will you do with all your money?'

'Live, I guess. What do you do with your money?' Harry was getting irritated, but was glad he was wearing old clothes.

She ignored his question, and fired the next one, 'Do you think all your money will be able to help the poor?'

'Please,' he said, 'I'll let you know if something new happens.' He was still in his doorway, and quickly shut and locked the door.

'Damn,' he thought, he was going to have to work out some way of not answering questions. Once started, reporters didn't stop.

The doorbell rang again, and he switched off the bell mechanism. He was grateful for the filter on his cell phone.

After a while he packed his bag, grabbed his car keys and gingerly opened the front door. There was no-one in sight, and he quickly went down the stairs to the secure basement parking. He blessed his 10-year-old white City Golf – you couldn't get much more inconspicuous than that. When he drove out he saw the reporters still hanging around, and they only recognised him when he had passed.

As usual at UCT he battled to find parking, and then merged into the mass of students. Fortunately it wasn't raining, and he quickly made his way to the Physics Building. It was only when he reached Mrs Shaw that he was recognised.

'Harry! Welcome back!' She hugged him: very unusual for Mrs Shaw, who generally kept her distance from students and staff.

She held him at arms length, looking at him with pride, 'You have turned things upside down here! You should have told us.' Harry decided not to tell her – again – that he had told them.

'Professor Swain wants to see you – he said to tell him as soon as you came in.'

'I'll just put my bag away.'

A minute or two later Mrs Shaw ushered Harry into Professor Swain's office. Swain was sitting behind his desk, and motioned to

Harry to sit down on the chair opposite. Mrs Shaw closed the door behind her.

'Welcome back, Ehlers,' Swain said coolly.

'Thank you.'

'As I indicated last week, I'm disappointed you didn't tell me – or anyone else in the department – what you were doing. We could have helped you, and at least we would have known what was going on.'

'I submitted my paper, and you approved it.'

Swain ignored Harry's comment, 'Then you used the department labs without permission.'

Harry decided not to reply, as no-one seemed to listen anyway.

Swain waited a moment, but when Harry said nothing he continued: 'Then there's the whole question of the patent. The fact that you did the work here at UCT automatically means the university owns the patent rights. That was implied when you came here, and you can see it in your contract agreement.' He picked up some papers on his desk and offered them to Harry.

Harry looked at the papers in Swain's hand: 'If that's my appointment contract, it's the first time I've seen it. As you know I haven't been given anything to sign.'

Swain stared at him: 'The contract was finalised in our e-mail correspondence that brought you back here. This is just a formality.'

Harry was quiet, then added slowly, 'Professor Swain, I formulated the theory in Nepal – UCT doesn't have a claim.'

Swain smiled grimly, 'That's not what our legal experts say.'

Harry was feeling frustrated and angry. He stood up, 'Let them say what they like. I have a lot to do, please excuse me.' He walked out the door without looking at Swain again.

Once in his office he locked the door, and stood at the window where he could see the pine trees on the slopes of Table Mountain. For the first time he noticed a broken latch on the window.

What a difference to Caltech! In fact, what a difference to everywhere else. He stood a while, burning, but realised he had to calm down, turn his mind to something else.

He sat at his desk and connected his laptop onto the university system. Immediately the e-mails started rolling in, eventually stopping at over six hundred. He looked aghast – what the hell was he supposed to do with all that?

He had no desire to talk to anyone about the gravity machine, and he scanned through quickly, marking the few he recognised at first glance; the rest he deleted.

One of the first ones he saved was from Andile Mangope, with *Cederberg* as the subject matter. It was short and to the point:

Hey Harry, remember the Cederberg this weekend – going Friday, back Sunday. Or are you too famous now?

He leaned back in his chair, smiling, relieved at something normal and exciting. It was just what he needed. He quickly penned a reply:

Yes! I'll be there.

He was still busy an hour later responding to mail when there was a knock at his door.

Mrs Shaw had a brief message, 'The Vice Chancellor wants to see you. She suggested lunch.'

Harry stopped: now what? However, he had no other commitments, so replied, 'OK.' It was arranged that he be at the VC's office just before one'o'clock.

When Mrs Shaw had gone he wondered what the VC wanted: more of the same, making him feel guilty about what he had done? Wanting the patent? She was a noted academic, a sociologist, but he had never met her, so didn't know what to expect.

He was at her office with five minutes to spare. The board on her secretary's office said in big gold lettering: Professor Precious Mahlangu, Vice Chancellor. He looked in at the half open door.

Professor Mahlangu was talking to her secretary, but quickly noticed Harry.

'Ah, Dr Ehlers,' she said, smiling broadly and coming over to him. 'May I call you Harry?'

He nodded as she shook his hand. She was a petite lady, with her black hair in a bun showing streaks of grey. She wore a casual cardigan over a smart pair of slacks, though it was her sparkling black eyes that welcomed Harry.

'I'm so pleased to meet you. And on behalf of the university I want to say congratulations. You've done us – and the country – proud. It's a truly remarkable achievement.'

'Thank you professor,' Harry responded; she was the first one at the university to actually congratulate him.

'Call me 'Pre',' she smiled.

'Come, Harry,' she continued, 'let's go to lunch. I want to hear all about the gravity machine.'

They went to the staff cafeteria, and joined the registrar and a dean at a table. For the first time since returning to South Africa Harry relaxed. Pre was genuinely interested in what he had done, and also knew the west coast of the USA, so could relate to the area. He again thought wryly his mother would have been furious with him for his choice of clothes, but he didn't know he was going to lunch with the VC.

'Of course I saw it all on TV – I would have loved to have been there,' Pre said. 'To see history being made'. She stopped, looking at Harry.

'The glob – the first one. Where is it?'

'At home.'

'Fantastic! I want to see it. Can you arrange a demonstration?'

'Yes ... but when?'

She turned to the registrar: 'What do you think of tomorrow morning. We'll have a private demonstration here in the staff cafeteria.'

'Could be quite hectic,' he replied. 'We'll have to keep it quiet.'

'Good, it's arranged,' she responded. 'Ten'o'clock.'

They finished the first course, and Pre became serious: 'Harry, I'd like to know what you're going to do now. I'm sure every university in the world wants you on its staff, or perhaps you're going to join a big company? We would love to keep you here, but we can't compete with places like Caltech.'

'I don't know, Pre. I came back here because I felt I belonged here, that I could do something here. Do I have to decide soon?'

'No... we can see what we can offer you. Just as long as we know you'll consider staying.' He nodded.

'There's one other thing,' she continued. '... the patent.'

When Harry didn't respond, she carried on, 'I'll give you my ideas on the matter, since I don't believe it's cut and dried one way or the other. I don't want the university to be involved in a court case fighting you. There's an awful lot of money in the whole thing, and what you've just said makes me believe you have South Africa at heart.

We need trust in this country – can we can trust you to do good by the university and the country?'

Harry looked at her, not sure what she meant, 'Do you want me to sign something?'

She shook her head. 'No ... trust. That's what I'm talking about. You seem to be ... well, genuine. Can we trust you to support the university and the country? I'm not sure how you are going to organise the proceeds of the patent, even a small percentage will be big money here.'

Harry thought about it, 'You mean you will trust me to do what I want, and that it will benefit the university.'

She smiled, 'That's right. In any case, a court battle will just alienate everybody, and I don't want that. It will only benefit the lawyers.'

'I'd like that – but it's not what professor Swain said this morning.'

She sighed slightly, 'I think you must understand professor Swain suddenly came under a lot of pressure, in particular because he didn't know about the gravity machine. However, he doesn't make the decisions.'

She continued, 'Have you decided how to handle it? What you want to do, and what to do with the income?'

He shook his head, 'No, I don't know yet what my options are – we had an offer to take over the whole patent.'

'For a lot of money, I should imagine.' Harry didn't volunteer any numbers, and she continued, 'Remember we have good people here who can help you.'

When Harry returned to his office he was much more positive: Pre Mahlangu had helped to welcome him back to South Africa.

Later when he went to the faculty cafeteria for afternoon tea he was mobbed by students and staff. There was a rumour he would be demonstrating the gravity machine on Friday, and everybody wanted to see it.

'I've been asked to demonstrate it in the staff cafeteria,' Harry responded.

'That's no good – what about the rest of us?'

One of the heads of department undertook to see if he could change the venue to accommodate more people.

Harry managed to talk to Andile, and confirmed he would be going to the Cederberg that weekend.

'I'm not sure about transport, Harry, we're pretty full up. Accommodation is available. Can you take your own car?'

'Sure – it's actually better if I'm independent.'

'Okay. You'll probably want to join the group going to the Maltese cross on Saturday. Rock climbing's all arranged. It's not a difficult route, and you should handle it.'

Harry hesitated: 'Let me see how I feel. I don't want to commit myself to anything – I don't even know if my rock shoes are still okay.'

Andile nodded, 'Sounds like a good idea.'

Harry left UCT soon after tea to pick up provisions for the weekend: the arrangements always were that everyone catered for themselves.

He was glad to see there were no reporters outside his apartment building. Once in his apartment he dug out an old box containing all his camping gear from the back of a cupboard. Fortunately most of it was still intact, even though he last used it before he went to Cambridge; his red rock shoes still gave a tight fit. Everything was set up for the weekend.

Stephen phoned, indicating he would be back on the following Tuesday. Harry mentioned the reporters at his door, and Stephen was concerned.

'That's not good, Harry – you need some protection.'

He was quiet a moment, then continued, 'We deal with a security company who have personal protection services. I'll contact them to see what can be done.'

Harry thought it was overkill, 'Do you think it's necessary to go that far? I mean, I can't be under that much threat.'

'Harry, there are some weird people around – rather be safe. Remember you can afford it.'

On Friday Harry was at the university relatively early, ready to set up the glob. However, he found the 'private demonstration' had developed into something much bigger when more people heard the glob would be on show. It was now destined for one of the large auditoriums on the campus.

'I'm not giving a talk,' Harry objected. 'People can have a look at the glob, not at me.'

'In fact, what is required is a continuous demonstration,' somebody suggested. The idea was taken up, and eventually it was arranged that the glob would be constrained within a cage, and people could walk by and inspect it. A suitable cage was quickly constructed and bolted onto a table, while a small door enabled access for both the generator and glob.

Half an hour behind schedule Pre Mahlangu introduced Harry to the packed auditorium. She mentioned this was history in the making, and that the audience would be able to tell their grandchildren they had seen the original glob.

Harry did not give a speech, merely describing the generator and the glob. Then he pumped in the gravity energy so the glob floated about a metre above the table. Thereafter it was put in the cage, and the audience invited to file past and have a look.

Knowing the value of the exhibit, not only from the gold inside the glob, but also from the historical perspective, security was tight, and ushers controlled the queue. The most common comment seemed to be: 'It's so small!'

Harry knew the glob would lose its energy in less than a day, and he would not be present to pump in more energy. He therefore instructed Dale, the technician who had originally helped in the glob's construction, how to transfer more energy when the glob came down. Dale was delighted to get the credit for his work, and Harry was confident the exhibition would be a success. News travelled quickly, particularly when radio stations picked up the story, and it seemed the whole of Cape Town would be visiting the auditorium over the weekend.

When Harry finally returned to the Physics Department he found Andile waiting for him.

'Harry, can you give someone a lift to the Cederberg? All the other cars are full, and there's this late request from one of the Yemeni international students. He wants to experience different parts of South Africa while he's here. His name's Abdur.'

'Sure.' While Harry would have preferred to go on his own, he felt he couldn't refuse such a request.

Back in his apartment, Harry packed his rucksack. While they would drive up to the mountain hut and would actually not need to hike with the rucksack, he had to pack his gear in the right container: it would not do to arrive with a suitcase.

Harry picked Abdur up at the university residences, and they were on their way to the Cederberg well before four pm.

Abdur did not talk much, asking a few questions about the gravity machine and what Harry would be doing. He said he was studying English at the university. Beyond that, he lapsed into silence, and Harry was happy to be wrapped in his own thoughts.

After driving about 250km along a good road, soon after six Harry turned off to the Cederberg Wilderness area. They drove past the main camp at Algeria, and continued along the road to the turnoff to their camp. Fortunately it was still not dark, and after a couple of kilometres of rough dirt road they finally reached their destination and Harry found parking in amongst some planted pine trees.

He and Abdur took out their bags and surveyed the situation: Harry hadn't been there before, but it was typical of camps where he had been. There were two main huts, each sleeping twelve in two barrack rooms with bunk beds, and a general lounge area with a table and a couple of benches. Outside there was a boma area, and already a column of smoke reached skywards into the evening light. A few of the mountain club crowd were around the fire, while others were settling into the accommodation.

Abdur was obviously uncertain of what to do, and Harry indicated to one of the huts.

'We can just find a couple of bunks – apparently it's not full, so we just take what there is. First come, first served.'

Abdur nodded, and followed Harry to the closest hut.

Suddenly there was a cry from behind: 'Harry!'

It was Andile, hurrying up to them. He gripped Harry's hand, 'Great to have you here!'

He turned and bellowed, 'Hey guys – who says we aren't famous. Look who's joining us: Harry Ehlers, inventor of the gravity machine!'

Activities stopped as everyone peered at the new phenomenon. Harry could have killed Andile for the unwelcome publicity, but waved a lame greeting and continued to the hut. At the door he looked back at the other hut and saw a face he recognised: Tracy was just coming out to check on the commotion. He stopped a moment and looked at her, and she smiled and waved.

'There's plenty of space, Harry – just find a bunk anywhere.' Andile indicated into the hut.

'Thanks.' For a moment he wondered if he could make it to the other hut. Then he thought 'Naaah, she's probably with other friends – likely a boyfriend.' In any case, he was there for the solitude, and there was Abdur ...

'Andile, this is Abdur – he's the exchange student from the Yemen.'

Andile smiled and shook his hand. 'So, you're looking for a mountain club experience. You've come to the right place.' He left them to settle in.

After selecting a bunk and dumping his bag on it, Harry went out into the lounge area of the hut. There were a couple of young students at the table, a boy and a girl, and she came up to him.

'Are you really Harry Ehlers – you know, have you just been to the States? On the Thommo talk show ...?

He smiled, she seemed so young. 'The same, just an ordinary person like you.'

The boy came up as well. 'Wow, nobody's ever going to believe this. Can we take a photo?'

In the end he had to pose between them while the boy took a selfie. He was beginning to realise he wasn't just an ordinary person. At least not in the minds of the public.

Harry only knew Andile – and now also Tracy – amongst the mountain club members present. He took a beer and a pizza he had brought and went and joined the group around the fire. At first he had to satisfy them he was Harry Ehlers, and then there were the expected questions about what he was going to do. It was by now a common question, and he was getting used to saying he would see how it would all pan out.

However, there was some genuine concern about their sport: 'Hey, man, Harry, some jokers just going to wing it up climbs using your machine. How're we gonna stop that?'

'Just make sure he hasn't got a gravity machine on him,' responded someone else.

'Yes, but the whole thing about climbing is the danger, the exposure, getting away from people. Now you can have some idiot floating just behind you, making stupid comments.'

'Make for some great photography.'

'That's not the point!'

'It will be a lot safer. You could rig up a belay system into the sky away from a climb, so when somebody peels he just falls away and hangs there.'

'Serious climbing's going to be compromised. Your invention's not a good idea, Harry!'

'One will be able to get to way-out, incredible climbs.'

Harry left them to their debate: he continued to be amazed at all the new consequences of the gravity machine.

He finished his pizza and continued sipping his beer. He saw Tracy sitting around the other side of the fire, also eating. At one stage he looked up and found her staring at him, but she quickly turned away. He thought he should get up and talk to her, but when he looked again she was gone.

She didn't come back, and he wondered where she had gone, or with whom she had gone. Yet when she was sitting there she didn't seem to be with anybody. He shook the thoughts from his mind; he was sitting in the darkening light at the edge of the fire, not participating in the ribald chatter, enjoying the company from a distance.

However, not being part of the groups or their planning for the weekend's climbing, the conversation began to pall, and after finishing his beer Harry quietly left the company. He went back to his hut, getting an anorak and a small LED torch. He wanted some time on his own.

There was a quarter moon giving some light, and he made his way to the farther end of the camp where the main path led away. It went through some of the strangely-shaped rocks typical of the area, and led in amongst the low fynbos.

The sounds around the campfire receded behind him as he made his way along the path, using the pale moonlight to guide him. It seemed to lead up to a small knoll on the immediate horizon.

It took him more than ten minutes to reach the knoll. As he approached the top he could see more of the jagged rock formations. The path wound its way between two large boulders, and once through he looked around for a place to sit.

He found it at the base of one of the large boulders, where he could sit and lean back comfortably. Beyond him he could see the general topography rising further, until in the distance another jagged ridge formed the horizon. The moonlight cast pale, indistinct shadows over the landscape.

He sighed in contentment: this was what he had come for. Away from everyone, and no-one who could contact him, since he had deliberately turned off his cell phone and left it in the hut.

The quarter moon did not dim out the stars, apart from one small section in its vicinity. Elsewhere the pinpoints of light were shining brightly on the black canvass of the sky, and he revelled in the way the stars came out when there were no competing lights. He looked at the constellations, identifying the way in which past civilisations had interpreted the heavens.

This was his universe, this was what he was trying to understand, how it all fitted together. Because he had to believe it did all work rationally, that there was some way in which the mind of man would be able to describe and understand it. At that stage he just let the majesty of it all sweep over him.

The stars were a constant in his life, something he could always turn back to. While he was still at school he had often lain on his back on the small rectangle of lawn in their yard in Wynberg, staring up at the stars. The surrounding city lights meant at times he could see very little, but it was enough to know the whole universe was out there. He had often read how insignificant mankind was in the great scheme of the universe, and yet it was at times like those when he felt most alive, when he felt a unity with creation. Not meaningless, but a part of everything.

'So, where does it all go from here?'

Harry started, and it took him a moment to register another voice in his silence. It was close by, and was half familiar. He looked up to his left, and saw a figure sitting on top of the boulder.

'Tracy ...?'

'Hello.'

His whole previous train of thought was forgotten, as he sought to respond.

'Been here long?' he eventually asked.

'Before you came.'

He digested her reply, now curious, 'What are you doing here?'

She didn't respond immediately, then said slowly, 'Getting my space. It's not only gravity machine inventors who need to get away.' Her teeth caught the moonlight as she smiled briefly.

He nodded and lapsed into silence, and she didn't volunteer any more conversation. However, he couldn't get back into his previous mindframe, not with Tracy so close. He didn't even mind the interruption.

He turned and looked up at her again, but he could see from her silhouette that she was staring out over the landscape.

'Stunning place,' he said. She nodded.

'What do you come to think about?'

It took a long time for her to answer, 'All sorts.' It was almost as though her voice broke a bit at the end.

Then she was much firmer. 'It's getting cold, I'm going back to the fire.' She stood up from her rock, and clambered down to the front.

Harry also registered he was getting colder. 'I'll come with you,' he said. She wrapped her sweater tighter around her shoulders.

They walked between the big boulders. She had switched on her torch, looking directly in front. Harry was fiddling to get his torch out of his pocket. The next moment she let out a little cry, and even as he looked up Harry felt himself grabbed from behind. A rag was put roughly over his mouth, and the last thing he remembered was the sickly smell of some volatile compound.

CHAPTER 10

It was the low droning sound that eventually woke Harry. He battled through a fog of inertia, trying to make sense of where he was. Eventually he could open his eyes, and focussed on a curved wall going over him. He felt a luxurious sheet gently draped over his body.

His head felt heavy, and he turned slowly to look to his left, where there was a window in the wall. He could see bright sunshine outside, and recognised what looked like a wing. It took him a moment to realise he was in a plane.

He looked quickly to his right, where he saw Tracy lying on another bed, adjacent to the other side of the plane's fuselage. She had thrown off her sheet, and was lying clothed in her camping gear, hands behind her head, staring up at the ceiling.

'Tracy ...?'

At the sound of his voice she turned to him. She looked a while and then asked slowly, 'Do you know what this is about?'

He was thinking better now, and slowly sat up, holding his head, 'Where are we?'

'I thought you'd worked out we're in a plane.'

He stared at her, disconcerted by her cynicism. 'I meant what's going on.' He was also still dressed in his denims and T-shirt from the night before. His shoes had been taken off.

She didn't respond immediately, looking at their surroundings. Then she said slowly, 'I guess we've been abducted. No doubt because of your gravity machine.'

He didn't answer, letting her response sink in. It was probably the only answer that made sense, but why was another question. They were in a luxurious compartment on the plane, and at the bottom end of the two beds there was a low table with two comfortable chairs, while at the top end there was a basin in a counter with a mirror.

There were closed doors on either side. He got up quickly to try the handle on the closest door – it was locked.

'The other one's also locked,' Tracy said dryly.

Harry sat down again on the edge of the bed. Then he went to the basin and splashed his face with water, drying himself using a neatly-folded embroidered towel. He felt a lot better.

'I'm sure they're watching us.' Tracy had turned again to look at Harry.

'Cameras,' she continued, pointing at the ceiling.

Harry nodded in understanding, trying to see if he could identify a camera or something in the structure of the compartment.

He gave up and smiled brightly, 'Well, we're not tied up. I'm hungry – let's see if there's anything to eat.'

Beyond the low table were a series of cupboards. The first one turned out to be a fridge, stocked with a variety of drinks.

'Anything you want?'

Tracy got up to see what was available, and chose what looked like a fruit juice can. She indicated to the writing on the can, 'Looks Arabic.'

Harry opened another cupboard, and found a smorgasbord of delicacies. He took it out and put it on the table.

'Certainly is middle-east – this looks like meze.'

She looked at him, 'Meze ...?'

'It's a whole lot of small dishes – from the middle-east. I drifted through the region earlier this year – I think this yoghurt, cucumber and spices dip is tzatziki. And this is halloumi cheese – quite salty.' It wasn't often that Harry could show off culinary knowledge, and Tracy seemed impressed.

There was sliced bread available, and they sat down at the table, tasting the different offerings. Harry opened a tin of juice, and leaning back in his chair he looked at Tracy delving into the selection.

She smiled at him, 'I know this one – it's hummus.'

If this was abduction, Harry thought, it really wasn't bad.

She looked at the food, 'I must admit this is much better than the breakfast I had planned in the Cederberg.'

He smiled, 'Yes, I packed cereal for this morning.' A thought struck him: 'I wonder if they're missing us, and what they'll do about it.'

She looked keenly at him, 'So you don't know what this is about?'

He shook his head, 'Haven't a clue.'

Suddenly there was a noise at the door closest to them. Both turned to see the door opening slowly, and a swarthy man dressed in a traditional long-sleeved white Arabic dress came in.

He bowed, 'Good morning Dr Ehlers. Good morning mademoiselle.'

Harry nodded, while Tracy just stared at the newcomer in anticipation.

He wrung his hands slightly, looking at them both in turn, 'You are wondering why you are here.' His voice was slightly lilting, his English pronunciation very good and measured, though with an unknown accent.

He turned to Harry, 'You must please not think ill of us, Dr Ehlers. We mean no harm, and in fact when you understand why we fetched you, I am sure you will agree with our actions.'

'Mademoiselle,' he continued to Tracy, 'I apologise that you have become involved, but unfortunately last night we had to bring you along.' She said nothing.

He looked at them both, and seeing no particular adverse reaction to his statements, continued, 'My name is Sameer. I will look after you until we land, and I will explain what will await you.'

'But first: you can freshen up – there is a shower.' He pointed at the other door.

'You may want to change? There are some clothes.' Sameer indicated to an array of drawers near the basin. 'It will be very hot where we are going, so you may want to put on a cooler shirt.'

'I'm afraid not ladies clothes,' he apologised to Tracy. 'All your camping clothes are under the beds.'

He waited for a response: Harry glanced at Tracy, but she said nothing.

'Thanks Sameer, I'll have a shower.' Tracy also nodded, and Harry continued, 'However, you'll have to unlock the door.'

'Good,' Sameer responded. 'I will leave you, and prepare breakfast.' He unlocked the shower, but when he left again they could hear him lock the door where he had come in.

'You shower first, Tracy.'

There were large drawers under the beds, and Tracy quickly opened hers and found her pack stashed inside. She rummaged through, and then ducked into the shower and came out a little later wearing a loosely-fitting light blue cotton shirt. There was a faint smell of fresh herbs, and she had combed her hair.

In the meanwhile Harry had inspected the shirts available, selecting a white shirt with wide sleeves. He looked up as Tracy came out, 'That looks good!'

She smiled briefly and sat down at the table, nibbling again at the meze.

The shower was remarkably functional, and Harry felt the last bits of wooziness washed out of his head. He found the herbal body lotion, and a little later he was much refreshed as he sat down again at the small table opposite Tracy.

Sameer came back carrying a tray with two plates, 'I have Kubideh kebabs with basmati rice and pita bread – it is ground lamb. Very tasty.'

It did smell good, with the slight fragrance of the rice mixed with the spiciness of the kebab. Harry was hungry, and tucked into the breakfast.

'This is good,' he said, smiling at Sameer. Tracy ate her breakfast in silence, though she did finish every scrap.

Sameer never sat down, standing quietly to one side while they were eating. When they were finishing off, he said quietly, 'We will be landing in the Seychelles in forty-five minutes. I must tell you what this is about.'

He hesitated a moment, and continued, 'The Prince would very much like to meet you, Dr Ehlers. He is a great student of history, and has recognised your invention as a turning point in the progress of society.'

Harry glanced at Tracy, and she raised her eyebrows.

'The Prince has always regretted not being a part of what he views as the great leaps forward. Now that this has happened, he would like to congratulate you, and to offer any help you may need in fulfilling your ideas.'

He let the idea sink in, 'The Prince felt he needed to see you urgently, Dr Ehlers, and we could see no other way to bring you here. Quite obviously you are very busy, but the Prince felt it was necessary that he see you in the initial stages of this development.'

'We will not keep you any longer than you want to stay, and we hope you will enjoy your time in the Seychelles.'

He turned to Tracy, 'That also applies to you mademoiselle.' She shrugged her shoulders.

'Thanks, Sameer,' Harry responded, 'I guess we're here now, so let's see how it goes. However, I don't want to stay long.' He looked at Tracy.

'No,' she said, 'I need to get back.'

A thought struck her, 'What about the situation in South Africa? People will know we've been abducted, especially with Harry being so high profile ...'

Sameer smiled, 'No, that has been taken care of. They think you've been called away.'

'Abdur?' Harry asked.

'He has done his work well.'

They let it be, and a short while later the plane banked sharply, and they could see Mahe, the main island of the Seychelles, spread out below. The first impression was of greenness, and then of a varying and rugged terrain; certainly not a coral atoll. The airport seemed attached to one side of the island, and as they came in they could see white beaches overhung with trees. The water was a clear blue, with offshore reefs prominent.

The tropical heat and humidity hit them the moment they stepped out of the plane. Obviously the Prince was well-connected, because they were quickly whisked through immigration formalities, even though they had no passports or other documentation. It was a relief to get into an air-conditioned limousine.

After a short drive along a tree-lined coastal road they turned abruptly into the interior of the small island. The road was narrow, and wound its way steeply upwards through tropical forest. Eventually they turned into a gateway which opened seamlessly as they approached. Ahead they could see a large, square building, prominently positioned on the ridge along which they were driving. The stark white structure contrasted sharply with the green of the surrounding forest.

Neither Harry nor Tracy had said much and he muttered quietly, 'Nice little pad he's got here.'

Sameer had been in the front of the limousine, and he opened the doors for Tracy and Harry. 'This is the Prince's new lodge,' he informed them. 'It has an unequalled view anywhere in the Indian Ocean.' Indeed, as they stood there they could see the main habitation on the island spread in a thin line along the coast below them.

'That is Eden Island' Sameer continued, pointing down at an island adjacent to the mainland. 'It is entirely man-built, on a derelict reef.' From the number of vessels, it was apparently a boat-lovers paradise.

'And that is the Prince's yacht,' Sameer said with a touch of pride, pointing at a sleek white boat dominating all else in the main harbour.

They entered the lodge through an ornate wooden door, into a wide hallway dominated by a marbled staircase. The air-conditioning ensured a pleasant temperature.

'The Prince will see you in the main reception room.' Sameer pointed up the stairs. 'Please go up, and I will announce you.' He left them to continue on their own.

They went slowly up the stairs. Everything still had a new look about it, inviting a more lived-in appearance. The maroon carpet deadened their steps, and at the top they entered the reception room through wide open double doors.

This area had had detailed attention. Rich wooden panelling covered the wall on the left, with a number of display cabinets at eye level and stuffed trophies decorating the higher levels. On the right numerous cupboards and below them a series of wide drawers in the same wood panelling indicated more specimens or trophies. The end consisted of floor to ceiling bookcases, filled with leather-bound tomes; the Prince obviously intended to impart a sense of learning.

On the left Harry could identify a kudu with a magnificent set of horns, and beyond that a lion growled malevolently at the air.

'Why do men always want to kill things?' Tracy muttered under her breath. Harry glanced at her, but she had moved off to get a closer look at some of the other 'things'. He carried on: up ahead the curved front of the room had floor to ceiling glass windows, and probably offered a magnificent view over the island and adjacent ocean.

A door on the right opened, and a man entered. He was dressed in the traditional Arabic long-sleeved white dress covering his whole body, with a small white close-fitting cap on his head. Of medium height, he carried a presence that did not brook dissent. This must be the Prince, thought Harry.

He smiled when he saw Harry, his even white teeth accentuated by his dark moustache.

'Ah, Dr Harry Ehlers.' He stretched out both arms in greeting.

They were interrupted by a cry from Tracy, 'This is a jambiya!'

The Prince looked across at her, impressed she had recognised one of his treasures.

'Yes, it is beautiful. I had it made a few years ago.'

Unfortunately he had misread the tone of her voice. She stormed across to where he was standing, tears welling in her eyes.

'You bastard,' she spat out brokenly, pointing back at a display case, 'you killed a rhino for that ... that thing!'

The Prince's mood changed in an instant. His brow darkened, and he drew his hand back and struck Tracy a full blow across the side of her head. She spun around and collapsed on the floor.

'Nobody calls me a bastard.' He looked down at her, 'especially not a woman.'

Harry was dumbfounded by the turn of events. He quickly went across to where Tracy was lying on the floor. The Prince looked at him for a moment, realising that all his careful planning had been undone in an instant. With a mutter of disgust he turned abruptly and hastened back through the door where he had just entered.

Harry helped Tracy sit up. A ring on the Prince's hand must have cut the skin on her cheek just below the eye, and Harry used the wide sleeve of his shirt to wipe away the blood.

'Why do men have to be so violent?' she asked, gingerly touching her eye.

'You're going to have a hellova shiner,' he tried to lighten her mood.

He looked around, but the Prince was gone and they were alone again. The instant of violence had given way to an oppressive silence, muted by the books and panelling. There were some comfortable-looking armchairs in an open area at the large windows.

'Let's go sit down.' He helped her get up, but she indicated she could walk over to the chairs on her own. Once they had sat down, Harry looked across at her: she was sitting forward in her chair, one hand on the weal that was beginning to appear on the side of her face, and staring straight ahead. She seemed to be tormented by a memory, and he said nothing; he did not understand what had just happened.

She sensed she had to explain, and started quietly, hesitantly, 'There's a jambiya in one of the display cases.' When she saw Harry didn't understand, she continued, 'It's a curved Arabic dagger – the saifani handle is made of rhino horn.'

Again Harry didn't respond directly, and she carried on slowly: 'Two months ago I sat next to a dying rhino. Poachers had hacked off its horns – just taken them off with a saw, or an axe … its lip was hanging in two pieces, with blood dripping down …'

She stopped, recalling the moment, and covered her face with her hands and convulsed in a sob. 'Oh god.'

Harry was silent. He felt he should comfort her, take her in his arms. But he wasn't a touchy-feely kind of person, and the moment passed.

After a while she turned to him again, her eyes full of tears, and he noticed again how brown they were. Her curly light hair was matted on her forehead, the weal already turning blue below her eye. She looked vulnerable, her eyes pleading.

'They had shot him,' she continued, staring at Harry, now more dispassionate. 'I could see his heart beating, and pumping out blood from the little bullet hole. And we could do nothing – just watch him die.'

She turned forward again. 'He looked at me the whole time. Why did we do that to him? What had he done to deserve such treatment? Then his eye just glazed over and he was gone.'

'Hell, Tracy, I'm sorry,' Harry eventually said.

She nodded imperceptibly: 'They had to kill a rhino to make that jambiya.'

Harry didn't say anything. They were quiet a while, until she suddenly stood up and walked in front of the large windows.

'I'm sorry I screwed up – I didn't ask to come here. I should be in the Cederberg right now ...'

'So should I,' he responded quietly.

She stopped and looked at him, and for the first time she smiled, a cynical smile, 'You're right. I guess you also don't want to be here in this Charlie's palace.'

He relaxed, thinking that, yes, he couldn't even organise a weekend away without some new interference in his life. He looked out over the tropical paradise at their feet, 'Still, you gotta admit it's some view.'

She was quiet, staring out, and asked slowly, 'I wonder what's going to happen now?'

The question brought Harry back to their situation; they had been alone since the Prince's sudden exit.

Almost on cue, the side door opened and Sameer came in. He walked slowly and deliberately over to where Harry and Tracy were watching.

"Dr Ehlers,' he said as he stopped in front of them, wringing his hands slightly, 'the Prince regrets to inform you he has been called away on urgent business.

He won't be able to see you now, but he hopes you may meet at some future date.'

Not likely, thought Harry. The whole while Sameer had looked only at him, ignoring Tracy.

'Can you get some ointment for Tracy's face?' he asked.

'No, no, don't worry about me,' she said quickly.

'If you don't require anything further, you can fly back to South Africa,' Sameer continued, ignoring Harry's request.

'That's a good idea,' Harry replied.

Without a further word, Sameer bowed slightly and left.

'Wow, what makes me think I'm not one of the Prince's favourite people,' Tracy said when he had gone.

Harry smiled: 'Well, at least we're going back home.'

It soon became obvious a decision had been taken to get them off the Seychelles and back to South Africa as soon as possible. An impassive character came into the room and introduced himself as Murad: he would be escorting them. Again, Tracy had the distinct impression she was deliberately ignored, but at that stage she couldn't care.

They were soon in the air, and the comfortable cabin felt familiar and luxurious. However, this time they were left to their own devices as they heard Murad lock the door to the main section of the aircraft.

'They obviously don't trust you,' Harry said jokingly, but then noticed an apprehensive look on Tracy's face.

'Harry,' she said, 'I'm getting a headache. If you don't mind, I'm going to lie down.'

'Of course – I'll see if I can find an aspirin.'

He did find some pills which gave instructions in English, and which seemed to be for headaches. Tracy took a couple and soon appeared to be sleeping deeply.

Harry took a drink out of the fridge and contemplated his situation.

It was quite bizarre, he thought. He had been abducted, flown to the Seychelles, and an hour later flown back again. He wondered what the Prince would have expected of him, and was actually quite glad for Tracy's intervention – he didn't want to be treated as some changer of history.

Then there was Tracy herself. He knew little about her, but she continued to surprise him. He looked across to where she was sleeping: she had turned to face the aircraft bulkhead, and her short curly brown hair was splayed on the pillow. He had been enchanted at how beautiful she had looked at times during the day, even though it was obviously not one of her priorities to doll up.

She must have issues, or otherwise why would she wander away from the camp to go and sit by herself on a rock? Harry didn't consider it strange in his own case because he had always done that, and in any case he had a lot to think about.

So she had to have a lot on her mind as well. The rhino issue was one aspect, and it was apparent she was passionate about wild life. Was that all? He shook his head: he would like to know more about her, but for the moment that would have to wait.

There was little to see out the plane window except endless expanses of ocean, and he lay down on his bed. Not to sleep – he had too much to think about.

It was some time later he woke and found Tracy sitting in a chair, nibbling at the meze.

'Hi,' she smiled at him, 'sleep well?'

'Thanks,' he responded. 'Where are we?'

'Over Africa already.' She indicated out the window.

He looked out the window, and could see a large expanse of South African interior, mainly flat and no sign of any city or built-up area. He couldn't identify where they were, and jumped off his bed and took another fruit juice out of the fridge. He sat down opposite Tracy.

'You've got a pretty memento of the Seychelles,' he said, indicating her eye which was taking on a decidedly blue colour.

She smiled, touching the weal gingerly: 'At least the headache's gone.'

He took a plate with a piece of halloumi cheese on a slice of bread, and leant back in his chair, 'Tell me about the rhino.'

She looked at him seriously. Then she frowned, 'It was on one of our neighbours' game farms in KwaZulu-Natal – in January. I've always worked there during my vacation periods, and these poachers came in and took out two of their rhino. Just like that. And I don't think they'll ever catch them, even if they wanted to.' She spoke dispassionately, quickly, and then stared up at the ceiling: it was apparent she didn't want to say anything more on the matter.

'Does it form part of your thesis?' he asked, and added quickly by way of explanation: 'You said you were doing environmental management.'

She seemed surprised he remembered, 'No, not really. Though it all forms part of what we're doing to the environment.' She stopped, and continued, slower and more deliberate, 'And to all the animals, plants and everything else. Screwing it all up – in the name of development.'

'You feel pretty strongly about the environment?'

She nodded, 'We – humankind – are going to find out very soon we are dependent on nature, on all the plants and animals we are killing off. Not the other way around. People are not the apex of evolution, we are just a part of it all.'

She was interrupted by the door being unlocked, and Murad entered.

'We will be landing in Cape Town in thirty minutes,' he informed them. 'Your car is at the airport, Dr Ehlers, so you will be able to drive home.' Then he was gone again.

They checked up on all their gear, packing it back into their cases.

'You going to keep your new shirt?' Tracy asked. 'It suits you.'

Harry looked at it, 'Yes, why not? It's very comfortable.'

They didn't get another chance to continue their conversation, and they soon landed. It was late afternoon in Cape Town, and through some unknown arrangement Murad took them in through the domestic arrivals. This meant they didn't have to worry about immigration and passports, and they went straight out to Harry's *City Golf* in the airport parking.

'Everything is as you left it,' Murad explained, giving Harry the car key. He pushed a hundred Rand note into Harry's hand. 'For the parking,' he said brusquely, before turning abruptly and heading back to the main airport building.

'It's a bit late to head back to the Cederberg,' Harry said, putting their packs into the car boot.

Tracy grimaced, 'Yes, they've screwed up the weekend. It's an omen to go and do some work.'

'Feel like something to eat?' Harry asked when they were driving back to Cape Town. He didn't want to just let her leave again.

'Thanks – I've had a lot to eat. I want to get back to my digs now.'

She directed him to where she was staying in communal lodgings in Milnerton, fairly close to the university. He helped her get her gear out of the boot of the car, but she said she could take it from there; he was getting used to being rebuffed.

However, as he was getting into his car she said hesitantly, 'Harry, I'm sorry if I've been such a pain. Perhaps ...' She bit her lip and let the sentence hang.

He turned to her, 'Tracy, is there something wrong?'

'No ... no, it's fine.' She bent to pick up her pack, smiled wanly and went off to her lodgings.

He watched her go, and drove back to his own little apartment.

CHAPTER 11

Sunday, and he should have been in the Cederberg. Harry felt frustrated and cheated, in particular since the jaunt to the Seychelles seemed so unreal and unnecessary.

He phoned Andile, and found he was about to start a climb.

'What happened to you Harry? Abdur said you'd been called away, but I don't trust him. Are you okay?'

'Yes ..., I guess so. I'll tell you about it when you get back.'

'Right. Good to hear from you. I gotta go – the guys are waiting.'

Shortly afterwards Stephen called with an update on what was happening: most specifically he had started looking into the process of lodging patents in signatory countries. It would be a drawn-out procedure, and they would to have to contract patent attorneys in all the relevant countries.

Sir Richard Straithwaite had phoned.

'He is a very forceful and insistent man, is Sir Richard,' Stephen commented. 'He says they've re-evaluated the gravity machine, and they've increased their offer to ten billion.'

'Ten billion pounds?' Harry asked, still amazed at the numbers being bandied around.

'Yes, but they want to know soon so that they can set all their structures into motion. It's a good offer, and I think we should accept.'

Harry was quiet a moment, recollecting his conversations with Hamish Prentiss, then the claims of the deputy minister and Mac Manyi, and finally the trust of Pre Mahlangu.

'No, Stephen, I'm more convinced now I shouldn't give up my rights.'

'Well, I think you need to consider it all very carefully, and don't make up your mind before knowing all the facts. Remember there is still room for negotiation, and it isn't as though they'll take over the whole operation. It would make things a lot easier to have the resources of a big organisation like B2O handling it. If we are going to do it all ourselves we are going to have to set up a company to handle all the business.'

'Is it all that much?' Harry was loath to get involved with things smacking of management and bureaucracy.

'Yes it is – we can discuss it further when I get back.

That brings me to the next point: you're going to have to run another workshop. I've been inundated by complaints of exclusion at the American workshop. The Europeans want a workshop, let alone the Asians and others. The competition is fierce, and nobody wants to be left out.'

'When?'

'Soon – I would guess in a week or so.'

Harry contemplated his options, and the way his life was being ruled by external forces.

'You'll be well paid,' Stephen added.

'Yes, well, I guess I have to do it.'

'Then there's the question of your safety: I've contacted *CF Security* - a personal security company. They said they would have someone come around on Monday – that's tomorrow. You need to be in to discuss what they will do.'

'Okay.' More constraints on his life.

Finally, Stephen added that he would be flying back to Cape Town on Wednesday, landing on Thursday afternoon. Harry didn't tell him about the Seychelles.

After hanging up, Harry read some of the Sunday paper delivered to his apartment, but felt he had to get out. He decided to go to the university to see if all was well with the glob.

The public viewing was in full swing, and it seemed that all Capetonians had decided they wanted to get a view of this remarkable new invention. This new gravity machine invented by one of their own.

The glob was floating in its cage, and a fan had been put on one side to blow air into the cage to move it around. Dale was in his element, pushing it back when it came to a side of the cage, and occasionally letting one of the audience also push it around. He had re-energized it on a couple of occasions already, apparently with all the showmanship of a magician.

Harry was immediately recognised and mobbed by the crowd. He had to sign autographs, have photographs taken and answer questions. It was with some relief that he eventually got away back to his apartment.

He also thought about Tracy. A lot. He realised he still didn't know her surname, and the only contact was that he knew where she lived. At times she had seemed very distant during their time on the plane, and had declined to go with him for a bite to eat after they had returned. Yet she had half apologised when she reached her lodgings. There seemed to be something she wasn't telling.

He wanted to see her again, yet even with all his new-found fame he was hesitant at being rebuffed – again. He had a desultory lunch, finished reading the paper and generally moped around his apartment. By late afternoon he finally made up his mind: he put on the shirt he had worn for the *Thommo-Talk* interview, went down to the garage, and drove to Milnerton where Tracy lived.

He parked outside in the road, and hesitated a moment, looking at the house. It could be described as fairly typical student accommodation, with a small but quite neat front garden with a gate on a latch, a small porch and a front door with a security gate.

However, he had come all the way already, and so walked to the door and rang the bell. He heard some female voices inside, and then the wooden front door opened slowly. A girl he didn't know peered at him through the security gate.

'Hello,' he said, 'I'm ...'

He didn't get a chance to finish the sentence. 'Harry Ehlers!' she squealed in delight. She opened the door and yelled back into the house.

'Traceeee ... Harry's here to see you!'

'Come in, come in,' the girl continued, unlocking the gate and ushering him in. She closed the door behind them.

'I'm Anne,' she added as she guided Harry to the lounge, where there were a couple of others sitting on some comfortable but non-matching armchairs. She introduced them as Judy and Mpho.

'Unmistakeable,' Judy said, 'especially with that shirt.' She was a big woman, and she leaned back in her armchair, inspecting Harry. 'Incredible, the man of the moment, all over the world.' She turned to the others, 'Nice looking, don't you think?'

'Do you think he's real?' asked Mpho. 'I mean, to look like that, and have brains!'

'I want to take him home with me.' Judy grinned at Harry.

'You'll have competition,' said Mpho.

'Why don't we kidnap him,' added Anne, 'and keep him here. Apparently he's used to it.'

'Oh, come on girls, you're embarrassing him.' Tracy came to his rescue, smiling as she came into the lounge. Harry grinned, almost blushing, and not quite knowing how to respond.

'No, I think it's a good idea,' Judy continued, 'though we don't have a plane or a pad in the Seychelles.'

'Just ignore her, Harry,' Tracy interrupted, 'she's a man-eater. Do you want some tea or something else to drink?'

'Uh, Okay – I'll have some coffee.'

I'll make it,' Anne said quickly. 'Some more tea, girls?' Harry and Tracy sat down on two other armchairs, sinking right down on well-worn springs.

'We didn't know whether to believe Tracy when she came in here last night saying she'd just had a day's holiday in the Seychelles – with the inventor of the gravity machine.' Judy said. 'It was a totally weird story.'

'Especially with her shiner,' Mpho added. Harry looked at Tracy: the left side of her face was swollen, with a small skin-coloured plaster over the cut. There was a slight blue tinge to her skin around her eye that she'd obviously tried to hide with make-up.

'How is it?' he asked.

'Fine,' she smiled. 'I'll get over it.'

'We thought it was probably some mountain type that had done it,' Mpho continued. 'And when she came with her story we thought she was delirious as well.'

'It was bizarre,' Harry agreed. 'But then the world seems bizarre right now.'

'You've done your bit in that respect,' Anne said, coming into the room with the drinks.

The coffee and the conversation relaxed Harry. All four of the girls were postgraduate students, though Judy and Mpho were part-time with jobs in the city. It was apparent they were a close-knit supportive group of friends.

'Harry,' Judy said when the cups were low, 'you didn't come here to talk to us. If you want to ask Tracy anything, go ahead. We're her advisors.'

'Oh, sushh, Judy,' Tracy said quickly.

'No, that's right, Harry,' Anne confirmed. 'Go right ahead.'

Harry looked at them, and at Tracy, who had her head bowed slightly. He smiled, and decided to play along.

'Well,' he said, 'I was wondering whether the lady in question would like to have dinner this evening.'

'She has dinner every evening,' Judy said with an inscrutable face. 'You'll have to be more specific. Do you want to take her out to dinner?'

His smile broadened, 'Yes.'

Judy turned to Anne and Mpho, 'Well, ladies, what do you think? The gentleman seems quite reasonable, and his prospects of being the richest man in the world are promising. So I would say we give our approval.'

'Provided there's no kidnapping involved,' added Mpho.

'I agree,' said Anne.

'Well, that would be our advice, but what does the lady in question think?'

They all looked at Tracy, who raised her head and stared at her three friends: there was almost a pleading look on her face. Then she briefly closed her eyes, and smiled wanly at no-one in particular.

'Okay,' she said faintly, 'I'll go get a jacket.'

They watched her leave the lounge, then Judy turned to Harry. She was serious now.

'Harry,' she said quietly, 'Tracy's a great girl. But she's had some terrible ordeals recently. I meant what I said about being reasonable. Treat her gently.'

'What do you mean?'

'She'll tell you in her own time.'

Tracy came back with a jacket on, which she clasped tightly around her shoulders. As they went out the door Judy said, 'Harry, I'd advise you to put on a sweater. With that shirt you'll be recognised everywhere you go.'

They walked quietly to Harry's car, and once in he drove in the direction of Wijnberg.

'I thought of going to Kalk Bay – there's a restaurant almost on the harbour wall. Food's good, and there's a great view over False Bay.'

She nodded, not venturing an opinion. He glanced briefly at her: she was still clasping her jacket around her shoulders, and looking straight ahead.

'You know, I still don't know your surname,' he ventured after a while.

It took her a while to answer, 'My surname's Freese. As I said on the plane, I'm from KwaZulu-Natal, KZN. The Wartburg area. My family's been farming sugarcane for generations.'

'When did you come to UCT?'

'Just over a year ago. I wanted to do a Masters, and they have a very good environmental management department here.'

The talking seemed to relax her, and she smiled at Harry, 'Thanks for asking me to supper.'

'It's a pleasure,' he smiled back.

'You also confirmed my story to the others. They thought I was nuts, saying that I'd gone to Seychelles for a day. And with you of all people.'

'They seem like a good bunch.'

'The best,' Tracy said firmly. 'They've been very good to me.'

It was still quite early when they reached Kalk Bay. The wind had dropped, but it was becoming cool and Harry took up Judy's suggestion and put a sweater over his *Thommo Talk* shirt.

They took a walk to the end of the quay. There were a number of fishermen trying their luck from the quay wall, and they walked quietly, enjoying the evening.

'Have you decided what you're going to do, once you start getting money?' she asked after a while.

'Not really – there's a possibility of selling the patent, giving someone else the headaches. Stephen wants that.'

'Stephen is the patent attorney?'

'Yes.' He told her about Stephen, how they had met and written up the patent.

'The other option is to set up a company, or possibly a trust or foundation. To me that sounds like a better option – I'd keep more control, but it would mean more management and stuff.' He grinned wryly.

'I also promised Pre Mahlangu that I'd work with the university.'

'Pre Mahlangu – the Vice Chancellor?'

'Yes – but I don't want to rush things until I know what it means.'

The restaurant was still fairly empty that early in the evening, and they had no problem in getting a table at a large window overlooking the sea. Fortunately Harry wasn't recognised, and after they had sat down and been given the menus he looked at her and smiled.

'What ...?' she asked when he didn't say anything.

'I'm just thinking,' he said, half introspectively, 'I don't often go to restaurants – primarily because I've never had the money. Now, over the last couple of weeks I've been paid over three million Rand. More than I've ever seen in my life. So, order anything you want.'

'Three million ...? Wow!' She smiled briefly, and continued, 'The newspapers have been mentioning all those big numbers. I guess they don't mean anything until you use the money.'

However, she didn't order anything extravagant, and after Harry had ordered a schnitzel she continued with her ideas.

'You know, you could do so much good with the money from the gravity machine.'

'Such as?'

She hesitated: she didn't know how he felt about subjects she was passionate about. However, she had to try him.

'Environmental matters.'

'Rhinos?'

'That's just one aspect. It's important, but there are so many different angles, so many assaults on our planet.' The words came out quickly, as she looked at him for a response.

'I've been following the climate debate,' he replied slowly, 'so I have an idea of what is forecast – temperatures, sea level rise and things like that. What are you thinking?'

'Those are the physical aspects, and of course they're serious. However, there is so much else happening, in particular the way we are decimating all the other species on the planet. Ecological systems we don't even know about are going extinct.'

When Harry didn't respond she continued, 'Everything is people-orientated, and all the big foundations – Gates, Rockefeller, Kellogg – specifically focus on people. They don't realise people are actually the problem.'

'We have enough people – they're taking over all the habitats, destroying so many species.'

'And money would help?' Harry asked.

'Yes – one could set up much better family planning programs. Empowering women will mean fewer unwanted babies. Getting lawyers to fight bad developments and legislative ideas. Operating international campaigns against big business, and particularly big oil.'

The words came out in a rush, and Harry was left in no doubt where her interests lay. But he enjoyed it, and Tracy told him about all the things she had become involved in. The battles with her family to stop planting sugar cane on the banks of rivers, and how she had eventually shown that it was financially better to have trees and vegetation to stop erosion. The campaigns she had run, and the recent incident with the rhino.

He found out that she was a Scuba diver, having done all her training in KZN. She had started again in the colder waters around Cape Town.

'I did the PADI open water course in my first year,' Harry responded. 'But didn't do any more, there was too much else…'

He smiled, 'It would be fun to dive again.'

After the main course they had dessert and a leisurely coffee. The sun went down behind the mountain, and the restaurant slowly filled up. They could see False Bay through the window, with the rays of the sickle moon glistening on the water. It all added to a restful, intimate dinner, even with the babble of voices from the tables around them.

'Harry,' Tracy eventually said, 'I'm sorry I'm talking so much. I've never said all those things to anybody. Normally I listen – you wouldn't say so...'

He smiled, 'I've enjoyed it all. It's obvious you're passionate about these things.' She was very beautiful, even with the plaster and the eye beginning to turn blue-black.

Harry asked for the bill. Till then they had been quite private, but it all changed when Harry tried to pay with his credit card.

The manager at the counter looked at the card, and then at Harry, 'You're Harry Ehlers – you're the gravity man ...' Harry had to nod, hoping that was where it would end.

But it didn't. 'Dr Ehlers, we're privileged to have you dine here,' he continued. Then he turned to Tracy, 'And of course, your beautiful companion, Miss ...?'

'Tracy,' Harry filled him in.

'Miss Tracy,' he said approvingly.

'To show you how much we value your custom, and for what you've done for South Africa, we would like to offer you your meal gratis.'

Harry recollected what Prentiss had said about fame and money, and getting things for nothing. 'Thank you, but it's not necessary,' he replied.

'It's our pleasure. However, would you mind if we took a photo ...?' Prentiss hadn't said anything about paybacks, and Harry looked at Tracy. She shrugged her shoulders, and a short while later they posed with the manager for the photo.

This attracted other patrons, and a few more photos were taken. It took them a while to get away, and Harry thought that perhaps it was better not to accept such offers in future.

Tracy was quiet on the drive back. She held her jacket tightly around her, and when Harry glanced at her she was staring straight ahead.

He parked his car in front of the house. He switched off the engine and looked at her.

'You haven't said a thing since the restaurant. Is something wrong?'

She kept on looking straight ahead. Then she seemed to make up her mind, and turned to him.

'Harry,' she said softly, 'I ... I need to tell you something...' Her voice tailed off.

'Yes?'

She was quiet for what seemed like an age. She bowed her head, and continued softly, 'I owe you an explanation ...'

'It's okay ...,' he began.

'No,' she continued, firmer now. Her eyes searched his, and she said unevenly, 'Harry, I may have AIDS.' Even as she said it her eyes filled with tears, and she heaved a deep sob. She buried her head in her arms against the dashboard, her body wracked with further sobs.

Harry sat in silence, looking at her. He tried to put his arm around her shoulders to comfort her, but at the first touch of his hand her body went rigid and she turned again to him, her eyes wide.

'Harry, please ...'

He withdrew his hand. He knew about the AIDS pandemic in South Africa, but it had always seemed far away, happening to someone else. And now this ...

'What happened?' he asked eventually.

She didn't answer as she struggled to get control of her emotions. Then she turned to him, her eyes wide, the make-up on her face streaked with tears.

'I was raped,' she said. She was calmer now, and she almost spat the words out.

Harry stared at her. 'When ... how ...?' he asked hoarsely.

'About a month ago,' she said in a monotone.

'Who did it?'

'It doesn't matter, you don't know him.'

Harry leant back in his seat. He felt shattered: how could anyone do that?

'Hell, Tracy, I'm sorry,' he eventually said.

She didn't know how he would react, whether he would be furious, violent or whether he would blame her. All she saw was compassion and a helplessness as he now looked at her. She felt she had to explain further.

'Mac had been badgering me to go out with him,' she began.

'Who?' Harry sat up, staring at her for an answer.

'Mac Manyi,' she said, surprised at his sudden intensity.

'He did it?'

Her wide eyes gave him his answer.

'The bastard,' he said vehemently.

'You know him?'

'I met him when I returned from the US.'

She nodded. But now she felt an even greater necessity to explain.

'We went to a nightclub.' She hesitated, and suddenly she was cross, 'He knows the owner, and they have a room at the back. They held me down ...'

She stopped, recollecting the moment. 'God!' she said, 'damn, damn, damn!' She hit the dashboard with her fist, and burst into tears again.

Harry put out his hand to comfort her, but she again withdrew involuntarily as he touched her and he pulled his hand back.

'What did you do?'

It took her some time to regain control. 'Afterwards ... afterwards two others brought me back. They were laughing and joking, and said Mac had AIDS.'

'Did you report it to the police?'

'Hah,' she said contemptuously. 'Mpho was here, and took me to the nearest police station. It was quite late, and there were two officers, and they weren't interested at all. Mpho could talk to them in Xhosa and insisted they take a statement. When they heard it was Mac Manyi they laughed and said I was lucky – I should go back and ask for more.'

Harry felt himself seething, but wanting to hear more. 'And then?' he asked quietly.

'Mpho threw a book on the counter at them, and said things I didn't understand. They got nasty, and we left quickly.'

She took a deep breath. 'Judy has a doctor friend close by – a lady. She helped me.'

Tracy seemed totally deflated now, her emotions drained by the telling of her story. She stared down at her hands, clasped tightly on her lap.

Harry felt totally helpless. He looked at Tracy, cursing Mac, and wondering how a man could be so totally base. Yet he didn't know how he could help her now.

Eventually she turned to him, her face impassive. 'So, now you know ...'

He smiled gently, 'I can understand why you needed space in the Cederberg.'

Her lips twitched a faint smile in reply. 'Yes ...'

Then she was more definite, 'Now I need to go.'

She made to open the car door, but he took her arm, 'Tracy, I'm here if you need me.'

She turned and her eyes searched his face. She nodded briefly, opened the door and got out.

Harry walked her to the front porch, where she quickly unlocked the door. She went in and turned and looked at him. Then she leant over and gently kissed him on the cheek.

'Thank you, Harry,' she said quietly, and closed the door.

He drove home slowly. Well, now he knew her story, but it was not something he had wanted to hear. He touched his cheek where she had kissed him, and felt another surge of anger: he would have nothing to do with Mac Manyi in the future. In fact, he wondered if it would be possible to open a case against the youth leader – he had enough money to do it.

CHAPTER 12

Harry slept fitfully. He kept churning over Tracy's story, feeling his own helplessness with the situation. He wondered about Mac – the person he had met at the airport didn't seem so vile. How could he do something like that?

At the same time he realised the deed had been done. He just didn't understand the reasons why.

What made a man rape? Lust? Power? Vindictiveness? One act like that could destroy a life.

Why did he want to hurt her? She was so beautiful and trusting, so genuine and passionate about her interests. He resolved he would do everything he could to help her – somehow Tracy had become a part of his life, even though he had only known her for a week or two. He realised that he wanted to see her again, and there was no way in hell that he would – or could – just walk away.

And Mac? Harry remembered he said he would come to see him about the patent. How should he react? Harry had never espoused violence, and had always rationalised his way through problems: if that didn't work, he just walked away from them. In his past there had been nothing he considered so serious that he could not just leave and carry on with his life.

But now?

There must be some way Mac could be brought to justice. After all, rape was a serious crime, and he should rot in jail. On the other hand, Harry knew there were communities in South Africa where taking liberties with a woman was considered a man's right, and correspondingly the rights of women were trampled. Moreover, if a man had political clout it was very, very difficult to get justice done.

However, Harry now had money, and would have a lot more in future. He should be able to use that to get justice. Hire some smart lawyers to prosecute Mac.

What if Tracy had AIDS? That was the worst possible scenario. Mac didn't look as though he had AIDS, but he could be HIV positive. He wondered if Tracy was taking ARV's – they apparently helped to counter the AIDS virus. He would need to find out, and get any other kind of medical assistance available.

He still felt tired when he finally got up on Monday morning. He had a shower, standing under the stream of water and wondering what the day would bring.

However, it wasn't Mac who came to see him: while he was finishing breakfast his mobile rang on his limited access number.

'Good morning, Dr. Ehlers,' the man's voice on the other end said, 'this is *CP Security*. Mr Cambre said you would be expecting us this morning.'

'*CP Security* ...? Oh, of course.' Harry had forgotten Stephen's arrangements for his personal security.

Harry let the man in through the building's security door, and a short while later they sat at the kitchen counter to discuss his security requirements. The apartment had an open plan arrangement, where the wide counter at the kitchen was also the dining room table, and with the small lounge beyond extending to a minute balcony. A bathroom and the single bedroom completed the unit.

'You've got quite a small place here,' the man from *CP Security* said. 'You're not thinking of moving soon?'

'No ... no, I'm quite happy here.' It was obvious he thought Harry should be moving to something a lot grander.

'Well, security shouldn't be a problem,' the man continued. 'We'll put a camera up to monitor the front door of the building. If anyone buzzes your number we will interrogate them, and if they are on a list you give us, or if we think you may want to see them, we will contact you. You can decide whether to let them in. There will also be a camera at your front door.'

'You'll need a movement sensor in here and in your bedroom, and we'll put magnetic catches on all your windows and doors. And you'll have a panic button.'

He stood up and went onto the balcony. The apartment was on the second floor, and Harry had often thought someone with a modicum of mountaineering ability would be able to climb up by standing on the railings of the porch below and using windows and the rough facebricks to lift himself up to the next level.

CP Security also didn't think it was safe, 'We'll put a couple of beams here to monitor the outside,' he said.

'How long to set this all up?' Harry asked.

'Oh, we'll have it finished this morning – it's all wireless.'

'Do I have to stay here while you're working?'

'No, it would be best if you weren't here. If you have a spare set of keys we can lock up when we've finished. If you agree, we can keep a set of keys for access in case of emergency.'

'How do you respond to an emergency?'

'We have patrol cars in all the areas, and we can generally respond within five minutes of a call-out.'

It seemed pretty well organised, and Harry left *CP Security* to their work. He was given a pin number for the to-be-installed security pad, which he could change later. He was joining the great mass of South Africans with all their security safeguards.

At the university Harry found Andile anxious to find out what had happened over the weekend. Abdur said he and Tracy had left together, but neither of their cell phones were answering and Harry's car was also gone. The mountain club group had discussed the matter but decided nothing further could be done, and had continued with their climbing and hiking. He was relieved when Harry phoned on Sunday.

'What actually happened?'

'You'll never believe it.' Harry told him briefly about their trip to the Seychelles.

'Bloody hell,' Andile muttered. Then he smiled, 'That Tracy's quite something. But I'll have something to say to Abdur if I see him again.'

'Just leave it,' Harry said, 'it's done.'

At tea Harry found Dale regaling the staff room with stories of the Capetonians who came to see the glob. The display was continuing to be a hit with the public, and other postgraduate students were involved with looking after the glob and informing the spectators.

Harry stood at the side with his cup of coffee, watching the proceedings, where Dale noticed him.

'Hey, Harry, you need to go and talk to your public.'

Harry smiled, but shook his head.

'C'mon, they want to see you.'

'No thanks – you're obviously doing a good job.' He finished his cup and left the room. There was a lot of truth in the adage of too much of a good thing.

Mrs Shaw collared him as he went back to his office: 'Harry, I'm spending my time answering queries about you and the gravity machine. You're going to have to work out something so I can get on with my work.'

'Sure, Mrs Shaw, I'll see what I can do.' However, he actually didn't have the foggiest notion what he could do. And to a large measure he was beginning not to care.

Then, when he logged onto the university internet system he watched aghast as the unknown e-mails just piled up. He opened three or four, but as before most involved personal questions, requests for money and invitations to talk.

He started deleting all unknown e-mails, and then noticed one subject line which said: *Australian family – congratulations Harry*. He looked for a while, then opened it.

It was from his Australian grandfather and grandmother, whom he had never met, and had never even spoken to. They were suddenly aware of his existence, and the e-mail congratulated him and spoke of missed times and opportunities. They, and the whole growing family in Australia, would love to see him whenever he had time for a visit.

He leant back in his chair, looking at the computer screen. His father had spoken very little of his family who had emigrated some years before democracy in South Africa. Harry had been aware of an underlying tension, for which his mother seemed to blame herself. He could recall one occasion when his father had said words to the effect that *'if they don't want to accept you, then I want nothing to do with them. They can rot in Australia.'*

He made a sudden decision that they could continue rotting in Australia, and deleted the e-mail. He called Tracy to find out if she was going to lunch in the cafeteria. Yes, she was happy to go early.

Coincidentally, they found the same table as the previous time Harry joined her. Now she seemed a lot more relaxed. Harry told her about his new security system, which he hoped would be a waste of money.

'It's probably a good idea, now we know about some of the weirdo's out there,' she replied.

He smiled, hesitated, and changed the subject to something that had been bugging him.

'Tracy, have you taken ARV's?'

Suddenly she was serious, 'Of course. Judy's doctor made sure I had all the right treatment. I had a whole cocktail of ARV's.' She grimaced: 'Not nice – they had all sorts of side effects, headaches, insomnia ...'

'Are you still taking them?'

'No, I finished last week – that's why I could go to the Cederberg.'

'And?'

She looked at him inquiringly, 'You mean has it been successful?'

He nodded.

'I'll know in about ten days.' She looked away, and continued slowly: 'I'm being positive about the whole thing. I don't even know whether he has AIDS.'

He smiled encouragingly, 'I'm sure it will be OK.'

They lapsed into silence, and Harry wondered about the unreality of the whole situation. She just cannot have AIDS!

There was one more thing he had to know, 'And one other thing ...' He hesitated, battling to say it, but finally asked, '... pregnancy?'

'No, thank god,' she answered vehemently. 'That would have been ... the end. Too much.' She looked at him, trying to see if he understood.

It had all taken a load off Harry's mind, and he smiled sympathetically. Almost involuntarily he took her hand where it was lying on the table. But then he withdrew again quickly, grinning sheepishly as she looked and smiled at his bashfulness.

'I'm having my first game of squash this year,' he said quickly.

'Yes, I see you did pretty well at Cambridge.'

'I guess I can't have any secrets.'

'Not when you're famous, no.'

The squash game was not very successful for Harry. He had played for the Cambridge second team, the Ganders, but was rusty, and consequently had to do a lot of running. He also found out he was not fit, so by the end he was soaked in sweat.

His opponent, who played for the university second team, was conciliatory. 'You just need a bit of practice – you've got the shots.' He was happy to be able to inform his friends that he had just creamed the inventor of the gravity machine.

On the other hand, standing in the shower afterwards, Harry was also happy. He had managed to get rid of some of his frustrations on the little black ball, and the physical exertions had been just what he needed.

On Tuesday morning Harry decided to work at home, since the university situation seemed to be getting untenable. In particular, he didn't know what to do about Mrs Shaw's request: no doubt he could contact Pre Mahlangu, but he didn't get around to doing it.

Moreover, he was working on some ideas about possible ways to inhibit the sudden deflation of gravity energy. This would involve further investigations into the characteristics of specific molecular structures, and once he had defined what was required he would be able to ask physical chemists whether there were suitable molecules available.

He was surprised when his doorbell rang in mid-morning. He looked at the new monitor, and with a start realised it was actually the immediate door to his apartment that had rung, not the door on the outside of the building. With a frown he turned on the camera, and his heart sank as he realised who was outside.

'Come on Harry, open up – we've got some things to talk about.' The voice of Mac Manyi was unmistakeable, and the camera showed there were two others with him.

Damn! Harry actually didn't want to face the situation, particularly not after the lunch yesterday with Tracy. He was filled with loathing for the man at the door, and hesitated, not knowing what to do.

The doorbell rang again, accompanied by an insistent knock. Reluctantly Harry succumbed, and opened the door.

'Ah, Harry,' Mac Manyi greeted him. 'We need to talk.'

He was dressed in his trade-mark grey suit, and he marched into Harry's apartment, accompanied by his two cronies.

'This is a small place, Harry – not fit for your status. You should get something better.' Mac looked around, and went into the lounge and sat down on the big comfortable chair; the other two sat on chairs at the kitchen counter.

He put some documents on the coffee table.

'I've spoken to people in Foreign Affairs, and a whole lot of lawyers, and we've come up with a draft system for African empowerment for the gravity machine. We need to work through these papers.'

But Harry was just standing, staring at him, not wanting to do anything associated with the man. Mac turned and looked at Harry, a puzzled look on his face.

Then he smiled broadly, 'Ah, I get it. I saw the picture in the paper this morning ...'

Before he could continue the doorbell rang again. It broke into Harry's indecisiveness, and he quickly went to the door.

A big man stood outside. He was wearing a uniform, with a half-familiar badge on his left sleeve.

'Morning, Dr Ehlers. I'm Etienne from *CF Security*. Got a message to say unknown people had come to your apartment – they managed to get through the building security. Is everything okay?'

'Come in.' Harry could feel his hands wet with sweat as he turned back into his apartment with Etienne behind him.

'Who's this?' Mac demanded as he saw the security man.

'Please go,' Harry said to Mac, pointing at the door. 'I don't want to talk to you.'

Mac stared at Harry, and then leant back in the chair. 'Oh, come now Harry – is this about that girl, what's her name ... Tracy?'

Harry said nothing.

'She probably told you a whole pack of lies about me.' He looked inquiringly at Harry, and shook his head. 'No woman's worth that. There are lots more out there – forget her.'

'Get out!' Harry said hoarsely. All he could see was the bloated body of the man in front of him between Tracy's legs, as she desperately fought ...

Suddenly Etienne stood in front of Mac. 'Dr Ehlers asked you to leave,' he said quietly.

'Fuck off!' Mac looked at the man in front of him with contempt.

Etienne reached down and grabbed the tie and collar of Mac's smart white shirt. Without seeming to strain he lifted, and Mac came up out of the chair. A button on the shirt couldn't take the strain and popped off. A look of desperation came onto Mac's face, and he looked across at his cronies, but they didn't seem to be interested in helping him.

Etienne held Mac up, so that his feet were scrabbling on the floor. 'Do you want me to help you out?'

Mac eyes were wide now, and he was battling to breathe. 'We'll go,' he eventually gasped.

Etienne lowered Mac slowly, and stood and watched as the three unwelcome visitors made their way to the door.

Before going out Mac turned around, straightening his shirt and tie. 'Harry,' he said, 'you're a fucking disappointment. This is about Africa, and you're like the rest of them, just taking what you can, and giving nothing back. You don't have African blood – you're a fucking, bloody Yank.'

He looked at Etienne, 'You'll regret this.' He slammed the door as he left.

Harry found he was shaking, and he sat down at the counter. 'Thanks,' he said to Etienne.

Etienne didn't respond immediately. 'I probably shouldn't have done that,' he said eventually.

'Why?' Harry was surprised.

Etienne looked at the front door, 'Am I right in assuming that was Mac Manyi?' Harry nodded.

'Status is everything to that kind of man,' Etienne continued slowly. 'He lost face here, and he'll want to get even.'

He turned to Harry, 'Manyi mentioned another name ... Tracy. Who is that?'

'She's a friend,' Harry responded, a frown on his face.

'You may want to warn her.'

'You can't be serious...'

'I can't say for certain, but in my line we take precautions. I can arrange to have someone watch her.'

This was getting totally out of hand, and Harry couldn't believe what they were now discussing. Still, he had to admit he was happy Etienne came when he did.

'She needn't know about it. If anything, they'll try to arrange an accident, something to let you know they're in control,' Etienne explained, seeing Harry's reticence. 'Where does she live?'

'In Milnerton – with three friends.'

'That's probably okay. What I can suggest is that she has low-level surveillance – for instance her car when she's parked it somewhere. Or if she's somewhere on her own.'

He looked at Harry, 'I think you need the same.'

'I don't want to be watched!' Harry said, angry now.

'No, I don't mean a body-guard or anything like that,' Etienne said quickly. 'What I'm thinking of is a motion sensor and camera at your garage. We have people on the campus – they can keep a check on cars. You must give me Tracy's car registration and where she generally parks.'

'What I also suggest is that you have a portable alarm with you permanently – as a bangle or attached to your watch strap is easiest. When you set it off it sends us your position as well.'

Harry seemed unconvinced.

'It really is not intrusive,' Etienne continued, 'but it could save your life. Or Tracy's.'

'I'll think about it. What about you – he threatened you as well.'

Etienne smiled, 'It comes with the job.'

CHAPTER 13

Harry met Tracy for lunch again, but didn't tell her about the visit from Mac Manyi. He was still shaken by the events, and didn't know how she would react. He also wasn't sure what to make of the veiled threats identified by Etienne.

They settled in at another small table on one side of the cafeteria. Coming early as they did meant they generally had a choice of where to sit.

'Did you see the photo in the paper this morning?' she asked.

'No ... what photo?'

'The restaurant owner on Sunday – getting full value for the meal he gave us.' She smiled, 'Gravity man selects Kalk Bay eating spot. It seems you're a well-known gourmet now.'

'It's actually ridiculous,' he responded, 'and I suppose people believe it.' The photo was obviously how Manyi knew about Tracy.

She sensed some reticence in him, 'You're very quiet today, Harry – is something wrong?'

He smiled at her, 'No, no, nothing ...'

After a moment he continued, 'Stephen is coming back on Thursday. He let me know this morning he wants to arrange a workshop in Germany next week – probably Thursday.'

'Is it a lot of work?'

'It'll probably be similar to the last workshop.'

'How is it funded?'

'Everybody who comes has to pay, so that covers the cost.'

'And you?'

'I'm getting three hundred thousand Euros.'

She stared at him, 'You're joking – that's more than four million Rand. For one day!'

He smiled, 'I'm trying to get used to the numbers – as I said, I got over three million in the US.'

She shook her head, looking at him, 'I read some of the estimates in the papers, but they were paper numbers. You'll have to get an accountant.'

'I know – there are apparently all sorts of tax implications.'

She was quiet, digesting the information.

'You don't know the half of it,' he added. He told her briefly about Sir Richard and the offer from B2O.

'Wow!' was all she could muster. 'A hundred and eighty billion Rand! I can't even imagine that amount of money.'

Then she was serious, 'You're not going to accept, are you? You need to keep control, so you can decide what to do. That money will really be able to do something in the fight for our planet.'

She sat back, continuing speculatively, 'Although you know, your gravity machine has even changed that perspective. There's always been the argument the Earth's all we have, but now ... now we can possibly go and colonise the solar system. I've no doubt we'll screw up all the planets as well – but it will take time.'

'Ever the optimist,' he smiled.

She smiled back, 'No, the realist.'

He changed the subject, 'How's the thesis going?'

She grimaced, 'Final write-up phase – you know, the worst part: putting it all together.'

'So, does that mean you don't have time for a dinner-date?'

Her eyes sparkled, and he couldn't help noticing how radiant she looked – even the weal above her left eye wasn't angry any more.

'Thanks Harry – I'd love to, but can we leave it for the weekend?'

It was just as well, he thought afterwards, he had a lot to do. He realised he needed a demonstration glob for the coming workshop. Baseball glob may be available, however, it would be much more satisfactory if he could adapt his own glob. He spoke to Dale about ordering a low frequency modulator, or finding out if anything suitable was available at the university. Even though his position and status was still not clear, he could now initiate the process with the full cooperation of the department.

On Wednesday he met Tracy again for their customary lunch, but she had a meeting with her supervisor scheduled and couldn't stay long.

When he returned to the department, Mrs Shaw told him that Pre Mahlangu had asked to see him, and Thursday morning he was in her office, with the Registrar.

'So, Harry, have you decided what you want to do?'

'I'd prefer to stay here at the university,' Harry responded slowly, not sure what she was expecting. 'But I'm not sure in what position. Mrs Shaw says she needs assistance to deal with gravity machine business.'

'Yes, Swain has mentioned it.' She smiled, 'I'm glad you will stay. Now let me tell you what we can offer you.'

It turned out the university had already consulted the SASF with the objective of establishing an Institute for Gravity Research. Obviously Harry would be the Director, and it would be associated with the Physics Department. An initial amount of one million Rand had been sourced, to cover Harry's salary and relocation costs. Additional funding would become available as necessary, particularly when other staff and students started arriving.

'A suitable office has been identified, and of course you will need secretarial staff.'

Harry was amazed. 'Thank you,' he said, 'this has all happened very quickly. I'm still trying to find my way, particularly what to do with the possible funding from the gravity machine.'

He hesitated, 'I'm still trying to get my mind around some of the numbers, and I guess I'm going to need help in deciding how to handle it all. I've had an offer for the patent rights running into billions...'

Pre and the Registrar nodded, wondering where Harry was heading, because they could not compete with those numbers.

'I'm not keen, and want to investigate the possibilities of establishing a foundation or a trust or something like that for the income. In which case the foundation could sponsor such a gravity institute.'

Pre looked relieved, 'The university would welcome such sponsorship. Thanks Harry, that's actually better than I hoped.'

'I also don't need a salary,' Harry added.

'You can't already be paid for rights?' the Registrar asked.

'No, I've been paid for the workshops – more than I need. There's another workshop next week in Germany.'

'We can look at that as we go along – we don't want to do you down,' Pre said. 'There are obviously a lot of details to be worked out.'

She turned to the Registrar: 'We need to schedule another meeting, with everyone involved. And have an on-site inspection of what we propose.' The Registrar nodded.

She stood up, signifying the end of the meeting, 'Harry, thank you again for your cooperation – the university looks forward to a long and successful relationship. We'll let you know as soon as we can start with the new Institute. In the next week or so.'

As Harry was leaving she added, 'If you need any advice to establish the foundation, our legal department can help.'

Later, over lunch, Tracy was also amazed at the rate at which changes were happening.

'Are you ready for the big executive image?' she asked.

'I think so – big office, big desk, big secretary.'

'And a big ego.'

Harry smiled, 'Seriously, I don't think I can take all that.'

'Well, you have a big advantage – you can decide what you want. Everybody else will jump when you tell them.'

'You want a job?'

'I don't sit on the boss's knees.'

'Pity, it's the way to progress.'

They talked a bit about the foundation, and she indicated ways in which funds could be spent: research into endangered species, destruction of habitat, fighting environmental court cases ...

'Of course, your gravity machine also raises enormous problems in terms of access.'

He nodded: 'Yes, I've thought about that – there will have to be new controls established.'

It was exciting talking about the future, and what lay in store, but then Tracy reminded him about the present, 'I need to get back to my books and forge my own future.'

That evening, Harry wondered about the nature of the foundation and what objectives he should set. Many foundations were altruistic bodies, and Tracy had indicated some of the things that could be done, mainly in the environmental field. He was being persuaded that was where the problems lay.

He sat drinking his coffee, feet up on the coffee table. Perhaps his flippant offer of a job was not so far off the mark – he wondered if Tracy had ideas of what to do when she handed in her master's thesis?

Then Stephen sent an SMS to say he had landed, and that they needed to meet the next day.

'Harry, there's a rush to build the first manned gravity machine.'

Stephen sat on the visitor's chair in Harry's little office, bringing him up to date on what was happening.

'Even though they can't bring it down?'

'Doesn't matter – it's the prestige of the thing. Imagine Times Square – or Piccadilly Circus – or Tiananmen Square – and a gravity machine going up from there. And then hanging there with that green light, having spectators paying to go up and sit on it. What publicity!'

He leaned forward, 'The big companies are frantic to get there first, and the public is expecting it. They've seen the globs, and they want more. It's the topic of conversation everywhere, and it's built up its own hype. The newspapers are telling people what to expect, and they want to know why they can't go and buy a gravity machine – now!

I'm surprised you haven't seen more of it here,' he added.

'Well, I was amazed at the enthusiasm of Capetonians to see the glob,' Harry replied. 'I've read some of the newspapers, watched some TV and avoided other contact. I've got a limited access mobile, Mrs Shaw has been fielding phone calls, and I've deleted most e-mails. The security on my apartment also keeps people out.'

'A real isolationist.'

Harry smiled, 'Keeps me sane.' He told Stephen briefly of his Seychelles jaunt, not mentioning Tracy by name. He also didn't add anything about Mac.

'So you've had your share of excitement ... and this new girl-friend – Tracy – is she the one who went to Seychelles?'

Harry frowned, 'How do you know about Tracy?'

It was Stephen's turn to smile, 'Harry, you're famous. Have you googled your profile, or looked at Facebook and Youtube? Twittered?'

'You've got to be joking – I'm not telling anyone what I have for breakfast.'

'I'm not saying you have to. Just that there's a lot of interest in you out there. You and Tracy having lunch are on Youtube.'

Harry stared at him, 'That's ridiculous.'

'No ... that's today.'

Harry changed the subject, 'Stephen, I'm thinking of establishing a foundation to handle the proceeds from the gravity machine. The university will help to set it up.'

'Have you thought seriously about the new offer from Sir Richard? You know B2O have increased it to ten billion pounds?'

Harry nodded, 'Yes, but I still think I would like to handle it myself.'

'It would make things a lot easier to have such a professional organisation handling all the details. You could still do what you want to do – set up a foundation with the money – and not have to worry about who builds gravity machines and if they are paying for the rights.'

'They would also have to set up those structures – it could be done as part of the foundation's duties.'

'B2O have contacts all over the world. And the knowledge and experience to do a good professional job.'

Harry frowned, 'I need to assess the whole situation – I don't really understand why they want control and what they'll do with it.'

'Probably maintain the status quo – one doesn't want odd groups in the world accessing too much power.'

'B2O seems to be a very conservative organisation. Perhaps some changes will be good.'

Stephen sat back in his chair, 'Harry, this could affect all sorts of things – even international power blocks and treaties. There are many people who won't take kindly to change.'

'That's why we can't just trust B2O, we don't know their agenda,' Harry replied doggedly.

'Their values are good.'

'I don't know their values!

They can't just take over,' Harry continued after a moment. 'This whole thing must essentially be for the good of the planet.'

'Oh, come now, Harry – that's a wishy-washy idea. You must face facts. You could get autocratic regimes coming in, or religious fanatics. So it needs to be in the control of people who understand these things.'

'And you think B2O do?'

Stephen shrugged, 'Probably. Better than most, anyway. Remember you can negotiate with them – you must understand all your options. You need to consider the offer seriously.'

Harry stared at Stephen, and then abruptly changed the topic, 'What about the workshop?'

Stephen sat forward, 'Okay, we'll talk about B2O another time.'

He explained the workshop would be held on Thursday, and would be an all-day session as in Caltech. The venue was Frankfurt, where they had found a modern, interactive auditorium that would hold more than one thousand people. It had been advertised, and already was almost fully booked. He suggested they leave on Tuesday evening, so that they had Wednesday to acclimatise and get organised.

'There's a lot of interest from the east – China, India, Japan... All the participants will be given full videos of proceedings.'

Harry was more enthusiastic now, talking about familiar topics.

'I'm getting a low frequency modulator so we can demonstrate taking the glob down,' he added. 'I'm not sure whether we can get baseball glob.'

'Good – I was going to ask about that.' Stephen paused, and then continued, 'The notes from the last session may need some revision.'

'Yes ... I've actually been doing some work on identifying molecular characteristics to stop the sudden release of energy.'

He smiled: 'I've given it a name – I've called it *gravity energy deflation*. To stop the analogy with a nuclear power plant.'

Stephen stared at him, 'You've worked out a way to stop that ... that explosion?'

'Well, not entirely. All I've done is specify what sort of molecules are required in the gravity material. They will act to inhibit a chain reaction which leads to that catastrophic deflation of gravity energy. I'm not familiar with the different molecules available to be able to identify a suitable one – there are a lot more knowledgeable people out there.'

'We must patent that!'

'Can we?'

'Of course. It goes to a new process and technique.'

Stephen sat back, 'It means we can offer the delegates something new. We can also sell the video separately.'

Harry was intrigued, 'You said delegates would get a video as part of the attendance: surely it's out there, so you aren't going to sell more?'

'None of those delegates will give it away. Then there are all the people who haven't attended, and those who were at the first workshop – they will want the new information.'

'What will the video cost?'

'With this new information, probably five, ten thousand Euros. Something like that.'

Harry whistled, 'That's a lot of money.'

'Yes, we can probably push your payment up to four hundred thousand Euros.'

Here were the big numbers again. 'What about you?' Harry asked, 'We've never talked about your payments.'

Stephen smiled, 'I'm sorted – I get a percentage of the profits of all these activities. They also cover my costs.'

He hesitated, but then continued, 'I made a lot of money after the first day when the markets crashed. I guess you could call it insider information.'

Harry recalled what he had heard earlier, 'That's what Hamish Prentiss said.'

'Who?'

'Hamish Prentiss – I met him on the plane. He said he could have made billions with the information.'

Stephen was impressed, 'You get around. Prentiss is a sharp customer, one of the richest in the world.'

'I bought short,' Stephen continued, 'primarily automotive shares. Very profitable.' He smiled in satisfaction.

Harry didn't understand the financial jargon, and let it be. He obviously didn't have to worry about Stephen not being paid.

'So,' Stephen continued, 'does that mean we have another weekend patenting session?'

'It looks like it – perhaps we can start this afternoon?'

They agreed to meet at Stephen's office at about four pm; Stephen would order a take-away for supper so they could continue with the patent description.

Then, just when Stephen was about to leave, Harry's phone rang. He looked at it, not recognising the number: however, Mrs Shaw had obviously deemed the caller important enough to forward the call.

'Yes?'

'Dr Ehlers, I'm speaking on behalf of Deputy Minister Angie Ramabola. She would like to arrange a meeting as soon as possible to discuss the future of the gravity machine.'

That was the last thing Harry wanted. 'It's difficult,' he replied, 'I'm leaving for Europe on Tuesday.'

'What about Monday, ten am, in the departmental offices in Cape Town? It won't be a long meeting.'

Harry put his hand over the phone and looked at Stephen, 'Government wants to meet at ten on Monday – can you make it?'

Stephen was not enthusiastic, 'Not longer than an hour.'

Harry turned to his phone again, 'We can make an hour – Stephen Cambre will be coming as well.' He was given instructions where to go.

'Do you know what it's about?' Stephen asked after Harry had hung up.

Harry frowned: 'The Deputy Minister welcomed me back when I arrived at Cape Town. She went on about African empowerment through the gravity machine.'

'African empowerment?'

'The way I understand it is that they want Africans on the board of every company manufacturing gravity machines. This to ensure a portion of the profits go to Africa.'

'That's crazy.'

'Which is more or less what I said, but it seems they want to take it further.'

'We'll have to nip that in the bud right at the start. You see, this is the sort of thing that happens when different groups want to muscle in.'

Harry didn't respond, and Stephen stood up to leave, 'I'll make all the travel arrangements. We can come back on Friday after the workshop.'

When he was alone, Harry went onto Youtube, and found the video of himself and Tracy having lunch. The quality wasn't good, and was obviously taken from one of the walkways above the eating area. He shook his head that people could be interested in such mundane matters.

However, it was the first thing he mentioned when he met her for lunch.

'Do you know you're on Youtube?'

She looked at him coyly, 'You're also on.'

'So you've seen it?'

'There've been a couple.' She looked up to see if there were any new amateur photographers around, but there was nothing obvious.

'My kid sister phoned on Tuesday – wanting to know if that was me with you.' She smiled, 'So I'm afraid the whole of KZN knows that we've been having lunch regularly.'

Harry grinned: it made him feel good she was enjoying their lunch time meetings as much as he was.

'I don't mind,' he responded.

She looked at him, 'Harry, you must know that every girl in the world would want to be here in my place. And here I am. I'm very lucky.'

'So am I,' he said quietly. He moved his hand forward to where her hand was on the table, but she read his intentions, and looked up quickly to where there may be photographers. He caught her message and stopped, smiling bashfully.

'The price of fame,' she responded, her eyes laughing encouragingly.

He told her about his meeting with Stephen, and the developments with the glob. He said he would be spending that evening and probably much of the next day on the new patent description.

She shook her head: 'Stephen really does seem to want to milk everything he can out of it, doesn't he?.'

'I guess. That's what he does, as a patent attorney. Anyway, it's better to have the patent now, than to try and get it afterwards.'

As it was, the new patent description went a lot quicker the second time around. Both Harry and Stephen had a much better idea of what was required, and by lunch time on Saturday it was completed to Stephen's satisfaction.

However, Harry still had a lot of work to do, compiling notes for the workshop. That evening he took Tracy to a barbecue, with friends from his undergraduate student days. He was proud to show her off, and they were proud to show him off to others.

When he took her back to her lodgings, she kissed him gently at the front door. 'Thank you, Harry, for what you're doing for me,' she said before going inside.

On Sunday he continued with his work. The cold and windy weather, with occasional squalls of rain meant he wasn't tempted to go outdoors. However, he did take off time in the afternoon to have tea with Tracy and her friends. They invited him to stay for a quick supper before he returned to his work.

His life was getting onto a very pleasant, even keel.

CHAPTER 14

Stephen and Harry were at the offices of the Department of Science and Technology well before ten am on Monday morning. They were hoping to get the meeting over as soon as possible, since they had a lot to do before leaving for Germany the next day.

The Department was housed in a modern building in the City centre, and as they approached they were concerned to see a small press corps hovering around the entrance. Harry was recognised immediately.

'Dr Ehlers, is it true the proceeds of the gravity machine will be used primarily for the benefit of Africa?'

Microphones were thrust into Harry's face. The question was not totally unexpected, and he had formulated a general response, 'We haven't finalised how the proceeds will be handled. In particular, Mr Cambre is still busy with the patents and the implementation of those rights.'

'You must have some idea of who the main beneficiaries will be. Are you going to keep the money for yourself?'

'We will probably set up a foundation to administer the funds.'

'Where will it be based?'

'Who are the trustees?'

Stephen took Harry by the arm and steered him in the direction of the front door. He waved at the reporters, 'All this still needs to be finalised – that's why we're having these meetings.'

Security at the door allowed them into the building, and they were taken to the boardroom on the fifth floor. It had an elliptical conference table that could seat about fifteen: they were the first to arrive, although there were staff fussing with the arrangement of seats and putting out soft drinks and glasses.

They sat down. Stephen looked at his watch: it was a couple of minutes to ten. He poured glasses of juice for himself and Harry, and said in a loud voice, 'I hope we can begin at ten, as arranged.' However, nobody took any notice.

Three or four departmental officials drifted in, introduced themselves and sat down. Then the door opened again, and Mac Manyi and two others came in.

Mac caught sight of Harry, 'Hey Harry,' he said with a wide smile, 'nice to see you again!'

Harry froze. He stared at Mac, and said grimly, 'I'm not having a meeting with you.'

'Oh, come on Harry, lighten up!'

'Either you get out, or I'm going.'

Stephen grabbed Harry by the arm, 'What's wrong? Why are you acting like this?'

Harry turned briefly to Stephen, 'The man's a rapist – he should be locked up in jail. I want nothing to do with him.' Other conversations in the room stopped as they heard what was said.

'That's rubbish.' Mac stood looking at Harry, making no attempt to leave.

Harry stared back, 'Okay, then I'm leaving.' He stood up and started gathering up some papers he had put on the table.

'Wait, wait.' One of the departmental officials quickly stepped in, 'I don't know what this is about, but Mac Manyi is an important part of this meeting.'

He turned to Harry, 'Dr Ehlers, can he not stay?'

'Either he goes or I go.'

The official looked at Harry, and turned to Mac Manyi. He waved his hands in resignation, 'Mac ...?'

Manyi scowled at Harry, 'Okay, I'll go.' At the door he turned around and pointed at Harry, 'That man is not good for Africa.' The door slammed as he left.

It was quiet in the room as Harry slowly sat down again. Stephen muttered under his breath, 'Well, that's not a very auspicious start to the meeting.'

And so it proved. The Deputy Minister herself didn't attend, and sent the Director-General of the department, Dr. Qoboshiyane. He arrived soon after, and from his cool greeting it was apparent he had been informed of Mac's departure. He sat down opposite to Harry and Stephen, with a group of advisors.

After being introduced he tabled a document, and Harry and Stephen were both given copies; the other people around the table already had their copies. It was only about five pages, and entitled *Using the Gravity Machine to Empower Africa.*

'This is a first draft of an agreement to formulate utilisation of the proceeds of the gravity machine,' Dr. Qoboshiyane explained, 'and we can go through the general structures now and formulate any amendments or changes. These alterations can be worked into the next draft and finalised at a subsequent meeting.'

He looked at Harry and Stephen, and they nodded briefly, not knowing what the document contained.

'At the start, we need to agree on the general objective, and this is given on the first page: *The Parties agree that the proceeds of the gravity machine will be used for the well-being of Africa and all its citizens.*'

'To the exclusion of all other peoples?' Harry asked.

'No, not necessarily. But the first objective is to benefit Africa.'

'We want to see it altered to reflect that,' Stephen came in. 'Something to the effect that all peoples will benefit, with particular emphasis on Africa.'

Dr. Qoboshiyane spoke briefly to a man on his right, 'We can make some changes, but perhaps we can just discuss some of the processes. It will clarify what we propose to do.'

'We want to set up a foundation,' he continued, 'which will structure the use of the funds on an equitable basis. The Trustees will be broadly representative of African governments, since they will be able to identify where the greatest needs are.'

Harry and Stephen looked at each other, but did not say anything.

'Quite obviously there will be a need to police the manufacture of gravity machines, and what we propose here is that the Trustees appoint individuals to represent the foundation on the boards of the different companies. They will be able to ensure compliance with the patent rights and payment of the levies.'

'What position do you envisage for Dr. Ehlers in this structure,' Stephen interrupted.

'He will be a board member.'

'Chairperson?'

'Not necessarily – the board will have to vote on that.'

Harry was feeling frustrated by these decisions that had been made without his consent, or even knowledge.

'I've already been investigating the formation of a foundation,' he said. Well, it was true, he had thought about it.

Dr. Qoboshiyane looked at him, 'Good – so we just have to agree on the structure and objectives.'

'I want to see it benefitting all people, not particular groups,' Harry continued. Then he added, 'More than that, it must be for the benefit of the environment, for our planet as a whole.' He wondered if Tracy would agree with his rather ham-handed description.

However, that did not go down well with the department. The official to the right of the deputy minister took up the argument, 'Dr Ehlers, that is very noble, but there are already a multitude of groups fighting for our planet. There are organisations like Greenpeace, IFAW, and now all the climate groups.'

He leant forward, 'What we are talking about here is some redress for past wrongs, to help a whole continent get on its feet. We have an AIDS pandemic, we have thousands dying of famine, we have children who cannot get education.'

'That is not limited to Africa,' Harry interrupted, 'so each situation can be looked at in terms of its priorities. All over the world.'

'That ignores the basic reasons for the problems, and we must sort out the fact Africa has been neglected, Africa has been raped.'

The word hit Harry, and he found his anger rising. Fortunately Stephen came in.

'I think we need to establish some basics here,' he said slowly. 'In particular, it is important to realise Dr. Ehlers holds the patent rights to the gravity machine. So he is the only one who can decide what to do with the proceeds.'

There was a moment's silence, and Dr. Qoboshiyane responded, 'We understand that. However, we thought Dr. Ehlers would appreciate the needs of Africa, and that we could count on him to assist in building up Africa to where it belongs. We thought he would remember where he was born and where he was nurtured. That the gravity machine originated in Africa.'

Harry thought of telling him he was actually born in the USA, wondering if it was important to know where you first saw the light of day.

He found everyone looking at him. 'I do feel for Africa,' he finally said, 'but Africa is also part of the world. National boundaries are arbitrary lines, and we need to concern ourselves with individuals, not nations or continents. Everywhere.'

However, the man to the right of the Director was having none of it, 'As I've said, that sounds very noble, but it doesn't give any definite practical guidelines of how the funds will be apportioned. We need to establish the structures which can ensure the right people benefit. It sounds to me Dr. Ehlers wants to keep everything for himself.'

'Which he is entitled to do,' Stephen said.

'Then he mustn't claim to be a great benefactor. Or an African – he has no *ubuntu*, or of being part of the greater African community.'

Harry leant back, 'I've never claimed to be a benefactor, but I do see the funds as an opportunity to help. Not groups on the basis of a misconstrued birthright, but individuals who show they deserve it.'

Dr. Qoboshiyane quickly responded before the man to his right could reply, 'Dr. Ehlers, it's clear we are not on the same page. We were led to believe you had agreed to the general structures outlined in the document. It seems not, which is a great pity. Have you in fact formulated the structures of the foundation you said you're setting up?'

'No ... there hasn't been time,' Harry answered.

Dr. Qoboshiyane frowned, 'Well, at this stage there is little sense in continuing with this meeting: your objectives seem to be very different to ours.'

He stood up, picking up his documents. He paused, looking at Harry and Stephen, 'Read through the document, and you can incorporate the ideas – if you have any feeling for this continent you won't kick your heritage in the teeth.' Then he marched out, taking his officials with him.

Harry and Stephen looked at each other. 'I don't think we won the popularity parade,' Stephen said.

When they exited the building they saw the official who had been on the right side of Dr. Qoboshiyane talking to the group of reporters. They tried to duck off in the opposite direction, but a couple of reporters at the side came running over.

'Dr. Ehlers, is it true you won't be collaborating in programs to help Africa?'

Stephen turned briefly, 'We are still setting up a foundation – nothing is decided.'

'Dr. Ehlers, did you call Mac Manyi a rapist?'

Again Stephen kept Harry moving quickly. 'No comment,' he said.

The reporters stopped, and they managed to get away.

Once in Stephen's car Harry sat back in the seat, 'Geez, what a bloody runaround.'

Stephen looked at him before turning on the ignition key, 'OK, what's this whole rape story?' As they drove back Harry told him of Tracy's ordeal, and his two previous meetings with Mac Manyi. Somehow, he felt better with the telling.

Stephen whistled under his breath, 'Well, that explains your attitude, and I can't say I blame you. Manyi is obviously a bad piece of work, and I would guess he told Qoboshiyane you had agreed to the proposal. He probably thought he could just railroad it over you.'

Back in his office at the university, Harry read through the tabled document. It had all the ideas Mac had originally propounded, designed specifically for empowering Africans without defining who they were. It would be left essentially in the hands of politicians to dispense the largesse.

He leant back in his chair, staring up at the ceiling: for the first time he noticed paint beginning to peel off. He turned his mind back to his problem – he couldn't see himself agreeing to the proposals.

He found he couldn't concentrate on the gravity machine workshop, and he phoned Tracy for an early lunch.

As expected, she was appalled at the proposed foundation.

'Harry, you can't possibly agree to those ideas. Nowhere is there anything that concerns itself with the problems of our planet: sustainability, conservation – all those things that will finally dictate whether in fact people survive. It's a formula for enrichment of a few at the expense of everything else.'

He didn't mention Mac.

On Tuesday he was at the university soon after eight am. He greeted Mrs Shaw as he went past her office, but she quickly called him back.

'Harry, did you watch the news – have you seen this morning's paper?' He had actually been too busy working on his presentation to do either, and came slowly back into her office.

'No, why?' He didn't like the tone of her voice.

'Look.' She handed him the paper lying on her desk.

The headline hit him: *Ehlers accuses Manyi of rape.* The subtitle carried the message further: *Ehlers won't cooperate on African empowerment.* He started reading, but was interrupted by Mrs Shaw.

'There were lots of calls yesterday about the story. I couldn't contact you.'

He looked up, 'Yes, I was working at home, and forgot my cell phone in my car – sorry.'

'I believe you'll be getting your own secretary soon, Harry,' Mrs Shaw continued. 'I don't mind doing admin for you, but it's taking up a lot of time.' She paused, and continued softly, 'Professor Swain doesn't like it, and your new office is probably going to be at the other end of the building.'

Harry nodded, his mind elsewhere, 'Do you mind if I borrow the paper?'

'Of course not, just bring it back.'

Once in his office he closed the door and read through the main story, as given by the official who had sat on the right side of Dr. Qoboshiyane. Harry apparently did not acknowledge the right of Africa to the proceeds of the gravity machine, and wanted to keep the patent rights for himself. Moreover, he had refused to continue the meeting if Mac Manyi was present because – according to a source at the meeting – Manyi was a rapist.

Suddenly there was an urgent knocking at his door, and before he could react it opened and Tracy came in. She was looking grim, her hair dishevelled.

'Harry ... why?' she pointed to the paper in his hands. Her lips trembled, and her eyes were full of tears.

'Why ... why did you say that.' Her voice was barely a whisper, and she stood there, looking totally fragile.

He dropped the paper and came to her. She backed away, her eyes wide now.

'No, Harry ... please.' She seemed to regain some composure.

'Just tell me why ... you had no right to include me ...'

He looked at her, not quite knowing how to explain. Eventually he said 'I'm sorry, Tracy. I said that to Stephen, because he wanted to know why I was against Mac Manyi attending. The others must have heard it.'

She still stared at him, without saying a word.

'Manyi came to see me last week,' he explained further.

'You didn't tell me.'

'No, I didn't want to upset you.' Briefly he told what had happened, and what Etienne had done. Her face remained expressionless, even when Harry explained how Manyi had been thrown out.

'Have you read what he said?' she asked, pointing at the paper.

'No, I've only just seen the headlines.'

She nodded, 'Harry, please understand – I want nothing to do with Mac. I don't want to see him, I don't want to hear him, I never want him anywhere!' She was again getting overwrought, and she closed her eyes. 'Oh god,' she said, burying her head in her hands and starting to sob.

He reached out to touch her, but she backed away again. She stopped sobbing and stared at him.

'Don't you want to see him in jail?' he eventually asked.

Her eyes were wide, 'No, I never want anything to do with him.'

He said nothing, and suddenly she was cross. 'He wouldn't be prosecuted – less than ten percent of reported rape cases get convictions, and most aren't even reported.'

He didn't say anything, and she continued slowly, by way of explanation, 'You don't understand ... Mpho and I opened a case at the police the next day. Filled in all sorts of forms.'

She was calmer now, and continued flatly. 'We went back last week to find out if anything was happening – they said they had lost the dockets.'

'Lost the dockets?' Harry repeated, '... How?'

'It's apparently common ... it makes cases go away.'

'So you see, Harry,' she continued after a while, 'I don't want to go to court. Mac would laugh at me and get away scot-free.'

She said it lightly, but her equanimity left her, and her lower lip trembled again. She looked at Harry, and quickly made her way to the door. 'I have to go.'

'Will I see you at lunch?'

She stopped at the door and whispered, 'I can't go out there.' Then she was gone.

Harry stared at the open door for a long time before going out into the corridor. It was empty, and he closed the door again and sat down at his desk. He picked up the paper and read it further.

He soon reached the point where Mac Manyi was asked for comment on the rape allegation: it was supposedly associated with Tracy Freese, Harry Ehlers' regular lunch date.

Yes, we had sex, he was reported as saying candidly. *She enjoyed it – it's what women want. I have no doubt Harry Ehlers is jealous – he probably can't satisfy her.*

Damn! Involuntarily he wished Etienne had strangled the man. He could understand Tracy's attitude now.

His phone interrupted his thoughts. He looked at it: Mrs Shaw must have let the call through.

He picked up the receiver, not saying anything.

'Dr Ehlers?' the voice asked. 'This is Rob Adler from the Evening Times ...'

Harry put the receiver down again.

He felt totally deflated, and sat at his desk, staring at the paint peeling off the ceiling. He stood up and took the paper back to Mrs Shaw.

'Please tell anyone who phones I've left for Germany,' he informed her.

Back in his office he packed the glob and its generator and modulator into his bag and left the department. He didn't want to return to his apartment, so he went for a drive along the Chapman's Peak road. He stopped at an observation point on the winding road cut into the mountain, overlooking the wide Atlantic Ocean. At that stage on a weekday morning he was on his own, and he sat on the bollard protecting the parking area, absorbing the expanse and timelessness of the scene. It was a real pleasure to be away from the machinations of humanity.

However, after a while he realised he had to get back, and he bought a hamburger for lunch before returning to his apartment. He still had some details to complete on his presentations, but by mid afternoon he had packed his bags. Soon after Stephen picked him up to go to the airport.

CHAPTER 15

They flew first class to Frankfurt. Stephen rationalised it by saying they had to have a good rest before the workshop.

'In any case, why not?' Harry didn't argue.

Stephen sat at the window of the aircraft, and as they approached Frankfurt he indicated to Harry to look out. Harry leaned over, and could see a big cloverleaf, with cars seemingly going in all directions.

'That's the *Franfurter Kreuz*,' Stephen explained, 'one of the most heavily used Autobahn interchanges in Europe. I wonder what it will look like in ten years time ...'

'There'll probably still be cars around,' Harry replied.

'Yes, but at some stage they'll have to decide to stop maintaining such structures. Then, what do you do with it?'

Harry sat back: it was an interesting question, but not something he would lose sleep over. Others could make those decisions.

It was Harry's first visit to Europe after the APA conference, and the workshop the next day had gained prominence in all the news broadcasts. It was seen as Europe's opportunity to get on board the new *mode of life*, and he epitomised the new future. His arrival in Frankfurt was widely publicised, and as he and Stephen walked into the arrivals concourse they could see a host of reporters and cameramen waiting.

'Do you want to talk?' Stephen asked.

Harry smiled, 'Sure, why not?' He was actually finding it quite funny, all this attention. But most of all, he didn't know what more these people could possibly want from him.

As the reporters and cameramen descended on the two arrivals, Stephen went ahead, holding up his hands.

'Please,' he said loudly. The microphones and cameras were pushed ahead, but there was no barrage of questions.

'Dr. Ehlers is quite happy to answer questions, but let's have some order,' Stephen continued.

Harry stopped, and there was a scramble for positions as close as possible to him, with microphones waving in his face. He moved back, and Stephen came and pushed the crowd back, to form a semicircle a metre or two away. In this process, Harry looked at the reporters: few were smiling, most were just getting their equipment ready, and almost none made eye contact. He realised they were working at a job, and what they wanted was a story. He wasn't sure he could give that to them.

'Dr. Ehlers, when will the first manned gravity machine fly?' the question came from a gum-chewing reporter in the front.

Harry smiled – what was called 'an engaging smile' in the evening papers.

'I haven't a clue,' he replied, 'you'll have to ask the manufacturers.'

'But aren't you involved in getting a gravity machine flying?' From another reporter.

'Nope.'

'What are you doing then? What is the workshop for?'

'I'm explaining my theory, so the manufacturers can apply it. I am not involved in any of those subsequent developments.'

'Do you have anything new to tell the participants?'

Harry hesitated, 'Yes,' he said slowly, 'I'll be describing some molecular characteristics to counter the rapid release of gamma rays when gravity energy is removed.'

'To stop the nuclear reaction?'

Harry shook his head – it really did take time to get rid of pre-conceived notions.

'It isn't a nuclear reaction. We need to slow down the release of energy.'

'Will it mean gravity machines can then be made?'

'The theory is there to make gravity machines – you've seen that already. But there are still many practical problems to solve: an easy way to get the energy out, improve efficiency by using other materials and not gold. Then there is the design, and the propulsion methods to consider. No doubt there will be many other problems – so you can see a lot of work is still needed before practical machines become available.'

'Dr. Ehlers, do you know Mr. Manyi is going to sue you for calling him a rapist?'

The question came out of the blue, and Harry stopped.

'Is that about Tracy Freese?' another reporter asked quickly, seeing his hesitation.

Stephen stepped in, saying brusquely, 'Dr. Ehlers isn't here to discuss personal details.'

That didn't deter the reporter, 'Is it true you called him a rapist?'

Stephen used his big frame to stand directly in front of the reporter who had asked the question. 'If there are no more questions, we have a lot to do before the workshop tomorrow.'

A question from the far side changed the topic, 'There are complaints that Asian countries are being deliberately excluded from these workshops to promote western companies. What are you doing to help them?'

'Attendance has been on a first come, first served basis,' Stephen replied slowly. 'Complete coverage of both workshops is also available to anyone who wants it.'

'At enormous cost.'

Stephen shrugged his shoulders, 'The stakes are high.'

There were a few further questions which Harry answered glibly. It was apparent the reporters were wanting something new for their readers and viewers, and there were requests for a demonstration. It took some convincing they didn't have the time, and eventually they did get away.

After a short drive to the city Harry found himself ushered into a luxurious suite high up in one of the top hotels. Stephen had the adjacent suite, which also included a small boardroom – 'so we can work on any problems that come up.' Harry looked out over the Frankfurt skyline with its scattering of skyscrapers, and not too far away he could see the River Main.

A limo took them to the site of the Frankfurt Trade Fair, adjacent to the auditorium they had booked for the workshop. Stephen had done a substantial amount of distance organisation, particularly in terms of setting up the registration facilities and providing caterers.

They were shown around by Herr Steiger, who took great pride in identifying all the technical details of the auditorium. In particular, he pointed out the complex system of cameras, and they were introduced to the head cameraman hired to record the whole event. Harry's presentation was put onto the big screen, and he was shown how to operate the remote.

Stephen was pleased with the arrangements. 'Harry, I've also decided on teleconferencing the whole event – makes it more accessible. It won't change your presentation, though you may have to answer some TV questions.' Harry stared at him, but then shrugged his shoulders: there was little he could do at that stage.

The glob was set up for the demonstration while Stephen and Herr Steiger discussed other aspects of the organisation. They worked through a provided lunch, and it was mid-afternoon before Stephen declared himself satisfied with the whole setup.

They went back to the hotel for a shower and cleanup. Stephen suggested they have a quiet dinner at the hotel, and the next day after the workshop they could sample some of the nightlife.

Harry had some time to kill, and walked the short distance through the city area to the River Main. There were walkways along the banks, and he enjoyed just looking at the people, the bridges and the shipping. It was pleasantly cool, and with the approaching summer it was still quite light when he returned to the hotel.

They talked little over dinner, each busy with their own ideas for the next day. Harry settled for a small schnitzel, while Stephen ordered a full Eisbein and sauerkraut. The red wine helped Harry to relax, but he had to admit he was feeling nervous about his responsibilities for the next day.

Afterwards they retired to the hotel lounge for coffee and the possibility of a small dessert wine. They found a wide settee with a low table and Harry had just sat down when a man came to them, with an attractive blonde on his arm.

'Ah, Mr. Cambre,' he said to Stephen, 'this is Fily Ahlgren. As we had talked, she would very much like to meet Dr. Ehlers.'

Stephen smiled, 'Of course.' He turned to Harry and explained, 'Fily has been starring in some recent European movies – I said they could join us for coffee.'

Harry stood up, acknowledging the newcomers, but Fily came around and took him by the arm, sitting down with him on the settee.

She looked at him, 'Oooh, you are such a famous man. What do you do for fun?'

'I, uh, well ...' Harry was taken aback by the sudden proximity of a beautiful woman. Her blue eyes danced in front of him, and her perfume filled his senses. She had an awfully low-cut dress, showing a lot of cleavage.

'I know, you probably work for fun,' she laughed merrily.

Harry regained some composure, smiling at her exuberance, 'Working's good.'

'Yes, but you must also play.' She looked at him, suddenly serious: 'I can see – your mind must always be busy: bzzzt, bzzzt, work, work, think, think.' She laughed again, an infectious laugh.

'I also work, you know,' she continued, 'but a different kind of work. I also study characters – it's necessary to be a good actress.'

'Would you mind if I took a photo?' Fily's companion interjected, '... as a memento ... I can send it to you as well,' he added to Harry as an afterthought.

'No, that's fine,' Harry said, flattered by all the attention.

They posed for the photo, with Fily cuddling up to him. The man took a few for good measure.

Then the coffee came, with a glass of port for everyone. Fily was obviously used to being the centre of attraction, and she chattered away about her career, her movies and the people she had met. Whenever she dropped a name she turned to Harry and asked: 'You've heard of him?'

Invariably Harry shook his head, and she laughed and explained what he, or she, had done to be famous. Then, when he said he had heard of someone in the movie-world she stopped and said: 'There, I knew you had some life in you!'

Fily's companion excused himself to go to the toilet, and Stephen also stood up.

'I need to go as well,' he said.

Suddenly Harry was alone with Fily.

She smiled, 'I have been talking too much. Tell me about you – you have a girlfriend? Or perhaps many girlfriends?'

Harry's mind went to Tracy. He swallowed, 'I ... well, not really.' The presence of the starlet was overwhelming.

She smiled again, confident in the effect of her presence.

She put her hand on his knee, and leant forward, 'Harry, you must relax, have some fun.'

She hesitated a moment, and then continued softly, 'Harry, you want me to come to your room tonight? We can have a lot of fun.'

Harry's eyes opened wide and his mind raced. Wow ... this was it, this was the moment he had dreamed about. When all his fantasies would be realised. This beautiful girl had offered to come to his room, to stay the night, to do who knows what ...

All he had to say was 'yes' – coolly, and in control. She would come to him. That's what she said.

Instead, his voice choked, and he heard himself croak, 'I ... uh,'.

He stared at Fily, her blue eyes and her perfume seemed to be in every pore of his being. He looked down at her breasts, and he felt himself sweating.

In the distance he heard his voice stammering, 'Fily ... I, ... have to ... have to prepare for tomorrow ...'

She was quiet, looking at him. Then she smiled, 'You're a good boy, Harry. You have a girl friend, and you must remain true.'

They were interrupted by her companion returning, 'I see you two are getting acquainted?'

'Yes,' she replied, 'Harry is a good boy. But he has to work – he has a big day tomorrow.'

Harry said nothing. He felt cold. His moment had passed.

Stephen also returned, and Fily stood up and joined her companion, 'We must go now – it's been wonderful to meet with you.'

They all made their way to the hotel foyer.

Fily turned to Stephen, 'Thank you for letting us meet Harry – he is such a famous man.'

She took Harry's hand: 'I've enjoyed this evening, Harry – thank you.' She smiled at him: 'You need a good woman to look after you, to help you have fun.' She waved a finger: 'Not so much work!'

Then she leant forward and kissed him gently, turned, and went off with her companion.

At the door she looked back and smiled at the two men who were still watching.

'She likes you Harry,' Stephen said.

Harry said nothing. He was still feeling numb, trying to piece together what had just happened.

'No doubt she will add you to her list of people she's met.' Stephen added. He looked hard at Harry, and was about to say something, but turned to go to the elevator.

They retired to their rooms. Harry collapsed on his bed, staring at the ceiling and trying to rationalise his actions. He had always prided himself on being in control of his own situation, but Fily had turned him into a bumbling idiot.

What would they be doing now if he had only said yes?

He thought of Tracy, and felt half embarrassed by his ideas of Fily, though he tried to justify them by the fact they had no confirmed relationship.

Then the picture of what had happened to her filled his mind. He sat up on the bed, staring at the wall. He felt loathing in the pit of his stomach: Mac had defiled the sex act, made it into a vicious, cowardly assault. Somehow sex lost its romance – would it be fun again? Involuntarily he wondered, if Fily was with him, would he be able ...?

He shook his head to get rid of the conflicting ideas. Then he stumbled to the bathroom and had a long shower.

He slept fitfully, dreaming, thinking, not sure if he was asleep or awake.

He was finally woken by an urgent knocking at his door.

'Harry!' he heard Stephen calling.

He stood up slowly, feeling drugged. He opened the door, and Stephen came in, waving a paper.

'Have you seen the news?'

Obviously Harry hadn't, and Stephen continued: 'Switch on – get BBC.'

He remembered the paper in his hand: 'I've got an English paper here – have a look.'

Harry took the paper, wondering what on earth could have caused Stephen to be so agitated. He opened it up, and saw the headline: *'EHLERS STOLE MY IDEAS'*.

It took a moment for Harry to register what he had seen. 'Whaaat?' he said under his breath, and continued reading.

The sub-title read: *'Armenian scientist claims Harry Ehlers visited and took his paper.'* Further on, in the print, a bold headline proclaimed: *'Armenian Journal publishes gravity paper by Panos Abalian.'*

He sat down to get the story in more detail. More than two months before, a little-known Armenian physicist, Panos Abalian, had submitted a gravity paper to a local science journal. In the technical details it was almost word for word like Harry's presentation at the APA.

Abalian had been interviewed by an Armenian journalist, and claimed Harry had visited him in March. He had discussed his gravity ideas, and had even shown Harry a copy of the paper he was working on. When Harry left he could not find the copy. Of course, he had the original on file on his computer, and went ahead and submitted it.

He was amazed to find Harry had given a presentation at the APA, and had had the audacity to build a gravity machine. Even worse, Harry had patented the ideas as though they were his own.

'I demand my rights to the patent.' Abalian was quoted.

'Do you know him?' Stephen asked.

Harry shook his head, 'I drifted through Armenia in March. It's a beautiful country, lots of history. Mount Ararat used to be in its borders, but is now in Turkey.'

'So you could have visited Abalian?'

'I've never met Abalian!' Harry protested.

'Yes, but the fact is you were there.' Stephen turned on the TV, 'It's seven – let's get the news.'

As expected, the claims by Abalian were the main story. The gist was much the same as the newspaper, and they interviewed a science reporter for insight into the story.

'*At this stage it's difficult to know what is going on*', he commented. '*It seems the journal received the paper from Abalian before Harry Ehlers' presentation at the APA, and if that is the case he must have had the ideas beforehand.*'

'*And Ehlers' claims about working out the theory in the mountains of Kathmandu?*' the anchor asked.

The science reporter smiled, '*Well, that gets to look a little thin, doesn't it?*'

'*And what sort of a scientist is Abalian? How old is he?*'

'*From what we can find out, he's in his late thirties. A bit of a maverick, but he has only published two papers – and that more than ten years ago. Nothing substantial, run-of-the-mill kind of papers – certainly nothing like this.*'

'*The paper apparently is in English – why didn't he submit it to a better-known journal?*'

'*Well, he says he wrote it in English because he recognised its impact. He also says western journals wouldn't have accepted it because of its radical assumptions.*'

'*Any truth in that?*'

'*Possibly. One must recognise the fact the science establishment is not necessarily open to new ideas, Ehlers could do it because he had been to Cambridge and had a working machine.*'

'*How is this going to be settled?*'

'*Well, of course, the first thing to do is to get to Abalian and find out if he could have written the paper. There is the question whether he could have written it in English, and then there is the content ... you have to realise this is very complex, almost philosophical stuff, and to understand the details requires remarkable insight into the latest advances in theoretical physics. Not something your ordinary physics lecturer at most universities could hope to cope with – except in very broad terms.*'

'*So, would he be interrogated by some top physicists?*'

'*Maybe. Or he could just be asked to give a presentation – I would guess the top guys would soon know if he understood what he was talking about. Of course, Ehlers has already done that, and there is no doubt he understands the theory – in fact he's had to teach the top guys. But where the original ideas came from, well, that could be another story.*'

'*There is also the journal, and the editor of the journal,*' the reporter continued. '*They will have to give confirmation of when the paper was received.*'

'*Is it a reputable journal?*'

'*I don't know – it's listed as an occasional journal, which means it gets published when they have enough papers. So certainly not top-flight, but quite a few smaller countries work like that.*'

The anchor was about to close the interview when the science reporter continued: '*It's interesting that Ehlers is already getting support. Apparently his ex-supervisor, Professor Fred Morton from Cambridge, phoned in this morning and flatly declared he didn't believe Abalian.*'

'*That is good support!*'

The anchor thanked the science reporter, and finished off: '*We'll keep you informed on what is going on. We haven't yet been able to get any comment from Dr. Harry Ehlers – today he will be giving another workshop to industry leaders on the workings of the gravity machine. That's in Frankfurt.*'

The news carried on to other stories, and Harry looked at Stephen, a perplexed frown on his face.

'You say you've never met him?' Harry nodded.

Stephen sat down on one of chairs. 'So why is there this claim?' He paused a moment, and then continued: 'It can only be for the money – somebody or some organisation wants to muscle in.'

'So what do we do?' Harry was feeling irritated and apprehensive.

'Nothing – at the moment. As the commentator said, Abalian is going to have to prove he could have thought out the theory. I have no doubt at this moment there is a whole horde of reporters heading for Armenia to find Abalian. And get hold of the journal and its editor.'

'So we carry on with the workshop?'

'Of course. You can say something at the start – deny you've ever met Abalian. And carry on as before. This changes nothing for today.'

'OK.' That made Harry feel a whole lot better.

'Now I'd better get back to my room – I have no doubt there will be more calls for me to comment on this.' He smiled: 'That's how I found out, being woken by a call from some news channel.'

After Stephen left Harry read through the article in the newspaper again. The claims were preposterous, but at the same time he could see they would have to be disproved. Somehow.

He turned down the volume on the TV, but left it on in case of any more breaking news. But there was nothing further. He got dressed and prepared for the day.

After a quick breakfast Harry and Stephen proceeded to the auditorium, where they found a group of reporters waiting. They were essentially there to cover the workshop, but with the new story they wanted comment directly from Harry.

He was brief: 'I just want to emphasize this is all new to me. I have never met Abalian, and I deny I ever received any ideas from him.'

He repeated the denial at the start of the workshop, and did not refer to it again.

In some ways the workshop was easier because he had already done it before. On the other hand, some of the questions were more incisive, since the participants had obviously had more time to study the theory. There were also a number of questions on practical applications he could not answer, to the obvious irritation of some of the listeners.

'I don't know all the answers,' Harry emphasized, 'and there's still a lot of work to be done before gravity machines become a marketable reality.'

However, interest became much more focussed when he delved into the new aspects of his theory, since it led the way directly to practical applications. Moreover, it was something that hadn't been covered in the first workshop, and the participants appreciated they were getting something new.

'These proceedings should not be made public,' one of the Asian groups complained. 'We have come here, we should have the advantage.'

'We are trying to be fair to everybody,' Harry responded. 'The concepts are new, and the knowledge must be made available. It must, after all, benefit all of humanity.'

Harry finally got away after six pm. Stephen was left to wind up the administrative details, and he made his way as quickly as possible back to his hotel room. He wanted some quiet, and moreover, he wanted to find out if there was any more news on Abalian.

It had taken some looking, but Abalian was eventually found by a local Armenian reporter. The interview was grainy and indistinct, and was conducted in Armenian. He came across as a volatile character, with a balding head and compensatory black beard; Harry didn't recognise him.

A translation at the bottom of the screen followed the interview.

'*Of course – those are my ideas,*' the subtitles said, as Abalian gesticulated wildly. '*Ehlers has no right to them. I demand the patent.*'

He was asked when he had submitted his paper, and he said a few weeks before Harry's APA address.

'*You can ask the editor,*' Abalian emphasized.

Which the reporters did. Professor Hagopian was the head of Physics at an institution for higher learning in Gyumri. He was an older man, also balding, but much more circumspect and controlled than Abalian. He could speak reasonable English, and confirmed Abalian had come to him with the paper a month or two before – he couldn't remember the exact date.

'You published the paper in English – why?'

'I realise impact, this is necessary to get wide circulation,' Hagopian replied.

Nothing more definite came out of these interviews, and Harry was gratified with the support he was getting from other physicists. Both Ken Flugle and Abel Fynwich stated they would be surprised if Abalian's claims were true, as they had practical knowledge of Harry's insight of the theory – something which would have come from formulating the ideas themselves. His new advances showed how deeply he understood the theory and its consequences.

Fred Morton was more forthright, saying he'd met Abalian at a conference the year before, and seen some of his work.

'*He could never have produced the theory,*' Morton ended off.

The interviewer took on a different tack: '*Was Ehlers at the conference?*'

'*Yes, he was one of a group from the Department.*'

'*So he could have met Abalian?*'

Morton looked at him: '*Perhaps, but that doesn't change my opinion of Abalian.*'

'*Thank you, professor.*'

Stephen came back soon after, saying he had booked a table at a restaurant for supper. Herr Steiger and his wife, as well as another couple involved in the administration of the workshop were also invited.

They went to the Fressgasse, the pedestrian-only street in the inner city known for its gastronomy. After some sightseeing they found the exclusive restaurant where Stephen had made the booking. It was meant to be a celebratory supper at the end of a successful workshop, but Harry was exhausted by the day's work, and the story of Abalian added to his sense of fatigue.

He excused himself after dessert, and walked back to the hotel. As in the past, he could relax and regain his equanimity by just being by himself in the crowds, watching people as he made his way back. He was happy when he could just lie down on his bed.

He wondered what Tracy was doing, and whether he should phone her. When his cell phone rang he was disappointed not to see her name, and he wondered who could have his number.

'Hello,' he said tentatively.

'Harry – Fred Morton.'

'Oh ... hello, professor.' Harry was relieved, recognising the voice of his Cambridge supervisor.

'Harry, I've told you before, don't "professor" me.'

Harry smiled: Morton was very forthright, but he found it difficult to drop the title when he talked to him.

'Now,' Morton continued, 'tell me straight: did you meet Abalian?'

'No ... um ... Fred. I've never met him. I don't even remember him at the conference.'

'And in Armenia?'

'No, the last thing I wanted was anything to do with a university.'

'So we were that bad?' Morton chuckled.

'No – that's not what I meant ...' Harry was embarrassed. 'I was trying to find something else ...'

'Yes, I understand. Well, it seems you certainly did find something.'

There was a moments silence, and Morton continued, 'Harry, while I'm talking to you – what are you going to do with the patent? I've heard rumours there are powerful organisations that want to take it over.'

'I've had offers ... a lot of money.' Harry didn't know where this was heading, but he had always admired Morton's basic distrust of the establishment.

'Harry, be careful. You need to give your ideas to all groups. At the moment you are far ahead of everybody else, and some organisation may want to buy your silence. They would want to make sure your ideas stay with them only. It could give them tremendous advantages and lead to new power blocks – which we don't want.'

'I agree. In fact today I presented some ideas on toning down the power release. It was available to everybody attending.'

He thought a moment, 'And to others ... at a price.'

Morton was intrigued, 'Is this something new?'

'Yes.'

'You really have got the bit between your teeth,' Morton mused. 'Amazing stuff.'

Harry didn't say anything.

After another moment Morton continued, 'If you've got something new then you must publish it – that takes it out to everybody. You say you presented it today?'

'Yes.'

'Have you written it up – notes or something like that.'

'Yes – quite rough, but presentable.'

'Good. Send it to me this evening. I'm editor of *Physics*, and with today's date it won't mean it has already been presented. I'll publish it as soon as possible.'

After Morton had hung up Harry e-mailed the rough copy of his new paper to get the days date on it; he would brush up the details for publishing when he had time.

CHAPTER 16

Harry stayed in the hotel the next morning. He had breakfast with Stephen, but then worked on editing his paper into a more presentable form.

He had no desire to go out into the city. In crowds he felt as though everyone was looking at him, calling him a cheat. He felt frustrated, not knowing what he could do to clear his name.

He did spend time looking at the news bulletins, but the story of Abalian was getting to be old hat, with no new information coming in. In particular, there had been no further contact with the elusive scientist.

Googling also did not help. Most of what was listed on the Internet was a rehash of what had already been aired, together with a lot of personal comment. He was both defended and abused in the blogs, and rapidly realised that he should not pay attention to the comments of unknown individuals. Easy to say, but some of the barbs hurt.

At lunch Stephen informed him that the workshop had been tied up, and could be rated as a great success. There were people who wanted to see Harry, but Stephen said he was not available.

Harry smiled, 'Thanks, that's the last thing I want.'

'I've also spoken to some German patent attorneys, to get the rights tied up here. However, the latest additions are giving some problems. At some stage we're going to have to sort it out.'

Harry nodded: however, it was not something he was in a hurry to do.

In mid-afternoon Harry finally submitted his edited paper to Fred Morton. Then it was time to leave for the airport and their flight back to South Africa.

They arrived at Cape Town airport on Saturday morning after an uneventful flight. There were no reporters around, and Harry was beginning to rejoice in his anonymity when he saw a newspaper billboard:

In big black letters it proclaimed *HARRY AND THE STARLET.*

He stopped and stared – now what?

There was a newsstand at the billboard, and after a moment's indecision he walked over and asked for a paper.

The newsvendor bent down to pick up a paper, but then stared as he passed it over.

'Hey, you're him! You're Harry Ehlers!'

'Give me the paper,' Harry said brusquely. He put down the money and left as quickly as he could.

'Nice!' the vendor called after him, '… she looks like a goer, man.'

Stephen had stopped ahead when he realised Harry was no longer with him.

'What's that about?'

Harry indicated to the billboard, 'I'm trying to find out.'

He opened up the paper, and on the front page was a picture of him and Fily, cuddling on the couch in Frankfurt.

'Shit!' Harry muttered.

Stephen chuckled, 'Nice photo.'

'What do you mean: nice photo?'

'Harry, don't get upset. It's just a photo of you and a girl.'

'It must have been that damn friend of hers. Probably set it up.'

He turned to Stephen, 'Where did you meet him?'

Stephen shrugged, 'I don't know – at the hotel? He just wanted to come and have a drink. You're a famous man, people want to meet you.'

'Not for this!' He jabbed his finger at the photo.

They didn't talk again until they were in Stephen's Mercedes, on the way to Cape Town.

Harry opened up the paper, and read the full story on the front page.

'Shit,' he muttered again, 'listen to this.'

'Fily met Harry after supper, and they sat together on the wide comfortable couch. Harry was obviously entranced by the beautiful starlet, and they cuddled close as she told him about the film scene in Europe. The drinks kept coming, and later Harry and Fily were seen going off together to his luxury suite.'

'Harry, it doesn't matter. Get over it. It's just a girl and a newspaper story.'

Harry stared out the window, 'Of course it matters. Nothing happened, and that makes me out as some … some womaniser.'

'It's that girl, Tracy, isn't it? You should forget her. You have a new life.'

Harry turned and was about to respond, but then decided against it. He stared ahead and didn't speak again until Stephen dropped him off at his apartment.

'We need to meet next week,' Stephen said.

'Okay, I'll contact you.'

The first thing Harry did was make a big cup of coffee. He wanted to phone Tracy, talk to her, see her, explain to her, but wasn't at all sure how she would receive him. Not after that damn article.

He fretted around, but then finally sat down in his big chair and decided he had to do it.

Her number rang for a while before she answered.

'Yes?'

'Tracy, it's me, Harry. How are you?'

'Okay.'

'Can I see you?'

She was quiet a moment, 'Not now Harry, I've got a lot of work to do.'

'Tracy, that story in the paper – don't believe it. It didn't happen like that.' He was urgent, pleading.

'It doesn't matter, Harry – you have your life to lead.' She was cool, circumspect.

'When can I see you?'

'Not now.'

'When?'

'I'll call you.'

It was clear their conversation was heading nowhere.

'Okay,' he said.

She hung up.

He sat on his chair, finishing his coffee. How could his life make such a turnaround? Just last week it was all so smooth ... Now, the world saw him as a cheat, a womaniser. The girl he wanted to see most didn't want to have anything to do with him.

What to do? What did he normally do when his life had no clarity? He went away, somewhere where he could think about it all. Where he couldn't be disturbed.

There had been an occasion long ago when he spent a few days with his parents at a hut on a wide open lake. He remembered the tranquillity of the area, close to the sea. That would be fantastic.

Suddenly he felt energised. He googled *Cape Nature*, and soon found the hut: *Mvubu* on Groenvlei. Was it occupied for the weekend?

He put in his requirements: Saturday and Sunday nights. He used his mother's last name, Grootboom, for the booking.

Then he waited for what seemed a long time before the message came back: it was available! Thank god something was going right.

He quickly confirmed the booking and paid for it by electronic transfer.

It didn't take long to pack a couple of bags, and then he was on his way. Sedgefield was about four hours drive away, and he was soon out of the city limits. He settled down to a comfortable drive on a good road.

The sound of his wheels had a soothing effect, and he felt himself relaxing. His City Golf went well, but it was underpowered, and he began to wonder about another car when he was passed on hills. Perhaps he should have a look: certainly Stephen's Mercedes was very comfortable. And powerful.

He reached Sedgefield in late afternoon, and stopped at the local supermarket to buy provisions. He had made sure that he had cash, and didn't have to use his credit card. Moreover, he had brought along his hoodie sweater, which he put on to go into the store.

Nobody paid any attention to the coloured man in his hoodie, and he soon had all his purchases. He smiled: if he had a big expensive car, people might have noticed. But not his Golf: everything had its advantages.

He collected the key for the *Mvubu* hut at the nearby hotel. Again, there were no queries, and he heaved a sigh of relief when he reached the hut parking area. He took a couple of small items and made his way down the boarded path to the hut.

It was as he remembered it. The sun was going down to his left, and the wide patio looked out over Groenvlei lake. It wasn't completely isolated, and he could see and hear the traffic on the highway in the distance. But it was far enough away from civilisation to forget about all his associated troubles. He switched off his cell phone.

The next two days revitalised him. On Sunday morning he woke with the sun streaming onto his bed, the lake still in darkness below him. He had breakfast on the patio, watching the birds in the reeds and lakeside forest, and with not another soul in sight.

Later on he went for a long run through the forest. Eventually the path took him down to a wide sandy beach, and he took off his shoes to wade into the sea. The water was too cold to swim, but he allowed the swash from the long swells to run over his legs. He looked over the expanse of shining sand, with nobody else in sight. It was all his own.

He slowly made his way back along the beach. In places there were cliffs on the landward side, with a soft friable rock, but it was low tide and he had no difficulty rounding a couple of headlands.

As he approached the road leading to the beach the signs of people became more obvious. Some discarded plastic bags and a tangled knot of line lay along the wrack.

Then ahead there was a lone fisherman. He was standing ankle-deep in the swash, and Harry deviated slightly to pass close to him.

'Catch anything?' he asked pleasantly when he was close enough.

The man turned to look at him.

'Wat maak jy hier?' he asked.

'Sorry – I don't speak Afrikaans.'

The man stared at him, 'Van waar die fok kom jy?'

Harry was taken aback by his attitude, but knew enough Afrikaans to understand he had asked where he came from.

'Cape Town...'

'Fok off, Engelsman.' As he spat out the words Harry got a strong whiff of alcohol, and decided to take the advice. So much for getting back to people.

There was a group of tourists at the road, but this time Harry didn't try any further pleasantries.

In the afternoon he took the canoe and paddled to the far end of the lake. In amongst the reeds there were plenty of waterfowl, and he was happy just to drift and watch them feeding. There were occasional aggressive social interactions, indicative that in bird-world it was also not all smooth sailing.

Harry thought a lot. About his situation, and what he should do about it. He decided he was being much too sensitive to other people's opinions and demands. He had to do what he wanted, not what somebody else thought was best for him.

And Tracy? He sighed: he wanted to tell her that nothing happened with Fily. At the same time he realised that her rape could leave serious scars. But more than anything he just wanted to talk to her again.

On Monday morning he dallied until he had to vacate *Mvubu* at ten am. There was a restaurant on the road out and he stopped for a leisurely breakfast.

There was nobody else on the porch, and when the waitress came out with his bill she stood a while looking at him.

'You know you're missing?'

'What?'

'You're Harry Ehlers, aren't you?'

Harry stared at her before nodding briefly.

She smiled, 'There was a report on the radio this morning that no-one knew where you were. You weren't answering your cell phone.'

'I turned it off.'

'Well, that would explain it.'

'Why do people want to know what I do?'

'Because you're famous?'

He grinned at her, 'Maybe – but that shouldn't matter. It's crazy.'

He left her a big tip.

It was only when he was halfway back to Cape Town that he switched on his cell phone. He listened on the hands-free system to the recorded messages, primarily to see if Tracy had phoned.

There were messages from Stephen, Mrs Shaw, the Vice-Chancellor's secretary and what sounded like a few reporters. But no Tracy.

His phone rang again a few minutes later: he didn't recognise the number.

'Hello?'

'Dr Ehlers?'

'Yes.'

There was a moments silence, 'The VC wants to talk to you.'

A short while later Pre was on the line, 'Harry – where've you been?'

'Away.' he replied irritatedly.

But then he felt he owed her an explanation, 'I took a couple of days off.'

'I understand.' Harry wondered what she thought.

Then she continued, 'We need to talk. When can I see you?'

'I'll be back at university tomorrow.'

'Good – we can have lunch.'

Almost immediately after there was another call.

'Harry Ehlers?'

'Yes?'

'Where are you?'

'In my car.'

'Where've you been?'

'Away.'

There was a moments silence, 'Who with?'

'Me.'

'You think I believe you?'

'Do you think I care?'

He hung up.

Harry phoned Tracy when he was back in Cape Town, but her cell went onto automatic voicemail. He didn't leave a message, because she would in any case see he had called.

One of his new resolutions made at *Mvubu* was to listen to news whenever convenient. So, at suppertime he switched on the TV.

There was breaking news:

We have just had a report come through that Panos Abalian has been killed in a motor car accident.

Harry sat up as the presenter continued:

Abalian was the reclusive Armenian scientist who accused Harry Ehlers of plagiarising his ideas for the gravity machine. Nobody has been able to find him, and it appears that a grim discovery at the bottom of a canyon will now reveal why.

Armenia is a mountainous country, and roads can be tortuous. It seems Abalian was driving alone on one of the roads in the Zangezur mountains when the accident happened. The wreckage of his car was discovered first - his body was found later some distance away. Presumably he was flung out when the car went off the road and into the canyon.

At the moment there is little further news, and we still await confirmation that it is indeed Abalian who was killed. However, people on the scene are convinced it is him.

We will bring you updates as soon as they come to hand.

The news channel called in an expert for comment, particularly in relation to Abalian's claims against Harry.

This doesn't take away Abalian's claim to the patent rights – at this stage we don't know whether he has signed any patent papers.

However, his death means it will not be possible to find out whether Abalian was capable of writing the paper as he claimed. As you know, there were proposals that he should subject himself to a panel of experts.

This takes away that possibility.

Wow! Harry sank back into his chair. Now what?

He didn't have long to wait: his cell phone rang.

'Dr Ehlers? Ted Magoba from the *Despatch*.'

'Have you heard the news about Abalian?'

Harry breathed in deeply, 'Yes, I've just heard it now.'

'And what do you think?'

'Well, I … don't know.'

'Are you glad he's dead?'

'That's a hellova question to ask!'

'And …?'

'Of course not. How can I be glad because someone's died? I've never met the man, but somehow you expect me to respond to his death.'

'Well, now you've got the patent again.'

'That's not the way I understand it.'

'Why? What do you expect will happen?'

'I think you need to ask the lawyers.'

'What are you going to do next?'

'The next thing I'm going to do is hang up.' Harry terminated the call.

He wondered about talking to anyone else about the situation, but the only one who would know anything was Stephen. And somehow he didn't feel like discussing events with him.

CHAPTER 17

It felt like a long time ago when Harry walked into the Physics Department on Tuesday morning. Mrs Shaw welcomed him when he walked past her office, but somehow her greeting didn't seem as genuine or friendly as in the past.

When he reached his office he tried to analyse it: did she think he was a cheat or a womaniser or both? Or perhaps he just imagined it – part of his own self-doubt.

He shook his head and opened the newspaper he'd bought on the way in.

The story was all over the front page:

ABALIAN DIES IN CLIFF PLUNGE

The accompanying grainy picture showed the underside of a car lying at the bottom of a deep chasm. The story had little more than what he had already heard on TV, including speculation on what it meant for him. Again nothing much that was new, though the consensus seemed to be it would cloud the whole patents picture rather than offer any clear-cut easy solution.

At the bottom there was a short note on Harry's so-called 'disappearance', noting he had been out of communication somewhere. It was not clear who was with him.

Harry smiled wryly – you couldn't win with the media: the report implied he was not on his own. He wondered briefly what Tracy would think.

At the departmental tea-time, Andile was typically forthright in his opinion.

'Harry, you know this bastard Abalian?'

Harry shook his head, and Andile continued, 'That's what I'm telling everybody, it's a bloody setup. All about money.'

'And those with the money get the girls.' Harry didn't know who made the remark, but a chuckle went round the room.

Later he had lunch with Pre Mahlangu, and he found her much more circumspect.

'I phoned professor Morton,' she said, and stopped, looking at Harry.

'He must be one of your greatest fans.'

She smiled, and continued, 'Anyway, he left me in no doubt what he thinks of Abalian's claims. So we must assume this is some contrived means to get at the patent rights. And of course Abalian's death just complicates it further.'

Harry nodded.

She was quiet a while, chewing on a mouthful of food.

'Harry,' she finally said, 'I play open cards, and I accept the gravity machine is your idea. But what is it with this Fily Ahlgren?'

Harry looked up at her, grimacing. 'It was a setup, Pre.'

'And?'

'Stephen said they could join us for a drink, and afterwards they left. Nothing else happened!'

She smiled again, 'Okay, it seems you need to be careful – about everything. There are a lot of different interests involved.'

Then she was serious, 'Have you thought further about what you're going to do – you're still staying here?'

'I'd like to donate money to establish the new research institute. Only trouble is there's no guarantee of any money now. I don't know how you see it.'

She nodded, 'It doesn't actually change the university's commitment. If you stayed we had decided to establish an institute anyway. We've got the initial funding from the SASF, so we will continue with our plans. Any additional donations will be a bonus.

We first had to find out if Abalian had a case, and if you were a fraud. We phoned more than just professor Morton, and the consensus is the ideas are yours. Of course at this stage we don't have certainty...'

Harry looked at her: this was serious stuff about his credibility.

'It's a matter of finding out the truth, and I think we've made the right decision.'

'Thank you,' he said quietly.

'You've obviously been through the mill as well, and it isn't finished yet by any means. What are you going to do about the patent rights?'

'I'm not sure – there are some issues which still need to be clarified. Nobody's said whether Abalian has actually patented anything, and if so who's got the documents now.'

'Okay – we'll have to see how it all plays out. On a more practical level, we need to go and look at your new offices –you must decide what you want. Perhaps Friday?'

Harry had little idea of the detailed planning of a research centre, and when he returned to his office he sent off e-mails to everyone he could think of for advice. In particular Ken Flugle, Abel Finwych and Fred Morton.

A while later he received a call from CF Security wanting to know if they could deliver his new emergency transmitter.

Half an hour later they were adjusting the little unit to fit onto his watch strap. He marvelled that technology could make something so small and versatile.

'This is the emergency button here,' the man explained. 'To trigger a signal you actually have to twist it – this stops accidental usage.' He showed Harry how to do it.

'The unit is coded with your name, and once triggered it sends your GPS position to our control centre, and we then take emergency action.'

He looked at Harry, 'You obviously travel all over the world – we have agreements with security companies in most countries, so it will work anywhere.

Any other questions?'

Harry sighed, 'No, not really. I just find it so depressing one has to take all these precautions.'

The man smiled, 'Well, it's called being prepared. It could save your life.'

Harry nodded, but a thought occurred to him.

'How's Etienne?'

The man's face clouded, 'You haven't heard?'

'No …?'

'He was shot last week.'

'How … what happened?'

'He was driving in Nyanga township on Thursday. It seems he stopped at a traffic light, and somebody came up and shot him three times through the car window. Then disappeared. He must have died immediately.'

Harry stared, 'Any reasons?'

'We don't know. Nothing was taken – he was just shot. Almost like a hit, though why him …? He was a good operator.'

Harry felt weak. 'Hell, I'm sorry …'

The man grimaced, 'That's why we need to stop those bastards out there.'

Later that evening Etienne's death was still on Harry's mind. He sat on his chair, remembering how Mac had been picked up, and the threat he'd made. Harry wondered if Etienne had reported it, and also whether he should have mentioned it that afternoon.

Even more, he wondered if Tracy was also in danger. Because of something he had done.

On Wednesday morning Harry found replies to his queries about a research centre. They emphasized that he needed good back-up staff, particularly an accounting manager. He would have to decide on office and lab space and who and what went in there – staff and students would line up to come, but those selections would be critical to the success of the institute.

At the end of his e-mail Abel Finwych added, 'Why don't you come here to Caltech – we already have it all set up for you'.

Harry sat back: it would be by far the easiest thing to do. Slot in with an established, brilliant team.

So why did he want to stay?

He actually couldn't answer that directly, and he was still mulling over his ideas when his phone rang. It was Stephen.

'Harry, do you have time? We need to talk.'

Stephen suggested Harry come to his offices, and he was happy to oblige.

A short while later he sat in Stephen's comfortable visitor's chair. Table Mountain looked as serene as ever, framed in the large picture window.

'There have been a lot of changes over the last few days,' Stephen started, 'in particular with Abalian's death.'

Harry nodded.

'Sir Richard contacted me last night,' he continued, 'it seems they knew about Abalian's claims before it became news.'

Harry stared at him: really?

'So they sent someone to check it out, and Abalian convinced him his claim predates yours. So much so they filed out a patent claim. B2O have Abalian's patent application in their London offices.'

It took a moment or two for Harry to respond.

'It sounds contrived,' he eventually muttered.

Stephen nodded, 'It could well be, but it actually doesn't matter. The point is there are two patent claims: yours and Abalian's. At the present time a court couldn't decide which has precedence.

Your provisional patent application could be challenged generally, as well as in any country where you've filed subsequent patent claims. And remember, B2O have money and lawyers to back up any of their claims.'

'And …?'

'And this kind of thing could carry on for years. It will cost a lot of money to fight, and you don't have that sort of money.'

Harry leaned back: somehow Table Mountain didn't look so friendly any more. He felt frustrated: he had worked out a theory, and now there were all sorts of people demanding a share of something to which they had contributed nothing. No, they didn't want a share, they wanted it all.

'Sir Richard put some new offers on the table …' Stephen continued.

Harry looked at Stephen again.

'B2O are still willing to buy your rights. They've got Abalian's application, and they would then have control of both. So there would be no requirement for any legal battles.'

Harry didn't say anything.

'However, with Abalian's claims as well, they need to pay for both. So they are now offering eight billion pounds instead of ten billion. Which is quite a bit better than half.'

Harry still didn't say anything.

'Well, what do you think?' Stephen asked.

'Hell,' Harry eventually said, 'I think it's a bloody con trick. I don't want to sell to B2O – I don't know what they stand for, and I don't know what they'll do with the rights.'

Harry was agitated now, because he had thought of another ramification.

'It's not just about the legal side – people are going to think it's Abalian's theory.'

By his nature, Harry had never trumpeted his own case, but this was actually too much. They were his ideas! Now there was even somebody wanting to take his mind away – and the man was dead!

'I'm sure history will see you as the inventor of the gravity machine,' Stephen replied soothingly.

'I doubt it – not if lawyers have anything to do with it.'

'Harry, you're obviously over-wrought with all the complications. You should go and think about it all – in retrospect you'll realise the offer from B2O is very fair. Remember it doesn't stop you from establishing a foundation or anything like that. It just gives you the freedom to do what you want to do.'

The next morning Harry reached his office no nearer to a decision what to do. He had had a sleepless night thinking about his options, and it seemed more and more that it actually didn't matter what he felt – the decisions were being made by other people based on unknown premises.

He had a list of items on the desk in front of him, items for the new Gravity Research Institute. Instead he doodled all over the page – why should he bother with all this?

He was being told to go and play with his toys while the big boys actually decided what should happen.

He could tell them to stuff off, and go and do what he wanted. But what was that, and wouldn't it just play into their hands? He wasn't at all sure if his greatest desire was to be head of the Gravity Research Institute at the university. There had to be more to life.

Suddenly an urgent knocking on his door startled him out of his melancholy. The next moment it opened and a woman came in.

It took him a moment to recognise Tracy's friend.

'Judy …?'

She stood in front of his desk, looking down at him. She was a big woman, but as he looked at her he thought she was remarkably attractive. However, just at the moment her face was set and determined.

She sat down on the chair.

'Harry – we have to talk.'

'Okaaay,' he said, wondering where this was heading.

It took Judy a moment to gather her thoughts.

'Tracy,' she said, '- do you want to see her again?'

'Of course … I've tried phoning but she doesn't respond.'

Judy smiled grimly, 'You don't understand women, do you?'

He didn't say anything.

'Harry – you don't know what she's been through, particularly since the rape story hit the news. She doesn't want to go out – she sits at home in her room most of the time. She says she's working, but I don't know …

And then … then there's the story of you and that bimbo, all over the newspapers.'

'Judy, nothing happened – I was set up!' He wondered desperately whether anyone would ever believe him.

She looked hard at him, 'I'd like to believe you – you actually seemed quite nice once.'

Bloody hell, he thought, what did that mean?

'Harry,' she continued, 'I don't want to interfere, and Tracy doesn't know I'm here – if she finds out she'll kill me.

I thought I must talk to you – to see if you care. She is going through terrible times. She needs your help.'

'What can I do?'

For the first time Judy smiled, a little smile, 'I'll leave that up to you.' Then she was gone.

Harry sank back in his chair. Judy had brought his mind right back to a subject he had been trying to avoid for the last few days: thinking about Tracy. Yet somehow it was better now. That Judy had come to see him must mean something.

He wondered about Tracy. He wished he could talk to her, tell her about all his problems. She would actually understand, and be able to give him advice. She always seemed to have a reasonable opinion about issues.

He phoned her again, but it went straight onto voicemail. He didn't leave a message.

Then he remembered something his father had told him, 'Flowers: it's amazing the power they have over the female of our species. If ever you have a problem, just get them flowers.'

On his way home he stopped at a florist. He didn't know what flowers to buy, and eventually settled for a big bunch of red roses. They would be delivered the next morning, together with his little card just saying *Love, Harry*.

Friday morning Harry spent with Pre looking at his new offices. With her was an Indian man she introduced as Pravin Ashwin.

As Mrs Shaw had indicated, the proposed new offices were on one of the lower floors, far away from Professor Swain. Fortunately a suitable office had become vacant, with an adjoining office for a secretary.

There were a couple of nearby offices, but they were filled by existing staff. It would take time to appoint staff and students to the new research centre, and when the time came plans could be made for suitable expansion. In the meanwhile Harry would have decent premises.

However, while they were in the office Pre sat down on one of the chairs and motioned to Harry and Ashwin to sit down as well.

'Harry,' she said leaning forward, 'Pravin is head of the Economic Planning department – he has some different ideas he'd like to put to you.'

Ashwin was a spare, tall man with a mop of black hair. He ran his hand through the mop before talking.

'Dr Ehlers,' he began, 'I've no doubt there's a lot of research you still want to do on the operation of the gravity machine. And there's no doubt a Gravity Research Centre continuing your line of research would be very successful at the university.'

He sat back, his black eyes intent, 'However, I think we must look wider than that. Your gravity machine is going to affect every facet of our lives, and there's a lot of work just waiting to be done to determine how society is going to adapt. In economics, planning, law, engineering, international relations … you name it, and it will be there. Even interplanetary regulations, I believe.

So if the university is going start an institute, why not broaden its impact? I know there are similar ideas in various parts of the world, but we have an enormous advantage.'

Harry frowned, not understanding the implication.

'It's you,' Ashwin explained. 'Whatever Abalian says, it's your name that's associated with the gravity machine.'

'That's right, Harry,' Pre added. 'We've done some brief surveys, phoned around, and companies will stand in line for the opportunity to be associated with the *Harry Ehlers Gravity Institute*.'

Harry looked at the other two, assimilating what they had just said.

'So, what do you suggest?' he eventually asked.

Pre smiled, 'The university owns additional buildings off the main campus, and we would look to utilise one of them for this institute. At a later stage we can build a whole new institute – designed specifically for the purpose.'

'Obviously it would be associated with all the different departments on main campus,' Ashwin added, 'but its objective would be specifically to investigate the implications of the gravity machine.'

He hesitated a moment, and continued, 'I understand the work you've done does not fall directly into any of the existing physics research directions – so you would be working essentially on your own anyway.'

Harry nodded.

'Well, then, you could build up your team in the new institute. The advantage would be you would also interact with other disciplines, and they would be able to find out first hand what new developments were being considered. Of the characteristics of gravity machines.'

Both Pre and Ashwin looked at him, waiting for a reply.

'It wouldn't affect my work?' he eventually asked.

'No, not at all,' Pre responded. 'In fact, I'm sure you'll find it exciting to see how the gravity machine will fit into society.'

Harry had to admit the idea was compelling. Then another thought occurred to him, 'The foundation could also be in the institute?'

'Yes,' Pre replied, 'it would be an additional bonus.'

The discussion continued over lunch, including which departments would be associated and the type of work that would be done. Apparently it would require a large multi-disciplinary team to handle all the different aspects. They touched on possible building sites and layouts.

When Harry returned to his office he felt much more positive. In spite of everything there was some direction to his life again.

Stephen phoned, 'Harry, I think we must go ahead with our patent applications – we can't wait for the Abalian debacle to blow over. Are you in your office?'

'Yes.'

'Good. I have a whole lot of documents for you to sign. The European application – also some individual countries – and the British, US and Canadian applications.'

A little later Stephen arrived with a whole bundle of documents in a small suitcase. They were carefully parcelled out, and Harry found his signature and initials getting scrawnier and scrawnier as Stephen put one document after another in front of him.

Eventually they were finished and Stephen put everything back into the suitcase.

'Good,' he smiled, 'this is going to keep me occupied for a while to get lodged.'

Shortly after Stephen left Harry's phone rang again. No name came up, and he wondered who had his private number.

'Harry?' A female voice.

'Yes?'

'Judy here.' He relaxed, wondering why she should be calling.

'Do you scuba-dive?'

'Yes …?'

'I thought you should know Tracy and two friends are going diving on Sunday. Out to Whittle Rock with *Diveout*.'

'Oh, … why are you telling me?'

'I'm sure she'd welcome it if you joined them …'

Harry hesitated, 'Does she know you've phoned me?'

'No … but I'm sure it will be fine.'

'Well, … okay …'

'Harry,' Judy started, but stopped and added, '… the roses were a very good idea.' She hung up.

Harry looked at the cell phone in his hand, musing whether he should take up scuba-diving again. It had been some time since his last dive, though that shouldn't be a problem.

On Saturday morning Harry phoned *Diveout*.

'I believe you've got a dive going out to Whittle Rock on Sunday?' he asked tentatively.

'Yup,' the man answered, 'still have space for four. Obviously weather-dependent. How many you have?'

'Just me.'

'No problem. What's your name?'

'Harry – Harry Ehlers.'

There was a moments silence, 'Yea, man, and I'm Donald Duck – quack quack!'

For a moment Harry was taken aback, but decided to play along.

'Well, Donald, I'll need all the equipment, wet suit, BC, DV, cylinder, everything.'

The man was obviously uncertain, 'Who did you say you were?'

'Harry Ehlers.' He was beginning to enjoy people's reactions.

'The gravity man?'

'Yes.'

'You qualified to dive?'

'PADI – the open water course.'

'That's okay – Whittle's about five to thirty-five metres. You can stay shallow.'

He hesitated again, 'You're going to have to fit a wet suit beforehand. Also check all the other equipment … and we need your PADI qualification.'

'I'll come down and sort it out now.'

Harry enjoyed his visit to the dive shop. Rick – alias Donald – apologised for his outburst, saying he hardly expected Harry to be a diver.

He also confirmed Tracy had booked to dive with two friends.

The new dive equipment was tantalising, and Harry decided to splurge with his new wealth. He bought top of the range gear: a buoyancy compensator or BC, demand valve or DV, flippers, goggles and thick wetsuit for the cold water. He loaded all the bits and pieces into the boot of his car. He could spend the afternoon familiarising himself with their operation, especially the dive computer.

His dive cylinder was labelled with his name – HARRY – and he left it at *Diveout* to be pumped up for the morrow.

CHAPTER 18

Launch time was set for nine on Sunday morning. Harry reached Simonstown well beforehand, parking his car in the public parking area at the back of the slipway. There was one other car with two divers getting their equipment sorted, and Harry nodded briefly to them before walking across to the slipway.

He could see Rick directing a 4x4 with a boat hitched on the front. It had a large *Diveout* logo on the side, obviously the boat they would be using for the dive. They manoeuvred it to the top of the slipway and Rick put some chocks behind the wheels, ready for loading.

He saw Harry, and came to greet him, shaking his hand.

'Glad you could make it.'

He looked up to the sky, where the morning sun was shining behind some wispy clouds. There was little wind, and the weather forecast indicated change only later in the afternoon.

'It's a great day for a dive,' Rick continued. 'Vis is good at Whittle, probably fifteen metres. Not too much swell.'

He smiled, 'Let me introduce you to the skipper.'

The driver of the 4x4 had climbed out of the cab and came across. He was a tall, angular man with sparse white hair, a dark complexion and parched skin from many days in the sun.

'This is Klaas.'

He smiled broadly as he took Harry's hand, 'Hey, I'm proud to meet you, man. That gravity machine is really something.'

'Thanks.'

'You must jus' remember to sign our visitor's book before you go.'

'Yes,' Rick echoed the sentiment, 'we have a record of famous people who dive with us.'

He motioned to the boat, 'Your dive cylinder is on board – you must just put on your wet suit, and bring all your other gear to the boat. Your valuables – car keys, wallets – can be given to me for safekeeping at the shop while you're out.

Harry ambled back to the car park, and could feel the excitement mounting at the prospect of the dive. It had been some time, and he hoped he remembered all the procedures and didn't make a fool of himself.

Two more cars had arrived while he had been talking to Rick, and his heartbeat quickened as he recognised Tracy at one of them. She had her back to him, bending down to take her wetsuit out of the boot of the car. He walked across.

'Hello Tracy,' he said hesitantly.

She stopped what she was doing, and turned around.

'Harry …?' There was a look of surprise on her face. '…what are you doing here?'

She didn't seem to be unduly upset to see him, and her consternation gave him confidence.

'I thought I'd go for a dive today,' he said, smiling.

'You're going with *Diveout*?' she asked, standing up and regaining some equanimity.

He nodded.

'Are you diving with anybody?' she asked, looking around.

'No, I just thought I need to get back into diving.'

'Well, you can join us if you want to.'

'Thanks.' He was surprised she was so forthcoming; he half expected she would ignore him.

In the meanwhile her two companions had also come around to the boot of the car to get their diving gear. An Indian couple, Tracy introduced them as Sudhir and Ela. Harry shook Sudhir's hand, and smiled at Ela in greeting

'You happy Harry joins us?' Tracy asked.

'Of course, great to have you,' Sudhir replied.

'They're friends from Durban days,' Tracy added by way of explanation.

'Have you dived a lot?' Harry asked.

'Not as much as we'd like to,' Ela replied. 'And you?'

'My last dive was more than three years ago, so I hope I can remember what to do.'

'I'm sure you'll cope,' Tracy smiled at him.

Harry was in great spirits when he went back to his car and put on his wetsuit and booties. He wondered at Tracy's apparent change in attitude, but loaded up all his other paraphernalia, slinging his weight-belt over his shoulder; he hoped Rick's weights assessment was good.

The other three had changed as well, and came over to his car.

'Brand new gear?' Tracy asked.

'Bought yesterday,' Harry replied, embarrassed by his display of expensive new equipment.

'We've hired our DVs, BCs and cylinders.'

They walked to the boat, where Rick supervised the loading of the divers' equipment.

'You all together?' he asked as he handed their equipment up to an assistant on the boat. They nodded, and he gave instructions for their equipment to be grouped.

With that done the divers milled around the boat: there were two other couples besides their group of four. Klaas climbed on board to test the engines, and just then another diver climbed off the boat. He was a squat, powerful-looking man, with muscles bulging under his wetsuit. He had cropped dark hair and a square face, with a flat-looking nose.

So that made for nine divers in all, almost a full complement.

Rick climbed into the 4x4 to get the boat down the slipway. He expertly manoeuvred it until the trailer and boat were in the water. Then the boat was unhitched, and it gently floated off. Klaas started the engines, and brought the boat up to the side of the harbour wall where all the divers could board.

The skipper's console was up front. The boat deck had a central rack structure where all the diving equipment could be attached; in particular, on either side the dive cylinders with BCs and DVs could be lashed on securely. There was also place for goggles, fins and additional personal items such as cameras.

The divers themselves sat on the buoyancy pontoons surrounding the central structure. There were rope attachments they could hang onto if the going became rough.

Sudhir, Ela, Tracy and Harry sat on the starboard side, with Harry farthest back. Their equipment fitted onto the rack opposite them.

'That your cylinder?' Tracy nudged Harry, indicating to the cylinder in front of them with HARRY boldly written on it.

He grimaced, thinking the letters could be a lot smaller.

Klaas stood by his console, and once everybody was seated he introduced himself. He indicated to the accompanying *Diveout* diver standing near Harry at the stern.

'This is Joe – he's in charge of the diving. Ask him if you have a problem.

Now please jus' introduce yourselves, so we know everybody on board.'

They went around the boat, everybody only giving their first names. The muscular man introduced himself as Borysko, in a guttural voice, adding he was from the Ukraine.

At the end, Klaas hesitated a moment, but continued, 'For those who didn't recognise him, Harry is Harry Ehlers – he's the gravity man!'

Harry smiled wanly at the others as recognition dawned in their faces. He saw one of them take out a camera for a photograph.

Klaas revved up the dual outboard motors and they slowly moved out of the harbour precincts. Once outside he turned straight out to sea, sending the boat scudding over the waves. There was a long swell running which came at them from the front starboard quarter, giving the boat an awkward motion. In addition the light wind had generated a small chop, but the large pontoons provided a very comfortable seat.

Harry looked at Tracy next to him: her eyes were shining, her short hair wafting back and looking quite blonde in the weak sun.

She turned and looked at him.

'Thanks for the roses, Harry – they're beautiful.'

He smiled in acknowledgement. He wondered if the roses had healed the breach between them, and quietly thanked his dad for the good advice.

It was about a twenty minute trip to Whittle Rock, and they enjoyed the ride. They passed two other dive boats at closer dive sites, and the Twelve Apostles making up the Cape Peninsula fell behind and they could see Cape Hangklip on the other side of False Bay becoming clearer.

Harry had to admit he was nervous about the dive, and he fiddled with his equipment, making sure he knew how everything worked. He had the latest dive computer, and Tracy checked out all the functions. Everything seemed in order.

After a while Klaas slowed down, checking on his position until he finally put the motors into neutral.

'This is it – Whittle Rock. We'll drift here while you get ready. Vis is good – look over an' you can see the rock.'

They peered over the side and could see the reef below. Even some of the fishes swimming lazily around were visible.

Now Joe took over.

'Right,' he said, 'has anyone dived at Whittle before?'

One of the other couples raised their hands.

'Okay, but today I want you all to follow me. I'll take you on a tour to all the good places – not too deep, because some of you aren't qualified to go all the way down. No-one should get lost with this vis, so always keep in sight of the others. Stay with your buddy, and if you get lost – surface. Klaas will be looking for you, so signal if you need assistance.

Air should be good enough for half an hour to forty-five minutes – keep a check on how much you have left. And remember: obey your computer at all times.'

It was standard stuff, and the divers started getting their equipment on.

Harry put on his weight-belt, and then, when he lifted up his cylinder/BC/DV combination, Joe quickly came across to help.

'Here ... uh, Dr. Ehlers, let me help you.'

Harry was about to say he could do it himself, but Joe had already grabbed the dive cylinder and raised it up so Harry could easily slip on the BC. The cylinder had a boot, and as Joe picked it up his fingers went into the boot hole at the base.

'Eh, what's this?' he said in surprise.

He was about to turn the cylinder upside down to see what he had felt in the boot when a harsh voice commanded, 'Leave it!'

Everybody heard the shout, and turned to see what was happening.

Borysko stood at the stern, a gun levelled at Joe.

Joe backed off into Harry behind him.

Borysko looked at the others on the boat: they were totally non-plussed at the turn of events.

'Stay away!' he said. Everybody moved back. Harry felt Tracy grab hold of his arm.

Borysko turned to Joe, 'You stupid man,' he shouted now, his face getting redder as he became more agitated. 'Why you interfere?'

'What'd he do?' asked one of the other men.

'Shaddap!' Borysko waved his gun at him and he took another step back. Something was making Borysko very unhappy.

He looked at them now, panning his gun over them slowly. He was assessing his options, but nobody else understood what was happening: why a pleasure dive should suddenly be changed into a life-threatening situation.

The gun ended up pointing at Joe again, and he cringed, not knowing why he was being singled out.

It seemed Borysko thought he owed them an explanation.

'That man!' he said keeping his gun pointed at Joe, 'he interfere. Ehlers' cylinder set to blow up – boom! – in thirty minutes. No-one else. Now I have to kill you all.'

Harry went cold, as he felt Tracy holding on tighter. This man had been sent to kill him.

As the import of Borysko's words sank in, a woman wailed, 'Why us?'

'Because now you know,' Borysko almost shouted back at her. He went on slowly, 'I kill Albanian and nobody knows. Now Ehlers must go. But nobody out there must know.' His black eyes levelled at Harry.

Harry stared back. This man had contrived Albanian's death, and now had him as his target.

Borysko turned on Joe again, suddenly furious.

'Is your fault!' he screamed. As he levelled the gun there was a sharp retort and a puff of smoke appeared at the barrel of the gun.

Joe's face took on a look of utter surprise, and his eyes widened as he grabbed at his chest. Before Harry could do anything he toppled over the pontoon and into the sea.

'No…!' a woman sobbed, as she hung onto her companion. Nobody else moved, too shocked by the extreme assault on Joe.

'Now – you do what I say!' Borysko commanded after a moment.

The ocean surface is a complex result of waves coming together from all directions, and these combinations sometimes give higher waves than the norm. Over a shallow reef, these waves can extend even higher.

Such a high wave went under the boat now, raising the stern up, and then it abruptly came down again. A dive cylinder with all its attachments had been put onto the central rack by one of the divers, and this teetered and fell off, banging against Borysko. He was taken by surprise, propping up the heavy weight as it pushed him sideways.

Harry saw his chance, and made a lunge at Borysko, grabbing the hand with the gun. However, the assassin was a powerful man and quickly regained his footing, pushing both Harry and the cylinder away. Harry clung on, and as he did so his grasp slipped down Borysko's arm and dislodged the gun from his hand.

It fell on the deck of the boat, and with the stern under the next high wave it slid forward, stopping at Tracy's feet.

She quickly picked it up, holding it in both hands and pointing it at Borysko.

Another change had occurred in the whole scenario.

Borysko was free of Harry, sprawled out on the deck at the base of the pontoon.

The assassin started moving towards Tracy. Her face was ashen, but her hands were steady as she kept a bead on him.

'Stop! I can use a gun.' She said hoarsely.

'Come girly – you can't just shoot a man,' he said coaxingly.

He was only two metres away, moving slowly forward. The others on the boat seemed transfixed by the action. Then Tracy lowered her aim slightly, and there was another sharp retort as she fired.

Borysko looked down at his left leg in surprise. The neoprene of his wet suit had been ripped open by the bullet as it went through the outer muscle. Blood was beginning to ooze out of the superficial wound.

Now Tracy was calmer, keeping her aim on Borysko's chest.

'The next shot will be higher,' she said.

Borysko weighed up his options, and suddenly leaped over the side of the boat.

It took a moment for everyone on board to realise what had happened, and that the immediate danger was over. They rushed to the side of the boat, but could see no sign of Borysko.

Harry got up slowly and came across to Tracy, putting his arm around her shoulders: she was shaking like a leaf.

'Well done,' he said quietly.

'Fantastic you two!' Ela came up to them. 'You saved us.'

They were interrupted by Klaas, still standing at his console, 'Very good for now – but we must find Joe.'

It brought them back to reality: a man had been shot, possibly killed, and they needed to find him quickly. In addition, Borysko was out there somewhere.

Klaas started the boat's engines, and they cruised around the area, with all the divers ranged around the pontoons scouting the sea. The long swells took them up and down, but the wind had increased slightly, adding a bigger chop to the sea. Joe was probably only being kept afloat by his wet suit, and it was difficult to identify something just in the surface of the water. They also saw no sign of Borysko.

Harry stood next to Tracy on the port side peering at the waves, his arm around her waist. He was happy to stay like that forever.

Without warning Klaas suddenly stopped the boat.

'The cylinder!' he said urgently, 'we must get it off the boat.'

They had all forgotten what Borysko had said: somehow he had attached something in the boot of Harry's cylinder which would cause it to rupture. That was what Joe had found.

Sudhir leapt to the stern, where the cylinder lay on the deck. He started taking off the BC and DV, but Klaas shouted at him.

'Throw it off – everything!'

He picked it up and hurled it overboard. The BC hadn't been inflated and it quickly started sinking.

He watched for a moment, and then turned, smiling, 'I hope that's the last of it.'

Even as he said the words a deep 'Whooomp' seemed to come from the depths of the ocean below them. The next moment the boat was lifted up by a massive fountain of water under the stern. There were screams as everybody on board was flung off, or if they had something to hang onto they went with the boat in an arc through the air.

Harry tried to keep his grip on Tracy but she slipped out of his grasp. He was dumped into the sea, and battled to surface again: a maelstrom of water seemed to be holding him down.

When he finally did reach the surface he gasped for breath. Around him was chaos. The boat was lying upside down in the water and there were all sorts of paraphernalia drifting around. Also heads bobbing in the waves.

'Tracy!' he shouted, hoping she was safe.

No response, and he shouted again.

'I'm here, Harry.'

He looked around and saw her waving to him. Thank god, he thought, after all that had happened already.

They all swam to the boat: fortunately the buoyancy of their wetsuits made it a lot easier. The stern was low in the water, and they clambered onto the hull. Eventually everybody was up. There were no serious injuries, with one dislocated shoulder and a possible broken forearm. Klaas knew enough first aid to put the shoulder back, though it was a painful process.

'What a bloody day! And I thought we were going for a dive,' one of the men said.

'We're not out of it yet,' Klaas said, 'we still have to get back.'

They all looked at each other. In the distance they could see three sides of False Bay.

'Can we contact shore?' Ela asked, worried now.

'How?' Klaas responded. 'Radios gone, and I couldn't switch on the emergency beacon.'

'Somebody must see us – perhaps a plane?'

Harry remembered his watch – he hadn't taken it off in his dive preparations.

'I can call emergency help.'

They looked at him and he indicated the little attachment on his watch strap. He turned the little lever, and hoped the signal reached *CF Security*.

'How do you know it works?' the man who had dislocated his shoulder asked. He held his elbow gently in place.

'I don't – we've just got to wait.'

'Well, it better work – all this shit is because of you, so you better get us out.'

'Oh, come on – he saved us on the boat with that gunman.'

'Who wouldn't have been there if he wasn't on board.'

No-one responded. They realised there was nothing else they could do except wait and hope.

With the waves making sitting on the hull uncomfortable, Harry and Tracy found it easier to lie down across the beam, hanging onto the keel in the middle. Others followed suit, and soon they were spread out along the length of the boat.

She was very close to him: there was something he had to tell her.

'Tracy, that story in the papers, with that girl … nothing happened.'

She smiled, a smile which turned up the corners of her mouth. God, she was beautiful.

'I know,' she replied.

'You know …? How?'

Her smile broadened, 'Fily told me.'

He looked at her in consternation, 'You spoke to Fily?'

'Yes, she phoned me.'

'What did she say.'

'She said her agent had set her up. She's dismissed him now.'

Harry didn't answer, wondering about women, and she continued, 'She also said you were very cute.' She smiled broadly now, but didn't add Fily had told her to hang on to him at all costs.

He conceded possibly it wasn't just the flowers which had caused the change in her.

They were interrupted by a shout from Sudhir, 'Look, a chopper!'

Coming from the Cape Town side there was a speck in the sky, and they could identify the harsh sound of the helicopter engine. It soon reached them, hovering over the boat and sending a blast of air down. A winch lowered a man down, and with help from the divers he stood on the hull.

'Everything okay here? Dr Ehlers, where are you?'

'Here – I'm fine.'

'Anybody injured?'

The woman with the broken forearm and the man with the dislocated shoulder were winched up to the helicopter. In the meanwhile the pilot radioed *Diveout* to send another boat to pick up the other survivors and tow in their boat. The National Sea Rescue Institute could also assist, because they needed to find Joe and Borysko.

They finally reached Simonstown in mid-afternoon. However, it was a different scene to the one they had left that morning: there were hordes of reporters, cameras and curious onlookers on the quay. The story had obviously hit the news.

Harry was recognised and badgered.

'Dr Ehlers, do you think Albanian was assassinated?'

'That's what the man said,' Harry replied as abruptly as possible, as he, Tracy, Ela and Sudhir tried to make their way to their cars.

'So what does it mean for you?'

Harry stopped and looked at the reporter, 'I don't know – you think about it.'

The other divers were all interviewed by the press corps for their versions of the story. Photos and videos were made and transmitted.

However, they couldn't just leave. A man, possibly two, had probably been killed, and they all had to make statements to the police. By the time that had been done the reporters had their stories and they could finally get to their cars. They took off their unused wetsuits.

'All my new equipment, all at the bottom of the sea,' Harry moaned.

'You'll get insurance payout,' Sudhir responded, 'I wonder if I can claim for anything?'

'What about supper tonight?' Tracy asked, 'why don't you all come over to my place?'

'Good idea,' Ela replied, 'we'll bring something.'

'Harry?' Tracy looked at him.

'Of course,' he replied, 'I'll bring pizzas.'

CHAPTER 19

Harry had a lie-in on Monday morning. There was no great urgency for him to get up, and he pondered on Borysko's revelations. In particular, why had Abalian been killed, and why was he also targeted?

Abalian's death was probably easier to understand, because dead he couldn't be interrogated on his gravity theory. However, developing events over the next few days would be interesting, particularly concerning the patent rights.

He switched on the TV as soon as he went into his living area: *The assassin at sea* was still the main news item. The whole group of them had watched it on TV the night before at Tracy's communal lodgings: all the interviews and the speculations. Harry and Tracy were the heroes of the whole event, with the other divers revelling to a greater or lesser extent in giving their impressions. The man with the dislocated shoulder was still not happy, muttering about his injury and wanting compensation from *Diveout*, Harry, and anyone else for his pain and suffering.

Joe's body had been found, but there was no sign of Borysko. Much was made of Tracy shooting him in the leg. Was it a serious injury? Would he be able to survive the sea and make it back to land?

CF Security ensured nobody badgered Harry at his apartment. They received very good publicity as the security firm that had been able to coordinate the final rescue, and were only too happy to be known as Harry's personal security.

Slowly the TV discussions turned to the question of who would benefit from Abalian and Harry's deaths, and fingers were being pointed at B2O. Initial queries were met by curt denials: 'Why would B2O want to kill a holder of patent rights to the gravity machine if he had already signed over those rights?'

After breakfast Harry drove to the university, and made his way as quickly as possible to the Physics Department.

'Harry!' Mrs Shaw called out as he tried to get past her door. He stuck his head back in.

'Yes, Mrs Shaw,' he replied as she came across and gave him a hug.

'My, you do know how to get publicity,' she admonished him. 'All this intrigue – you must be careful.'

He was glad to finally get to his office and close the door.

There were more than the usual number of e-mails and facebook comments and queries in his in-basket. Many had lighthearted jabs at his new hero status, but through it all was the realisation it was actually quite serious: there were some powerful people who wanted him dead.

It continued in the mid-morning tea break.

'You need to be careful of B2O,' Andile advised him, though there were other opinions as well.

'There are some people who've already lost a lot of money because of the gravity machine – I doubt you're very popular with transport and roads companies,' somebody intoned.

'Yes, but murder?'

'It's been done for less.'

Pre called when he was back in his office, concerned about his safety.

'It's unfortunate, but it seems you need to be careful where you go – at least until the patents question is cleared up. Have you heard anything new?'

'No, Pre – I know as much as the news bulletins are reporting.'

A little later Stephen phoned.

'Harry, glad you came out of that mess yesterday. The reports are horrific.'

'Yes, Joe being shot next to me was frightening – particularly when I realised it's me they actually want dead.'

Stephen didn't respond immediately.

'Have you heard whether they've found Borysko?' he asked.

'No – chances seem slim he'll make it – it's a long way to shore. The reports are he's a known assassin, with lots of survival skills.'

'Not good.'

'No.' Harry hesitated, then added, 'Stephen, have you any idea why they're after me? And who "they" are?'

'No.'

'Could it be B2O?'

'No – of course not! They can't benefit if you're killed.'

'Fingers are being pointed at them about Abalian.'

'I don't know why – as I said, court cases could go on for years. And they've got Abalian's patent.'

After a moment Stephen continued, 'There are also other stories about wills and family estates in Albania. Apparently some family conflicts.'

He changed the subject, 'Have you got a will?'

'No ...'

'Well, perhaps I better see if I can get one drawn up for you.'

After hanging up, Harry thought about this new complication: drawing up a will! But it made sense – he wondered who he could put as his beneficiaries.

Harry had arranged to meet Tracy again for an early lunch. After collecting their food they found a table for two.

'You're looking happy with life,' he remarked.

She smiled, 'My shooting Borysko has brought up all sorts of strange responses. I've had girls coming up and saying things like "Good for you, shows them what women can do". It's a whole feminist thing.'

'So where did you learn to shoot?'

'My dad made sure we could all shoot – on the farm that was important.'

He told her about the reactions he had experienced, and they could sense people in the cafeteria looking at them. Or even filming them. But somehow it didn't matter now.

When she finished her meal she leaned back and said, 'There's something else happening today.'

'What...?'

She grinned, 'My thesis! It's finished!'

'Really? That's great!'

'Yes – I'm getting it printed this evening. Bound tomorrow, and then I'll hand it in. You're invited to a thesis hand-in celebration tomorrow evening.'

That afternoon Harry had a couple of phone calls from news channels, wanting to know if he'd signed away any of his patent rights to B2O. His reply was an emphatic "No!".

Later, when he went to his car he found another newsman waiting for him with the same question. He gave the same answer.

Intrigued, he watched the early news bulletin, but it was only towards the end that a short item aired involving gravity patent rights.

'There have been unconfirmed reports B2O have secured Harry Ehlers' patent rights to the gravity machine. It is not clear where these reports originated, but they have been emphatically denied by Dr. Ehlers.'

Not much clarity there, and he continued with his work. The fact that a new gravity research institute was proposed for the university was now common knowledge, and he was already getting queries from potential staff and students. He didn't know any of them, but he had to read their cv's for suitability. He would have to make decisions on the precise direction of research the institute would follow, while there were also opportunities for collaboration with other institutes.

However, he kept on coming back to the question of the patent rights and B2O. There were issues where he needed answers.

On Tuesday morning Harry phoned Stephen, asking if he could come and see him.

'I've got clients until eleven – after that is fine.'

However, Harry had to wait another fifteen minutes before he entered Stephen's office. He was motioned to sit down.

'So, what can I do for you,' Stephen asked.

Harry thought a moment, collecting his thoughts.

'Stephen, I want nothing more to do with B2O,' he finally said. 'I'm not sure if you're still in contact with them, but I don't trust them.'

'I'm sorry to hear that, Harry – they're the one group who could really manage the gravity machine properly.'

Harry shook his head, 'There's that story yesterday I had signed away my patent rights to them.'

'Yes, I heard it – I don't know where it came from.'

'You didn't tell them?'

Stephen shifted in his chair, 'Of course not. I've always hoped you'd see reason, and join up with them – they may have thought I had persuaded you.'

'What did I sign the other day – when you brought all those forms?'

'Those were patent applications – as I told you.'

Stephen leant forward on his desk, his heavy brows furrowed, 'Are you insinuating I made you sign your patent rights over to B2O? You want to see the documents?'

Harry waved the accusation away.

'I'm going to form a foundation to handle the gravity machine, with a board to decide on management.'

Stephen leaned back in his chair, 'I heard you were thinking of it.'

He stood up, turned around and looked out the window at the Mountain.

When he turned back he said in cold, measured terms, 'Harry, you're an arsehole, an absolute fucking arsehole. You have it all in front of you – everything: money, power, position, control. You can do what you want. And what do you choose? To start some goody goody fucking foundation. Do you think it's actually going to achieve anything?'

Harry stared at him, and he continued, 'You think you can change the world? People will continue to rape and pillage and take everything they can for themselves. That's what it's all about – looking after number one.'

Harry said nothing, and Stephen grasped the back of his chair with both hands, 'I know that pistol-shooting bimbo of yours has told you otherwise, but you'll see in the end. You can't change society, and what we actually need in this world is strong control and order. That's the kind of thing B2O would do. Now ... your machine is going to give new freedoms to idiots who can't handle it – it's going to cause a lot of trouble.'

They looked at each other. Harry nodded slightly, stood up and walked out. He was shaking when he got into his car.

At lunch with Tracy Harry was still thinking of what Stephen had said, but he didn't tell her of their meeting.

She was exuberant: her thesis would be bound that afternoon, and she would then hand it in.

'All done!' she smiled.

'And then?'

She was more serious, 'Not sure. I've applied for some positions, and received responses. But nothing definite.'

'What do you want to do?' he insisted.

Now she was more serious, 'I'm not too sure – something where I can curb this attitude of take everything you can out of the environment. We – as people and fellow citizens of Earth – have to learn that we must live in harmony with nature.

But you know that – why do you ask?'

'Just to make sure you haven't changed your mind.' He wondered at the approaches she and Stephen advocated. Both recognised there had to be control, but one was altruistic and the other for personal gain. Even if Stephen had some points in his favour, he had to go with Tracy's sentiments: apart from being basically good, they just felt right.

That evening Tracy provided a grand dinner for her fellow lodgers and a few friends, including Sudhir and Ela. Anne was the main cook of the group, though Tracy claimed she did help with dessert. It was laid-back and pleasant, with wine and good conversation in full supply.

The party was still going strong at eleven when Tracy received a phone call, 'Have a look at the news – there are some new developments with the gravity machine.'

She told Harry, and switched on the TV. Other conversation dried up as the picture came on and everyone realised another stage in the gravity machine saga was about to be revealed.

A balding elderly man was being interviewed: he was speaking in an unknown language, but there were subtitles of the conversation.

The man was vaguely familiar, though Harry couldn't place him. He was very nervous or afraid, or both, wringing his hands, with his eyes darting from side to side, avoiding the camera.

The interviewer asked a question, which the subtitles interpreted as *Professor, can you confirm the date when you received the paper from Abalian?*

Then Harry remembered: this was Professor Hagopian, editor of the journal that had published Abalian's paper. But now he wasn't trying to speak English.

It was a few weeks ago, the subtitles interpreted Hagopian's answer.

After the Ehlers talk in America? The interviewer asked.

Yes, Yes. He wrung his hands again.

Then why did you say it was before?

People say I must.

Which people – did they say why?

I don't know … they kill Panos. Now they kill me as well.

You don't know where these people come from?

He shook his head, and a whole stream of words followed. The subtitltes continued: *I ask Panos, and he says it's all fine, no problems. I trusted him, and now he's dead. Murdered. Now they kill me.*

The interview was cut, back to the anchorwoman.

'Well, that's the latest in this whole sorry saga,' she said. 'It seems there can be no question now about who owns the patent rights to the gravity machine: undoubtedly Dr. Harry Ehlers. However, there are a lot of questions that still need to be answered, and B2O – specifically Sir Richard Straithwaite – will have to explain how they managed to get the patent rights from Dr. Panos Abalian.

We'll keep you posted.'

Another story followed, and Tracy switched off the TV. She turned and looked at Harry.

'That's fantastic for you,' she said, 'but that man is very afraid.'

'Yes,' Harry agreed soberly, 'but it looks like it's all coming out. Probably he's okay …'

Nonetheless, he felt a weight lifted off his shoulder.

The next morning Pre phoned again.

'This whole patents question is being resolved quickly now, and it's all good news for you. It means we can go ahead with planning the new institute without all sorts of issues hanging over us.'

'It also means the Foundation can be established,' Harry added.

'Yes, indeed. However, we have to move fast, and use all the public interest for our own benefit – we can get a lot of corporate involvement now.

Can you come to a meeting with Pravin at ten here in my office?'

Tea was provided, and Pre reported that a building had provisionally been identified to house the new Harry Ehlers Gravity Research Institute.

'It's a large double-storey old house, and will need to be modified before anybody can move in. Probably take a month or two.'

'Which will give us enough time to plan how we want to structure the institute,' Pravin added. 'And obviously we must be circumspect with appointments.'

He hesitated a moment, and then continued, 'we have already been able to source over eight million Rand – corporations want to get into this whole new venture at ground level.'

Pre smiled at Harry, 'it's exciting stuff. The SASF has increased its funding to two million, but that will be specifically on the science side – your physics research.'

Pravin presented an organogram of how he envisaged the institute. They discussed various aspects, and Harry took a copy to study at his leisure.

However, there was another matter he had to discuss.

'The Foundation must also fit into the whole structure.'

Pre nodded, 'Yes, you need to decide on its structure. To a large extent the decisions are yours, what you want it to do, who is on the board, whether you want an advisor, the beneficiaries, etc.'

'Would there be a CEO?'

'Yes, to see to the daily running – that could be extended at a later stage.'

'Can I propose a CEO?'

Pre looked at Pravin, and shrugged her shoulders, 'Again, I think that's up to you. Do you have someone in mind?'

'Well, yes,' Harry replied, half embarrassed, 'I'm thinking of asking Tracy Freese.'

It was a moment before Pravin asked slowly, 'That's the gun-toting girl...?'

'Yes, she's just finished her masters in environmental management, which is where I want the Foundation to work.'

Pre smiled, 'I believe there's also a romantic attachment involved?'

Harry grinned shyly, 'Uh,... yes, ... I guess.'

'Harry, that's your decision,' Pre replied firmly. 'But remember, if it doesn't work out between the two of you it could be very awkward.'

Harry nodded, and then continued, 'there's someone else I'm thinking of for the board.'

He looked at Pre and Pravin, 'I would like to ask Hamish Prentiss.'

'Hamish Prentiss!' Pravin said in surprise, '...do you know him?'

'I met him in America – he said he would be happy to help me if he could.'

'Fantastic, he would give your Board a lot of credibility.'

Back in his office Harry took out Prentiss' card, wondering whether to call. However, he had nothing to lose and dialled the listed number.

'Of course Mr Prentiss remembers you, Dr. Ehlers,' his private secretary said when he gave his name. 'I'll see if he can talk to you now.'

'Harry? Harry Ehlers? Is that you?' the voice came over the phone a moment later.

'Uh, ... yes – if you remember we met on the plane a few weeks ago.'

There was a chuckle on the other side, 'Yes – how can I forget. What can I do for you?'

In principle Prentiss was happy to come onto the board of the Foundation, however, he needed more information on its objectives and structure. He was actually in China at the time, and would be flying back to the USA the following week.

'Why don't I come past Cape Town on my way home – it's one of my favourite cities.'

Prentiss wasn't sure of his dates, but Harry said he had no firm commitments and would be happy to see him at any time in the next week.

Harry took Tracy out to dinner that evening, and afterwards invited her to coffee in his apartment. She seemed hesitant at first, but eventually agreed to come for a short while.

It was the first time she had been there, and she walked around the little lounge/dining room/kitchen area while he made the coffee. He had a picture of his mother and father on a small table, and she picked it up, studying the couple she would never meet.

'They seem really nice people,' she remarked. He looked up from his coffee-making and nodded his head. She had heard their story, and he obviously didn't want to go there again.

One blocked print dominated the side wall. The base was a multitude of colours with a wide blue swath coming out of it, tapering as it curved away to a fine point at the top right.

'What does this mean?' she asked.

He came across to where she was standing, 'I don't actually know, but I liked it the moment I saw it. It reminds me of infinity.'

He put his hand out and touched her on her back. But she went rigid at his touch, and quickly walked to one of the counter chairs where he was making the coffee. She sat down and said as brightly as possible, 'How's the coffee?'

He looked at her and came slowly back into the kitchen, 'Nearly ready.'

He made the two cups, handed her one and went to sit in his big chair.

'I'm sure we can both fit in here,' he said invitingly.

She remained on her chair, her eyes wide now, staring at Harry. Then she bowed her head, and when she looked up again her eyes were full of tears.

'Harry,' she said, her voice trembling, '...I can't.'

She bowed her head again, and continued softly, 'when you touched me now ... I can't explain it, I just felt ...like ... like I was being smothered ...'

'It's not you,' she added quickly, '– it's me. Do you understand?'

She sobbed quietly, the sobs wracking her body. He stood up quickly, but she held up her hand.

'Please ...'

He stopped and looked at her, frail and beautiful. He sat on the other counter chair and allowed her to regain control.

Finally she smiled at him through her tears, 'Thanks.'

She picked up her coffee and had a few sips, which helped her composure further.

'There's something I wanted to ask you this evening,' he finally said.

She looked at him questioningly.

'Will you be CEO of my foundation?'

It took her a moment or two to register what he had asked.

'CEO? What do you mean?'

'Just that. I like the way you think, and I'm sure you'll take it in the right direction.' He smiled at her confusion, and in return she smiled back. She took a serviette out of a rack on the counter to dry her tears.

'This is very sudden,' she said.

'I heard you were looking for a job. Pay's not good, bad boss, hours are terrible, but interesting work.'

'Let me think about it – when do you want an answer?'

'Tomorrow.'

She took another sip of coffee, 'It sounds good, but I have to ask my advisers.'

'Tell them I pay good bribes.'

She laughed, a nervous, relieved laugh, and he smiled at her return to normality.

They finished their coffee, and he took her home. He walked her to her front door, and before she went in she took both his hands tightly in her hands.

'Thanks Harry.' She kissed him on the cheek and went in.

That night he lay in bed thinking about the evening. Mac Manyi had a lot to answer for.

CHAPTER 20

Harry switched on the news while having breakfast: it was something he was getting used to since the media seemed to be playing an increasingly greater part in his life.

It was no different now: Sir Richard Straithwaite was being interviewed.

'So, Sir Richard,' the interviewer was saying, 'B2O is known as a secretive organisation. Why is that, and what does it do?'

'Well, Helen,' Sir Richard replied pleasantly, 'we don't seek publicity, and prefer to work in the background. I would guess this policy of not being in the public eye might make some people think we are secretive.'

He was exactly as Harry remembered him, short-cropped hair, fit-looking and confident.

Helen continued with her questions, 'And what is it you do?'

Sir Richard thought a moment before answering, 'We are a group of like-minded individuals who have high ideals for the future of mankind. B2O is a voluntary organisation, and many of our members are associated with corporations and institutions all over the world. We communicate our ideas, and recommend actions in certain situations.'

'You're not a religious organisation?'

'No, not at all. However, many of our members are Christians, and we believe in the basic tenets of Christianity and upholding a lifestyle commensurate with those principles.'

'Are you anti-Muslim or any other religion?'

'No, most definitely not. Most of the world's major religions have similar ideals, and we work with whoever agrees with our objectives.'

'And what are those objectives.'

Sir Richard took a moment to answer.

'Essentially we need to maintain established democratic systems, with the accompanying legal structures and discipline. Unfortunately our society is under a lot of pressure from undisciplined groups who have little respect for systems that work. We know adaption and change is necessary, but we want it to proceed in an orderly fashion.'

Helen changed her tack, 'What is your interest in the gravity machine?'

Again Sir Richard took a moment to answer.

'We've recognised it will bring major changes to society, and again we want to ensure these changes proceed smoothly. You must understand that there are powerful groups who want to use the gravity machine to destabilize present structures, particularly if they gain technological advantages. Moreover the mobility that comes with use of the gravity machine could cause total chaos.'

'And Abalian?'

'We've been in contact with Dr. Ehlers, and believed he would sign over his patent rights to us. When we heard of Dr. Abalian's claims we thought we should get his rights as well to be sure.'

'You didn't set up Abalian?'

'Of course not. Our ethics wouldn't allow that.'

'How did you contact him?'

'We have networks in most countries, and they were able to make contact. However, with all the latest reports from South Africa our contacts have disappeared – we know as much as is reported on the news.'

Helen nodded, and continued, 'So what now?'

'Well, we will have to keep a close watch on developments, and treat all eventualities as they arise.'

Helen thanked Sir Richard for agreeing to the interview, and then carried on with other news.

Harry stared at the TV screen: Sir Richard had revealed nothing at all. What had been B2O's part in the whole Abalian affair? The way he told it now, that they had only contacted Abalian after he had already claimed the patent rights was very plausible. Who actually knew?

Pre contacted him later in the morning.

'Harry, we must think about launching the new Institute soon. Contributors want to know about formal structures, and we are getting new enquiries daily.'

'I've also had applications for positions,' Harry replied, '… I presume this launch will include the Foundation?'

'Yes – have you contacted Prentiss?'

'He's interested – coincidentally he can come to Cape Town next week, so we can finalise it when he's here.'

'Incredible,' Pre mused, 'Pravin will be over the moon, he's a great admirer of Prentiss' ideas. We must try and organise the launch for when he's here.'

'I'll see if I can get definite dates.'

Harry hesitated, and continued, 'Pre, I must establish a board for the Foundation, and I think you will be able to contribute immensely. Will you agree to come on?'

She chuckled, 'Of course, Harry – it will be a privilege. However, you need to set out what the Foundation stands for. I think I agree with your principles, but Prentiss will want to know before committing himself.'

Harry told Tracy of the new developments with the Foundation over lunch.

Then he asked, 'What's your decision?'

'About what?'

'CEO of my Foundation.'

She smiled at him, 'I discussed it with my advisors last night.'

'And?'

'You haven't actually specified duties, salary, pension benefits, medical aid or anything else.'

'I'll leave that for you to decide.'

'Very unusual.'

She couldn't help grinning, and continued, 'They recommended acceptance, subject to it being purely a business arrangement.'

He smiled, 'Yes, I've also been advised it must be purely business.'

His face softened, 'You know, I can't think of doing anything without you. You're part of everything I do.'

She took his hand, and when she raised her head to look at him there were tears in her eyes. 'Thank you,' she said.

He looked around, suddenly realising they were in a public place.

'Yes, well, we need to look at the business – are you doing anything this afternoon?' He kept his hand in hers, giving it a press.

'What do you mean?'

'Setting up the objectives of the Foundation. Writing out your service contract.'

'I'm available, now that I have a job.'

They continued eating, and after a while Harry asked, 'Did you see Sir Richard on TV?'

She nodded, 'He came across very sincere and confident. What do you think?'

Harry shook his head, 'I don't know. I'm convinced B2O set up Abalian. They've killed at least two people, but I don't see any way they'll be brought to justice.'

'They probably gave orders, and somebody else did the dirty work.'

Harry nodded, 'And there'll be no way it can be traced back. Sir Richard appeared innocent and honest when he said they'd lost their contacts. They were just trying to help – like bloody hell.'

'Do you think they set up Borysko?'

Again Harry nodded, 'It makes sense. I think Stephen made me sign away my patent rights – he brought in a whole lot of papers last week, and I didn't check what I was signing. So both the holders would have died in accidents, and B2O would have all the patents. Unusual to have two such accidents, but no-one would have been able to show otherwise – they'd already accepted Abalian's accident.'

Tracy had a few more mouthfuls, and asked, 'And Stephen?'

Harry took a while to reply, 'I don't know – he told me on Tuesday that I was being stupid with the Foundation. That it wouldn't solve anything, and more controls were necessary. He certainly supports B2O, but I don't think he was privy to what Borysko was sent to do.

At least, I hope not,' he added.

'Can you take him off the gravity machine patenting? It would mean he'd lose a lot of money.'

'I don't think it's that simple, since I signed a contract with him right at the beginning.'

Harry frowned, 'I think he's actually made a mint already.'

She looked at him questioningly.

'I've no idea about the financing of the workshops. But looking at what attendees were paying, and the number who came, they would have collected much more than he paid me. He's had a lot of expenses with patents up to now, and I guess all that needs to be sorted.'

Harry leaned back, musing, 'On the other hand, he is a good patents lawyer …'

He sat forward again, smiling, 'But we'll leave that to the Foundation and new CEO to sort out.'

'Sies!' Tracy exclaimed, 'you'll have to pay a lot to do your dirty work.'

They spent the afternoon formulating their objectives for the new Foundation. It was an exciting, but in many ways an unreal exercise as they realised that the money coming in would give them immense power to initiate all sorts of projects.

Tracy had a much better idea of what she wanted, having been involved with various environmental NGOs through her school and university years. Moreover, her masters had been specifically aimed at environmental management, biodiversity and species extinction, so she became more optimistic as the afternoon progressed.

'It's like a dream come true,' she enthused, 'there are all these groups out there fighting the big corporations and government. Now we can help them win.'

'We can't just give money away,' Harry cautioned. From his parents' stories and his own experiences he had become quite cynical about people's intentions.

'Nothing is ever black and white,' he continued, 'and more than anything else we need to be objective. Everybody has their own reasons for doing things, and often those reasons are selfish. Look at the problems we've had already with the gravity machine – they all stem from greed.'

However, by the end of the afternoon they had a much better idea of what they wanted, though it needed to be spelt out properly in a document.

They had supper at an upmarket restaurant, enjoying the privacy the venue provided. Afterwards they each drove back to their own lodgings; Harry had concluded Tracy needed to decide for herself when their relationship could move further.

It was mid-morning on Friday when Harry received the call from Cambridge.

'Hello Harry – Fred Morton here.'

Harry recognised the voice of his ex-supervisor.

'Morning … uh … professor.'

Morton chuckled, 'Some day you're going to have to learn to call me 'Fred''

'Okay, morning … Fred.'

'Better! But this isn't a courtesy call, it's an invitation. What are you doing on Sunday – in nine days time?'

'Nothing planned that I know of. Why?'

'It's time for the next stage in your gravity machine development. We're planning the launch of the first manned gravity machine in Trafalgar Square. Not sure if it should be called a launch – probably flight would be better. You know what I mean.'

Harry sat back, 'Wow! I didn't realise anybody was that far.'

Morton paused a moment, 'Yes, there are a lot of companies just about there, and we want to be first. More than that, we want you to be at our launch.

So, can you make it?'

It only took a moment for Harry to consider this new development.

'Yes, of course, there's nothing I'd like more.'

'Good, we were hoping you'd agree.'

'Who's doing it … you're obviously involved?'

'Yes,' Morton chuckled again, 'I had the advantage of being your ex-supervisor, so everyone thought I must know what's going on – I was in high demand.'

He paused, 'I've got your papers and videos of the workshops. I must say you've done remarkable work – very innovative. Congratulations.'

Harry didn't say anything: he knew it was high praise coming from Morton.

'Anyway, a group of British and European car manufacturers came together,' Morton continued, 'They formed a group called Amalgum. I've been heading their research division.'

'You've solved the deflation problem?'

'No, not really – we've circumvented it for this launch. I'll tell you about it when you get here. When can you make it? You need to visit Cambridge again.'

'I'm not sure – we've got the launch of the Institute and Foundation here next week. I'll probably only be able to leave at the end of the week.'

'That's good – you can come to Cambridge the following week. Let me know when you're ready.'

Harry was elated after Fred Morton hung up: it would no doubt be a spectacle in Trafalgar Square, and returning to Cambridge would be the cherry on the top.

He told Tracy about it at lunch.

'You'll have to be there as well,' he said, 'as CEO of the Foundation.'

Prentiss confirmed he would be arriving in Cape Town on Tuesday morning, and they set up the launch of the Institute and Foundation for Wednesday. It would take place in one of the university's auditoriums and the press and anybody else interested was invited. There were small reports in the Sunday papers.

On Sunday *Diveout* invited all the divers from the abortive dive at Whittle Rock to a repeat dive. Unfortunately the weather was not cooperative and the swell was too high in the middle of False Bay, so the dive took place at one of the sheltered coastal sites.

Tracy, Harry, Sudhir and Ela all dived, and though the dive itself wasn't exceptional, they were treated royally. This included lunch afterwards at one of the Simonstown restaurants.

During a lull in the conversation, Sudhir was suddenly serious, 'One thing I still don't understand is how Borysko knew about Harry's dive.'

'I can answer that,' Rick replied. Everybody looked at him.

'He came into the shop soon after you had left, Harry. Said something innocent like "*Wasn't that Harry Ehlers making a booking here?*"

I told him you were going out to Whittle – perhaps stupid in retrospect, but I didn't think anything of it. He also booked a dive – paid on the spot.'

'And he knew which was your cylinder, Harry,' Tracy added. "Couldn't miss it!'

They were quiet a moment, assimilating this new information.

'He was probably following you, Harry,' Ela eventually ventured.

Sudhir nodded, 'Scary stuff, Harry – you need to take care.'

Harry looked at him, 'Maybe. But everything seems to have come out now. I don't know how anyone can benefit now by knocking me off.'

In spite of what he had told Tracy, Harry wanted to clarify the situation with Stephen. While he had been surprised at Stephen's attack, he recognised the lawyer's management and legal capabilities. Moreover, he had been on board since the start, and Harry had learnt to depend on his expertise. Then there was also the whole question of the patents contract.

On Sunday evening Harry phoned Stephen.

'Yes, Harry,' he answered. Cool.

'Stephen, I'm phoning about the other day – what you said. I never actually responded.'

'No.'

'Well, we have a contract, and I need to know how we stand.'

There was no immediate response, and Harry continued, 'I value the work you've done, and would appreciate it if you would continue. But under the auspices of the Institute and the Foundation.'

It took some time for Stephen to reply.

'Did you see Sir Richard on TV?'

'Yes.'

'Well, I don't believe that he had anything to do with that assassin. And I still think you're making a mistake not bringing in B2O.'

'Maybe – but we'll probably never know about Sir Richard.'

'Perhaps.'

'We'll set up the patenting structures in the Foundation, so it'll all be together.'

'That'll take some time, so I'll continue where I am.'

'That's probably a good idea,' Harry responded, 'we can then see how it develops and finalise it all at a later stage.'

'Okay.'

'You know the launch of the Institute and Foundation is on Wednesday?'

'I saw it in the papers. I'll come along and see how it goes.'

After he'd hung up Harry sat back in his chair: it was probably as good an arrangement as he could get. At least there was no hiatus now, and they could see if they could continue working together.

Tracy and Harry spent all their free time together. She was obviously taking her position as CEO of the Harry Ehlers Foundation seriously, reading up about other foundations, their constitutions and how they conducted their affairs. More particularly, how they allocated money and what kinds of follow-ups were involved.

Harry was pleased with her attention to detail, and her enthusiasm for the work. She was becoming more relaxed in everything she did, and more specifically also in their personal relationship.

On Tuesday morning Harry and Tracy drove to Cape Town International airport to meet Hamish Prentiss.

Harry recognised him the moment he came into the arrivals concourse, and introduced Tracy as the new CEO of the Foundation.

He looked at her approvingly, 'Yes, I've seen you on TV – I believe you've already saved Harry's life on that dive boat.'

Tracy grinned, 'That's all I'm remembered for – shooting.'

'Well, it gets people's respect.'

They walked out to the parking area, and when Prentiss saw Harry's ten-year old Golf, he raised his eyebrows, 'You haven't bought a fancy new car yet?'

Harry laughed, 'I haven't had the time – but I believe the expression is 'this does what is required" He had found Prentiss used the term when asked why he was still driving an eight-year old Toyota.

Prentiss smiled, 'Touché.'

'There are also rumours doing the rounds that all cars will soon be out of date,' Tracy added.

They discussed the new Foundation on the drive in to Cape Town, and continued in the office of the vice-chancellor when they reached the university. Pre welcomed Prentiss as a fellow board member.

However, Prentiss also expressed interest in the proposed activities of the new Institute, particularly the investigations into the way society would have to adapt.

'It's probably one of the most important topics we have to consider,' he said, 'because we have little time – the changes are here, and society isn't ready for them.'

Pravin Ashwin joined them at lunch, happy that Prentiss was showing such interest in the Institute.

The discussions carried on for much of the afternoon, and Harry drove Prentiss to his hotel after their deliberations and a pleasant supper.

'You know, Harry,' he confided, 'I was wary when you introduced me to Tracy. Such a pretty girl, and I thought it could be a problem if you've already promised her the position of CEO.'

He smiled, 'For whatever reason.' Harry said nothing.

'But what an intelligent kid,' he continued, 'she knows what's going on, and she's got good ideas of how to handle the situation. I like the way she thinks about the future.'

He stopped, and added, 'and then there's Pre – I can see why she's vice-chancellor. So I think you have a fantastic board, and I want to thank you for asking me to be a member.'

'That's great, thanks Hamish.'

'You know,' Prentiss mused, 'as an old male chauvinist, for most of the afternoon I completely forgot they were women.'

The launch of the new Harry Ehlers Gravity Research Institute and the associated Foundation was scheduled for eleven on Wednesday morning. It was not a high profile event, and there were the usual reporters, a modicum of interested public and representatives from various organisations and corporations who expected to have dealings with the new bodies. Harry saw Stephen take a seat at the back of the hall.

All five of the previous day's group were seated at a table on the stage, facing the audience. Pre was in the middle, flanked on her right by Harry and Tracy, and on her left by Pravin and Hamish. There were microphones in front of each one to catch all the presentations and discussions.

At eleven everything was ready to roll, and Pre looked at Harry.

'All set?' she asked.

Harry nodded.

Just then a new group of four came in at the back of the auditorium. They walked slowly down the sloping aisle to the front row, where Harry noticed four seats had been kept clear.

With a shock he recognised Mac Manyi. He was dressed in his tell-tale grey suit with a red tie, and Harry thought he half-smiled as they briefly made eye contact. They took their time to sit down, and once comfortable looked expectantly at the stage.

Harry turned to Tracy: she had gone ashen, and was staring straight ahead.

'You okay?' he whispered.

She nodded, still looking ahead.

'Harry?' Pre questioned from the other side.

He turned to her, 'Go ahead, Pre.'

Pre tapped on her microphone to get the attention of the audience. The talking died down, and she welcomed all to the launch.

'The Institute is a response to a dramatic new need that has arisen in society because of the invention of the gravity machine by Dr

Harry Ehlers,' she said. 'It will affect almost everything we do, and it's important the way ahead is planned carefully.'

To demonstrate what she meant, she projected onto a large screen at the side the different ways in which society would change. The slides covered items such as transport in all its different aspects and the way this would impact on town and regional planning, environmental implications particularly in terms of access, national boundaries and people-movement, economic repercussions and stock exchanges, legal ramifications and finally interplanetary travel.

Then she continued, 'The Harry Ehlers Gravity Institute will be one of several institutes at the university – a separate body, but it will obviously interact with the different established departments.

Dr Ehlers will be director, specifically involved with continuing gravity research funded by the SASF. Professor Pravin Ashwin will be seconded from the Economics Department and will coordinate other activities until we have a more formal structure established.'

She stopped and looked at the audience, 'You will have noticed two others at the table, and wondered how they fit into the Institute. Well, let me first introduce Mr Hamish Prentiss, international benefactor, businessman and financier, who has agreed to be an advisor to the Institute.

And finally there is Tracy Freese, who has recently finished a Masters degree in environmental management. Dr Ehlers will explain further how they fit into the structure.'

Now it was Harry's turn. He found he was more nervous than during his workshops, since he wasn't now dealing with science.

'Associated with the Institute,' he began, 'I also want to establish a Foundation to manage the funds that will come from the gravity machine.'

He paused a moment, smiling slightly, 'I hope I'm not being premature, because there is no money yet. Everybody's talking about how much the patents are worth, but I've seen nothing …'

There were some chuckles from the audience.

'However, I've gone ahead and appointed Tracy as CEO – she still has to negotiate a salary.'

There were more chuckles and murmurs in the audience, and Harry felt he had to justify the appointment.

'It's not only because she can shoot a gun or because she saved my life, she has the right ideas about our planet, and what we need to do to continue existing as a species.

So, yes, the Foundation will concentrate on environmental matters, and specifically the place of humanity within that environment.'

He felt it wasn't well explained, and paused before continuing, 'There will be a board established to see this is done properly, and I've been lucky both Professor Pre Mahlangu and Hamish Prentiss have agreed to be board members. We may appoint more board members in future if the need arises.'

He stopped, and looked at Tracy: she nodded briefly, still not smiling.

Pre took over, 'Well, there you have it in terms of the formal presentation of the new Institute and Foundation. We will now accept any questions you may have.'

Before anyone else could start, Mac Manyi stood up at the front, facing the audience and with the stage at his side. Others in the audience noticed him, and quietened to hear what he had to say.

'I want to comment on both the Institute and the Foundation,' Manyi began. He had a deep voice and it resonated in the auditorium: he did not need a microphone for everyone to hear.

'I am very disappointed with what I've heard and seen here this morning. Here we have a so-called son of Africa' – he indicated to Harry – 'who has invented this marvellous new gravity machine.

And does he want to help his people with his invention?'

He let the question hang, and waved disparagingly at the stage, 'Look at them! Do they look like they have the interests of Africa at heart?

No! Not at all! There's Hamish Prentiss, an American. We know all about him: he's a capitalist who made all his money by exploiting the poor. And enslaving the people of Africa.

Then there's Pravin Ashwin, an Indian. No knowing where his interests lie – but he's a capitalist economist, so he will make sure the Institute looks at new ways to exploit the poor.

Pre Mahlangu? Ah … she was an African – before she went to America. She's lost her roots, and will do the bidding of her masters.

Harry Ehlers? Turns out he's actually an American. So we can't expect much from him.

And Tracy Freese? A little white girl who's out of her depth.'

The auditorium was quiet while Manyi spoke. Cameras were rolling to record the event.

He continued, 'Ehlers had an opportunity to help the situation, to ease five hundred years of slavery and colonialism. We proposed a system of African empowerment, which would have taken funding where it's needed to wipe out poverty and unemployment. The proposal wasn't even considered.

Now they've established the Institute and its Foundation. With what objective? More of the same, exploiting the poor and those who cannot help themselves. They will ensure those in control remain there. The poor will get nothing.'

Manyi looked at the audience, satisfied with the effects his speech. He slowly went back to his seat.

On the stage there was a shocked silence at his attack.

Harry heard Tracy say softly, 'I'll take this.'

He looked at Pre, but she had heard Tracy, and nodded slightly.

Harry turned again to Tracy: she was pale, staring straight ahead. He waited, and the audience waited, because they sensed she would respond.

Finally, she took the microphone in front of her.

'Mr Manyi,' she said, her voice trembling slightly, 'at the Foundation we will treat all people as individuals.'

Her voice got stronger, and she continued, 'Africa is a land mass, a continent, and it doesn't define a people or a culture. In Africa we have many people, some rich, some poor, some advantaged and some disadvantaged. It's like that all over the world.

The origins of these disparities lie in history. We can't change that, but we can look to remedy the inequalities.

However, they are all people, all over the world. So we will treat all people equally.'

She stopped. She was staring at Manyi now, still pale, her face resolute.

'Mac, I once thought you were a friend. But you took me on a date to a casino and raped me.'

The words came out quickly, and her voice broke, but she continued, 'you held me down, and … and had your way.'

There was absolute quiet. Harry thought of touching her in support, but held back knowing what happened last time.

There were tears in her eyes, but she wiped her face roughly with the back of her hand.

Then she was over it, and continued angrily, 'Everything you do is for self-gratification and greed. How can you expect me to believe anything you say – especially when you claim it is for somebody else's good. You don't think of anyone but yourself.'

She left it there, staring at Manyi and breathing deeply.

The attention shifted to Manyi, and he glowered at her from his seat.

'You fucking bitch, you asked for it,' he finally muttered. The audience was suddenly vocal as those who hadn't heard wanted to know what he said. The man beside Manyi grabbed his arm and whispered in his ear. Manyi nodded, but continued glowering at Tracy.

He stood up.

'That's defamation,' he said, shaking his finger at Tracy, 'I'll sue you.'

He turned to the rest of the audience, 'You see the kind of people we are dealing with. No good will come out of this.'

He indicated to the rest of his group, and they marched out of the auditorium.

Everybody watched them go. Harry took hold of Tracy's arm and gave it a squeeze, but she didn't react; she was too intent watching the departing group.

'Harry?' Pre questioned.

'I think we must carry on,' he responded, 'it will probably help Tracy.'

She nodded, and tapped on her microphone again.

'Are there other questions?'

After the drama it reverted to a question and answer session, much of it about structure and preferences. Harry fielded any questions about the Foundation or those directed at Tracy, as she sat back in her chair and observed passively. Pre forbad any questions about her accusations.

At the end the auditorium emptied quickly, particularly as reporters wanted to submit their stories.

Harry took Tracy's hand, and she turned her face to look at him: her eyes were brimming with tears.

'We must go,' he said gently.

She nodded, and stood up gingerly. Then, suddenly, she clung to him and started crying, great big sobs that wracked her whole body. He held her close, feeling her trauma.

Hamish came up to them, 'That's good Harry, she needs to get rid of those emotions.'

CHAPTER 21

The news value of the launch of the new Harry Ehlers Gravity Institute faded into insignificance next to Manyi's accusations against its members, and even more so Tracy's accusations against Manyi. There were discussions on TV and in the papers about the direction the new institute should take, and what actually needed to be investigated. In particular, voices were raised against the idea that environmental concerns would form the cornerstone of the Foundation's interests. Why should animals get preference over people?

Two women also came forward to say they had been raped by Manyi.

Hamish Prentiss left early on Thursday morning, promising he would be back as soon as he could.

'Amazing place, South Africa,' he said, 'always something interesting happening here.'

Ashwin took him to the airport – they obviously had a lot in common on the economics front. Moreover, his involvement in both the Institute and the Foundation was seen as a great benefit, in spite of anything Manyi and his cohorts might say.

Harry met Tracy for an early lunch; they seemed to have to go earlier and earlier to get a table for two.

'How're you feeling,' he asked.

'Great,' she smiled back. 'Somehow I'm just very relieved. I told the girls last night that I've read all about facing one's demons, but never really believed it. But it's true. I feel something's gone, something that was holding me down, smothering me...'

'I see two women have come forward with rape stories.'

Tracy nodded, 'Another three have contacted me personally. They're frightened of Manyi – it seems he does this on a regular basis.'

'Bastard.'

'Not only him,' Tracy added, '… also his whole gang. It seems I got off lightly – two of the women were gang-raped.'

'Well, with all this new evidence, it must be enough to prosecute Manyi – and his gang.'

'Maybe – one can hope. Politically he's been untouchable. However, in that kind of society if someone is seen to be going down, everybody drops them as well.'

Harry chewed on a mouthful of food, thinking how society functioned through patronage and favours. However, as far as Manyi was concerned, that wasn't the end of the story.

'There's something else as well,' he said quietly, 'possibly murder.'

Now it was Tracy's turn to be surprised. Harry told her about Manyi's visit, Etienne's response, and then his murder.

'Why didn't you tell me?'

'I couldn't at the time. But I'm not sure how this can be pinned on Manyi.'

She nodded, and they continued eating in silence.

'There is some other news – good this time,' he finally said.

She looked at him.

'Our flight to London is booked for tomorrow evening.'

She smiled, 'I'm looking forward to that – get away from all this for a while.'

'Yes …' he continued hesitantly, 'but there's also a decision to make …'

'What now?'

He grinned, 'Well, we've been booked into a Hilton hotel. They want to know how many rooms.'

'Ah… and I guess you think one is enough?'

'Well, it is a deluxe room, and it will mean saving some money …'

'I didn't realise money was a problem.'

'One shouldn't be extravagant.'

She grinned at him, 'I suppose it will mean I can check if you have any midnight visitors ...'

Fred Morton met them at Heathrow airport on Saturday morning. With him was a spare, gangling individual whom Morton introduced as 'Nezer' Stonebrook. They later found out he was actually Lord Ebenezer Stonebrook, chairman of Amalgum, the consortium which had built the gravity machine.

'Very pleased to meet you, my dear chap,' he said to Harry.

'And you, Miss Freese,' he said to Tracy, holding her hand, 'honoured, indeed.'

On the drive to London Lord Stonebrook held forth about the big launch.

'This is a tremendous achievement by British industry,' he said, '... and of course our European partners. To be the first to build a manned gravity machine.'

He was a stickler for detail, and outlined what would happen the following day.

'The launch will take place in Trafalgar Square in front of Lord Nelson, between the two fountains. The gravity machine is not big – it's round, with a diameter of four metres, and stands about one metre high. We've built a small podium – two metres high – as the launch platform. It will let the crowd see what is happening.'

'There's seating for ten,' added Morton, '- in a circle, looking out. With just a handrail in front. Also a driver – propulsion is with one large ducted fan, and two side-thrusters, like a ship.'

'We want to make this a memorable occasion,' Lord Stonebrook continued. 'The first group – that's us – will take off at eleven. We'll fly around Lord Nelson, and then over all the crowds who may be gathered in the streets around Trafalgar Square. So everybody can get a good look.'

'How high?' asked Tracy.

'Not too high,' replied Morton, '- about fifty metres, so people can see.'

He quickly added, 'I hope you're comfortable with this?'

'Sounds great to me,' Harry said, looking at Tracy: she nodded.

Lord Stonebrook took over again, 'after we've had our flip, there will be three more flights with invited celebrities. Finally, we've had a lucky draw to select another forty people for four additional flights.'

'The enthusiasm for the lucky draw has been incredible – unbelieveable,' Morton said, 'we opened the competition to the social media yesterday morning, and by last night more than twenty million people had entered. From all over Europe – they'll fly here if they win – just to get on that machine.'

He stopped for a moment and looked at Harry and Tracy, 'The draw will take place at eleven today, and the organisers have asked for you to be present. Will you be prepared to participate?'

Harry looked at Tracy again.

'I guess ...,' he said.

'Lots of publicity ...?' Tracy asked.

Morton nodded, 'That's what it's all about. Your presence will make a big difference. There's this little publicity gap for being first, and we want to make the most of it. It's actually exceeded our wildest expectations.'

'We're going to Trafalgar Square now,' Lord Stonebrook interrupted, 'we'll show you what's happening.'

A little later they were standing in front of the National Gallery, at the top of the little slope that runs down into Trafalgar Square. Below them, between the fountains workmen were putting up a low stage structure.

'That's where the launch will take place,' Lord Stonebrook said.

'And all those people?' Tracy asked, pointing to where there were groups just sitting around, with what looked like rolled-up sleeping bags.

'I would guess they're getting their spots for tomorrow,' Morton responded.

Just then there was a shout of 'Harry Ehlers! That's Harry Ehlers!'

Very quickly they were surrounded by a horde of people with cameras and cell-phones taking pictures. Tracy, Morton and Stonebrook were gently eased aside as one after the other people wanted to be in photos with Harry. One pretty girl came and stood beside him, and kissed him on the cheek while a friend quickly snapped the scene.

They said little to Harry directly, apart from phrases such as 'can you stand there', 'look here' and 'smile.' One or two added things like 'fantastic invention.'

However, after a couple of minutes Harry had had enough and extracted himself and joined the others in the car.

'You've got a lot of fans,' Tracy said, 'including lots of pretty girls.' He grinned at her and squeezed her hand.

The lucky draw prize-giving was held in one of the auditoriums at the BBC.

The mc shook Harry's hand enthusiastically, 'Great that you could make it, Dr Ehlers – your presence just tops off the show.'

He turned to the others, 'I'd like you all to come onto the stage before the draw. We can chat a bit, and build up expectations.'

'Chat about what?' Tracy asked.

'Oh, general stuff – associated with the gravity machine. Nothing too personal.'

The auditorium was packed. The mc went out and introduced the show and the guests. Cheers and clapping greeted each one as they came out onto the stage, with the biggest cheer when Harry came on at the end.

It was generally light banter, and Lord Stonebrook and Fred Morton had been primed about what to expect. Moreover, the mc had been given all the necessary background on Harry and Tracy.

She was asked about her vision for the new Foundation, and went to great lengths to explain the interdependence of all life on Earth.

'So you aren't necessarily advocating that animals are more important than humans?' the mc asked.

Tracy grinned, 'Well, I'm sure we all know some humans who we could quite happily exchange for animals. But no, it's all a matter of getting a balance, and at the moment humans are tipping over the balance.'

'And Harry – how has the gravity machine affected you?'

'Totally …' he replied, shaking his head, 'I never expected anything like what has happened. I thought I was just … you know, pushing back the frontiers of science.'

'Yes,' the mc added, 'it's been a very big push.'

They went on to the draw. With something over twenty three million entries a random number generator produced each of the numbers on a large screen. Tracy was asked to set each of the selections into motion.

Each of the forty winners was identified: most were in Britain, but there were some from Europe. At number twenty seven there was a squeal of delight in the audience as somebody realised they had won. She came up onto the stage to collect her prize, and was introduced to all the guests.

After all the draws had been made the audience was loth to depart, though for those on the stage it had become tedious towards the end. They were happy to make their way off.

The BBC channel manager provided lunch, and afterwards they were shown the preparations for Sunday, and the part they were expected to play in the proceedings. In particular Lord Stonebrook would give a short welcoming and introductory speech.

The manager turned to Harry, 'I'm sure the people will want you to say something.'

'What can I say?'

'Oh, just a couple of sentences … you'll think of something.'

Tracy grinned broadly, 'They're making you work for your ride.'

It was time for an early supper by the time they left the BBC, and Lord Stonebrook took them to his favourite restaurant. The maître d' obviously knew him well and arranged a private table where they had a quiet drink before ordering from an à la carte menu.

Something had been bothering Harry the whole day, and he finally had the opportunity to ask Fred Morton.

'How have you solved the deflation problem?'

Morton smiled, 'A bit of cheating, I suppose. We've actually got eighty small gravity machines spread around the perimeter of the craft. They can all be operated individually, so when we want to come down we deflate them in groups of two or four. That stops any sudden come-down.

It's quite a smooth descent,' he added, 'though we've had to cover over the bottom of the craft so people can't see the deflations happening.'

Harry thought about it a moment, 'That means you lose the energy – you can't store it and use it again?'

Morton nodded, 'That's right, but to get the first manned gravity machine operational is so important that we've gone ahead with it.'

He added, 'The whole deflation problem is something we want to talk to you about next week.'

The leisurely dinner was followed by dessert, port and coffee. Discussions ranged around the details of the next day's proceedings and the potential of the gravity machine.

A thought occurred to Harry, 'Do you have the rights to build the gravity machine?'

'You mean in terms of the patent?' Lord Stonebrook asked.

Harry nodded.

'We've been in contact with your patent lawyer, Mr Cambre, and he's given permission for development machines to be built. You don't know about it?'

'No, but it seems a reasonable concession.'

It was after nine in the evening when Harry and Tracy were finally taken to their hotel. They received a royal welcome from the manager, and were ushered up to their deluxe room. The porter put down their suitcases, and closed the door as he went out.

A large double bed dominated the room, and Harry lay down on it.

'It's been a long day,' he said.

Tracy said nothing, and walked across to the large window, up three steps to a slightly higher level.

She stared out, and eventually said, 'You can see Trafalgar Square from here. I wonder how all the construction is going?'

Harry didn't respond. He looked at her, wondering how the evening was going to end.

She turned around, wringing her hands and looking at him imploringly.

'Harry,' she whispered, 'will you give me my privacy tonight?'

Well, that was it.

He smiled resignedly, 'Of course.'

She used the bathroom first, and when he had showered he found her tucked into one side of the large bed. He got into the other side and smiled at her.

She looked at him with those large brown eyes and beautiful face.

'Thanks,' she said.

He nodded, still staring at her.

'I'd like to kiss you,' he eventually said softly.

It took her an age to whisper back, 'I'd like to kiss you too ...'

'But ...?'

'I don't know if I could stop.'

That didn't seem to be a problem to him, but clearly she wasn't ready for anything else. He put his arm out along the big pillows between them.

'Come, you can lie here next to me. I won't do anything.'

She hesitated, but came across, her head snuggled into his shoulder. He pulled her close, and she put her arm across his chest.

They lay like that for a while, feeling the proximity of their bodies. Then he became aware of her regular breathing, and realised she was asleep. He stretched out and switched off the lights.

When he awoke in the morning there was sunlight streaming in the window. He looked to Tracy's side of the bed and saw her propped up on one elbow, looking down at him.

She didn't say anything, just carried on looking at him. There was a faint smile on her lips.

'Whaaaat ...?' he asked.

In reply she leaned across and kissed him, long and passionately.

And she was quite right, she couldn't stop. And he couldn't stop either – but then, in truth, the thought had never entered his head.

They ordered breakfast in their room and watched the TV build-up to the launch from the bed. The weatherman forecast a warm day with sunshine and occasional clouds. From the window they could see a section of Trafalgar Square in bright sun, with more and more people evident.

'It's quite something,' she said, 'all those people.'

He nodded, 'It's surreal – somehow we have to go and be part of it.'

She hugged him, 'A very important part – have you thought what you're going to say?'

'No, not really. I don't think there's much I can say. Just some platitudes.'

They dressed well before time. Harry put on his standard denims and a golf-style shirt with a collar.

He looked at Tracy.

'Shweshwe!' he exclaimed when he saw her wearing a long indigo-dyed skirt adopted by Xhosa women in South Africa. 'My mother used to wear one to special occasions – caused a stir in the US.'

They were picked up at ten am and taken to Trafalgar Square, though with all the people it would probably have been quicker to walk. They were taken to an open area in front of the National Gallery where Lord Stonebrook greeted them.

'Good to see you,' he said.

He looked approvingly at Tracy, 'Splendid, splendid, you look beautiful, my dear.'

They were early, and Harry stood looking at all the people filling up the square, climbing on the statues and fountains to get a good view. The low stage they had seen the previous day was cordoned off, and on the farther half stood the gravity machine. It looked similar to a fairground carousel – a round object with a flat base and a railing running around the outside and enclosing a circular set of seats. At what was obviously the rear a higher seat looked forwards, with a cowling behind it. The logos of the five associated car manufacturers were emblazoned on wide boards attached to the railing.

The excitement in the air was palpable.

He felt Tracy tapping him on the shoulder.

'Harry, there's someone here to see you.'

He turned around, and stared in speechless amazement.

'Fily … what are you doing here?' he stammered eventually.

Tracy smiled, 'I invited her – she said she was in London, so I thought it would be a good idea if she joined us.'

Fily came up to Harry and gave him a kiss on the cheek, 'Tracy's a wonderful girl, Harry, you're lucky you found her.'

Harry nodded, not knowing what else to say.

Lord Stonebrook joined them, 'Ah, Harry, all the pretty girls are with you.'

'Oh, yes, Nezer, …uh … let me introduce Fily Ahlgren.'

He turned to Fily, 'This is Lord Stonebrook.'

She fluttered her eyelashes, 'A real lord … I am so lucky.'

Lord Stonebrook smiled, 'It's a pleasure to meet you, my dear.'

He turned to Tracy and Harry, 'Things are beginning to move, and we need to do all the introductions and scene-setting.'

Then to Fily, 'Excuse us please, my dear – you will get a very good view of everything happening from here.'

They followed Lord Stonebrook down to the low stage.

Harry recognised Fred Morton in an open-necked shirt amongst a group of men in grey suits around the base of the stage. With a start he also saw Sir Richard Straithwaite, looking composed and at ease in the group.

What was he doing there?

Lord Stonebrook turned to Tracy and Harry, 'Let me introduce you to the Board of Amalgum.'

Besides Lord Stonebrook there were five others, chairmen of the consortium of motor car manufacturers who had combined to construct the gravity machine. They were each introduced to Tracy and Harry.

Sir Richard came up last, and Lord Stonebrook commented, 'I believe you know Sir Richard, Harry? He's not one of the board, but is a valuable member of our think-tank.'

Sir Richard smiled and held out his hand, 'Harry, it's good to see you again.'

'Sir Richard.' Harry shook his hand, but said nothing more.

He turned to Tracy, 'Miss Freese, it's my pleasure to meet you. I believe you will do great things with the Foundation.'

Tracy was obviously impressed, 'Thank you, Sir Richard.'

Harry seethed, but knew there was nothing he could do – Sir Richard had obviously charmed Amalgum, and was now charming everyone else.

He looked at his watch: there were still about 5 minutes before they went live. He wondered what he could do, but then smiled as he thought of something: it may work.

Lord Stonebrook was talking to one of the TV organisers, and Harry went across.

'Nezer, can I ask you something?'

'Of course.' He excused himself from the organiser.

'I've been looking at this first group on the gravity machine.'

'Yes?'

'Well, they're all men, apart from Tracy. All rather older men. Don't you think that's going to be criticised?'

Lord Stonebrook looked around, 'Possibly … but what do you suggest? We can't change now - they're all chairmen and on our board.'

'What about another woman? A young, attractive woman to add a bit of glamour.'

Lord Stonebrook frowned, and Harry continued, 'There's Fily Ahlgren …'

He pointed to where she was now surrounded by a group of young men.

Lord Stonebrook looked, 'Well, perhaps … it would add spice to our group.'

He thought about it, 'Sir Richard could go in the second group – there is someone who's taken ill …'

His face brightened as he made his decision, 'Yes, by Jove, let's do that. You go and call Miss Ahlgren, and I'll talk to Sir Richard.'

With a smile on his face Harry went to call Fily.

She took it all in her stride, 'Oooh, Harry – that will be incredible.'

When they returned to the group Lord Stonebrook was waiting, 'Welcome Ms Ahlgren, it will be a pleasure to have you on board.'

However, he confided to Harry, 'Sir Richard didn't like it – didn't like it at all. But it's done now.'

The TV organiser came across, pointing at his watch.

'Yes, yes,' Lord Stonebrook said. 'Come Harry – we must go and talk to the people.'

There were stairs going up, and Harry was immediately recognised when he climbed up. There was a chant of 'Ha-rry, Ha-rry,' and he waved his hand and smiled at the mass of humanity. Never in his wildest dreams did he ever imagine being treated like a pop star.

They stood on the stage next to the gravity machine; the mc held up his hand and the noise abated.

'Welcome,' he said, and the crown cheered, 'Lord Stonebrook will give a brief introduction to the events today.' He gave Lord Stonebrook the microphone.

'Ladies and Gentlemen,' he began, 'Yes! It's finally happening – the first flight of a manned gravity machine. This is history being made, and we are all here to see it happen.'

He was obviously more of a showman than Harry had given him credit for, and he carried on a bit about what the gravity machine would do for humanity. He was building up the expectations, and the crowd enjoyed it.

He stopped and pointed to Harry, 'But let us hear from the man who made it all possible – Harry Ehlers!'

Lord Stonebrook handed over the microphone, and Harry had to wait while the applause died down. He hadn't decided what to say, but smiled as the crowd looked up at him: in a way he wasn't nervous, and was actually enjoying the moment.

'Wow,' he said, and the speakers over the square and over the world boomed it out.

'I never could have dreamt this – not ever. All I've done is find out a bit more of how our world functions. I guess it's going to cause changes – I hope good changes. How you react is up to all of you.'

He looked at the gravity machine, and took hold of the railing.

'This is exciting stuff,' he continued, 'I haven't seen this machine before, and I'm really looking forward to the ride.'

He grinned, and his boyish enthusiasm infected the crowd, and they roared their approval.

Then he was more serious, 'I hope the gravity machine will fulfil its expectations. It opens up totally new horizons, as Lord Stonebrook has already described. But there are also responsibilities, and I trust you will all be responsible.'

He looked at the crowd, where there were heads being nodded, but they didn't want to be told about limitations. Responsibility was furthest from their minds.

He felt the mood and smiled again, 'Change is good, and we will have massive changes. Lots of opportunities, lots of new experiences, lots of excitement.'

He raised his hand, 'Here's to the future!' The crowd cheered.

The mc took the microphone and organised the passengers for the first flight. The five chairmen sat around the one side, and Harry was positioned more or less at the front, with Tracy next to him. Lord Stonebrook, Fily and Fred Morton completed the passenger list.

Lord Stonebrook appeared to be particularly pleased to be between the two ladies, and Fily found a good listener in Fred Morton as she went on about the fantastic opportunity she had been given. She knew what this would do for her career.

'Now, tighten your seat belts,' the mc told all the passengers, '- the gravity machine is perfectly safe, but we have to take all necessary precautions.'

As she clipped on her belt, Tracy asked Harry softly, 'Did you get Fily on?'

He smiled at her, 'Yes – she's a lot better looking than Sir Richard, and not as devious.'

She grinned and squeezed his hand, 'Nasty...'

'Well, we're ready for take-off,' the mc announced. 'I want to hand over control to Mike, the pilot of this gravity machine.'

Mike, sitting at the back, waved his hand, even as the first chords of 'Chariots of Fire' blasted out over Trafalgar Square.

The crowd was quiet, watching, the music fitting perfectly to the occasion. This was the moment they had been waiting for. This would signal the new adventures awaiting them.

No-one really heard the low hum as the gravity machine absorbed energy. It was only when the closest spectators could see space between the stage and the machine's base that they suddenly realised it was in the air. It was floating! They shouted, and the rest of the crowd took it up as they saw the craft moving upwards. Slowly, without fuss, it ascended.

On board, Harry could feel the floating sensation as the gravity machine rose, and he looked down at the crowd around the base as they went higher and higher.

Then he caught the eye of Sir Richard, staring balefully upwards. He held on to Tracy's hand: no doubt life would continue to be interesting.

CPSIA information can be obtained at www.ICGtesting.com
Printed in the USA
LVOW06*1427091115

461711LV00011B/99/P